PATH OF SECRETS

KENLEY DAVIDSON

PAGE NINE PRESS

http://KenleyDavidson.com

Dedicated to Bethany Johnson, who like Lady Norelle is an inspiring mentor to young women who need role models now more than ever. For her commitment to sharing both her time and her wisdom with our daughters as they grow up and give shape to their dreams, we are forever grateful.

One day her mother said to her, "Go, my dear, and see how your
grandmother is doing, for I hear she has been very ill..."
Little Red Riding Hood set out immediately to go to her grandmother,
who lived in another village. As she was going through the wood, she
met with a wolf...

Charles Perrault, *Le Petit Chaperon Rouge*

~

PROLOGUE

*I*n the end, the old woman was not difficult to persuade. She had her objections, of course, and a rather large number of unreasonable demands. But the offer of a holiday in the south proved irresistible, and at length, she was packed off at the head of a caravan so large, one would have expected royalty be traveling somewhere in its midst.

He was, of course, informed in no uncertain terms that he would be held responsible for anything untoward that befell her precious—and utterly pretentious—house. Her threats regarding the windows alone ranged from having him horsewhipped by the king, to ensuring that he was never received by any reputable hostess again should the glass suffer so much as a single crack.

He doubted the king would be interested in attempting violence against his person, and he couldn't imagine being a guest in any place the old woman might consider respectable. But he could pretend well enough, so she'd departed with the smug conviction that she was aiding one of the king's most trusted courtiers in a matter of great importance to society.

Even if neither of those things was actually true.

The girl would be arriving soon. She would be well-protected, of course, but her safety was hardly his concern. What mattered was his knowledge of what she carried, and the message that had reached him only hours ago: *The basket is moving north.*

The basket, and its rumored contents.

Very few were privy to the knowledge of what had been seized from the hold of a seemingly innocent merchant ship while it lay in Andar's largest harbor. Very few, and none outside of the Crown's most trusted advisors, and yet, somehow, word of the discovery had spread. Curiosity was rampant, payment had been offered in exchange for information, and promises had been made—promises that had yet to be fulfilled.

Thankfully, even the curious did not yet understand the true nature of what had been found. If the full details ever became known, it would mean war, and it was therefore vital that the traitor be discovered before he or she made good on the promise of stolen information. Wars, after all, were almost always counterproductive, even in his line of work. Therefore, preventing them had generally proven to be the wisest course of action, if not always the most straightforward.

And anyway, he'd been paid for his trouble, so he set about making the house ready with deliberation and conviction.

The girl must not be allowed to realize that anything was amiss, other than the obvious—she'd been told that her grandmother was dying, so she would expect a dark, somber atmosphere. Even the lack of servants could be explained away, by the demands and crochets of an unreasonable old woman.

No one would realize the truth until it was far too late to do anything about it.

CHAPTER 1

No matter how hard she tried, Miss Batrice Reyard couldn't escape the apparently universal truth that unmarried ladies of a certain rank were expected to enjoy embroidery.

She didn't.

Not that she wasn't proficient. Need a rose frame? She knew the stitch for that. A pansy border? She could create one without needing any sort of pattern. In eight colors. But part of the reason she'd run away from home at seventeen was a decided distaste for anything involving needles.

So how could she have ended up here, more than two years later, in the drawing room of Lady Something-or-Other, bending her head over an embroidery frame in less-than-willing imitation of all the other young ladies in attendance?

Oh, right. Because she was supposedly being sponsored at court, and her sponsor believed it would be beneficial for her to polish up her public persona.

Batrice couldn't have disagreed more. There was nothing wrong with her personality, thank you. Or her accomplishments. She'd suffered through five years of an exacting governess and was perfectly adequate at etiquette and all of the other traditional skills.

Or had been, she reflected, as her needle stabbed into the tip of her index finger for the third time that afternoon.

Besides, her sponsor was actually supposed to be giving her spy lessons.

Or whatever it was called when one was in training to become a secret agent of the Crown. Batrice hadn't expected it to be all thrills and excitement all the time, but was it too much to expect at least a few thrills? Or even the tiniest of intrigues?

Thus far, her lessons seemed to consist primarily of learning to convince the world that she was the least interesting person alive, which required a temporary return to the incredibly dull life of a debutante. A life that Batrice thought she'd left behind when she ran away from home and became an actress.

As she muttered a decidedly unladylike word under her breath, Batrice glanced around the drawing room and almost giggled when she encountered at least two other rebellious glances. Miss Coralynne Smythe was stabbing her needle through her work as though determined to commit murder by silken thread, and Zolanda Fidgins had spent the past hour pulling out one stitch at a time with glacial slowness. As Zolanda was quite sprightly in all other circumstances, Batrice reasoned that it was likely a ruse, and she wasn't the only one wishing she were elsewhere.

It wasn't likely, though, that either Coralynne or Zolanda had considered the consequences should they suddenly flip off their chairs and walk across the room on their hands. In Batrice's experience, acrobatics wasn't something young ladies thought about with much regularity, and the general reluctance of society to celebrate such talents had made it difficult to find much time to practice since she'd arrived in Evenleigh.

Her mentor had assured her that this process of deception—of pretending to be a proper debutante—was necessary. To be an effective agent, Batrice would need to be reconciled with both her family and with society as a whole. Such connections would supposedly provide her with the perfect cover for future activities, but Batrice wasn't at all convinced that her mentor's reassurances were more than a load of complete twaddle.

The drawing room door opened and Batrice looked up from her work once more, hoping to find that it was finally time for tea. But no. An overfed and over-enthusiastic lap dog entered the room, panting and drooling on the carpet as it tugged on its leash in an effort to reach Lady—what was her name again? The dog was followed by a neatly starched servant who observed its behavior with a slightly curled lip, waiting only for the mistress of the house to cease fawning over his furry charge before he bent to pick it up and, theoretically, remove it from the room.

The dog, sensing an end to its fun, neatly eluded the servant's grasp and took off in a circle, wrapping his leash around the man's ankles and bringing him crashing to the ground.

A chorus of gasps erupted.

"I'm so sorry," her hostess started to say, but to Batrice's delight, it was much too late for sorry.

As the fallen servant muttered a decidedly impolite word, the startled dog began to pull away from the scene of its crime. And as its ruffled collar was entirely too loose, it soon slipped off, leaving the delighted canine to race around the room, barking madly while careening into furniture, embroidery baskets, and ladies' skirts as its claws slipped on the polished floor.

Gasps became shrieks, young ladies jumped to their feet, and embroidery frames were flung aside as two decorative tables went flying, accompanied by the sound of shattering porcelain.

It was the most fun she'd had in weeks, Batrice decided, as she observed the proceedings with a broad grin.

The flushed servant scrambled to his feet while the lady of the house split her phrases between berating him and calling futilely for her darling Bitsy to "stop running about and be a good boy for Mumsy, won't you lovey?"

It was in the midst of this carnage that yet another servant appeared in the drawing room doorway.

Batrice watched as his eyes widened, a brief smirk appeared, and then a proper, polite mask of indifference settled over his face.

"Miss Reyard," he announced over the din. "I believe your carriage has arrived."

Her carriage? She didn't have one. She was expecting to be delivered back to Evenburg by Lady—Heppelwhite! That was her name—after the day's activities were concluded.

But trust fate to intervene the moment her life became truly interesting. Batrice dutifully packed up her embroidery as the dog ran out of energy and flopped down beneath a settee, forcing his humiliated keeper to crawl under it in pursuit. She was just exiting the room when she heard Lady Heppelwhite marshaling the other young ladies to abandon the shambles of the drawing room for a restorative tea.

Batrice allowed herself a single martyred sigh as she marched towards the front door, regretting the missed tea and wondering what she'd done to deserve such injustice.

But her good humor was restored when she saw whose carriage awaited her in front of the Heppelwhites' town house—her noble sponsor had arrived to fetch her in person.

According to Batrice's parents, it was nothing short of a miracle that she'd ended up in her present position, but in reality, the situation was more convoluted than miraculous. It had begun by her running away from home at seventeen, and culminated in a series of fortunate circumstances involving spies, a countess, and several attempted murders, at the end of which she'd found herself a position with Andar's Ministry of Information. Which was really just Lady Lizbet Norelle—the most fascinating, brilliantly manipulative woman it had ever been Batrice's good fortune to meet.

Rather than announce her actual intentions towards Batrice, Lady Norelle had written to Batrice's parents, insisting that she be allowed to sponsor their youngest daughter, promising to introduce her to many eligible young men and see to her safety for as long as she was allowed to stay at Evenburg.

The Reyards had never been more than minor gentry, so despite having disowned Batrice after she joined a troupe of touring performers, they hadn't hesitated to abandon their moral high ground when presented with the possibility of a relationship with the king's sister-in-law. Such an invitation was an unexpected and nearly unheard of honor, so they had, predictably, returned a letter of their own filled with very proper sentiments of gratitude. It never once mentioned the last words that they'd exchanged with their wayward child.

On the day she first left home, her mother had sobbed uncontrollably and begged Batrice to just plunge a dagger into her heart that instant because it would hurt less than watching her ungrateful daughter throw away everything they'd lavished on her.

Her father had said something that began with "mark my words," and ended with "no daughter of mine."

They might have been reading a melodrama. With such examples as that, was it any wonder Batrice had decided to become an actress?

But her two years with a traveling company had ended when the owner insisted she marry him. At nineteen, she didn't mind a bit of flirtation but wasn't ready to settle down, and in any case, she wouldn't have chosen an often-drunk forty-year-old with excessive back hair who fancied himself a comedian.

A footman in royal livery opened the door of the carriage with a stiff bow and handed her inside, where Batrice collapsed on the rear-facing seat and subjected her mentor to a narrow-eyed gaze.

"You knew exactly how awful that was likely to be when you promised I would attend, didn't you?"

Lady Lizbet Norelle smiled, the very picture of serene and self-contained royalty. Not that she was royal by birth—her sister had been married to Andar's King Hollin before her early death—but Lizbet had been an essential part of Andar's government for so many years, no one really remembered that she was only the daughter of minor gentry herself.

Nor did very many people outside of Evenleigh realize that Lizbet was one of the main guiding forces behind the Crown, in no small part because she managed it without being either traditionally commanding or classically beautiful. Instead, she was an average looking, middle-aged mother of two with a deceptively gentle demeanor and imperturbable temper.

"I'm sure I have no idea to what you are referring," she replied, her hands folded neatly in her lap. "Today was an invaluable opportunity to be seen in the company of other young ladies who are a part of the society to which you aspire."

"To which you aspire for me," Batrice muttered, settling her embroidery basket beside her on the seat.

"Did you make any progress today?"

"In what respects, my lady?" Batrice asked innocently, holding up her embroidery frame.

Lady Norelle surveyed Batrice's attempts at embroidery and burst out laughing.

"My dear, I do believe you're even worse with a needle than Princess Trystan, which is saying quite a lot."

"Why thank you, my lady," Batrice replied brightly. "I assure you, this kind of failure does not occur without effort. My mother once proclaimed that I couldn't be any worse if I tried, and I can confidently report that I proved her wrong within a fortnight."

"It's healthy to have goals." Lady Norelle's eyes twinkled with amusement, which reminded Batrice of the only reason she hadn't long since left the palace behind. Lizbet Norelle was, in Batrice's mind, nearly perfect.

She was smart, practical, and laughed at things that were actually funny. Plus she didn't try to pretend that embroidery was good for anything except giving the appearance of doing something ladylike while surreptitiously listening to state secrets or plotting to blow something up.

Not that Lady Norelle would admit to having blown anything up. But Batrice rather hoped she had.

Lizbet held out her hand for the frame, and Batrice handed it across the carriage.

"It's a fascinating design, my dear. Are these..."

"Daggers," Batrice replied, blinking innocently. "Also drops of blood. They will eventually encircle a heartfelt saying of some sort or another. Probably 'Death To My Enemies.'"

"Subtle," Lady Norelle noted, with a commendably straight face. "I predict your future drawing room will be the home of notably direct discourse."

"And perhaps a suitably timed stabbing or two," Batrice added sweetly. "But unlike most ladies, I would use actual knives."

Lady Norelle handed the frame back without comment, so Batrice bent her head over it and focused her attention on creating a tangle so elaborate no one would ever expect her to undo it. It was her own invention, and she was quite proud of it.

"I've received a letter," Lady Norelle said, after the carriage had traveled a block or two in silence.

Batrice was determined to prove that she had learned her lessons and did not express even the slightest interest in the letter or its contents.

Lady Norelle chuckled. "You're being so deliberately studious, I'm afraid it's obvious you're up to something. But perhaps that's only because I know you so well."

"My lady, I am creating a work of great beauty that will be an ornament to my future home. Why would I be anything other than focused on my efforts?"

"The letter is for you."

Batrice neither bounced in her seat nor exclaimed for joy. Letters had very seldom been cause for rejoicing in her experience.

"Is it my mother demanding an account for my behavior or my father inquiring eagerly about the rank of my suitors?"

"Neither," Lizbet chided, "and it isn't as though I open your correspondence."

"Then how do you know it isn't from either of my parents?" Batrice countered.

"Why would you apprentice with a spymaster who couldn't tell where a letter was from without resorting to amateurish tricks like actually reading it?"

Batrice laughed and set her embroidery aside to open the seal on the single, tightly-folded sheet. Before perusing the text, she glanced at the signature at the bottom of the page. "You are correct in fact if not in function," she reported. "It is from my grandmother. Who disapproves of me even more strongly than my parents, if such a thing is possible."

"Have you ever received a letter from her before?" Lizbet asked, brow arched curiously.

"Not that I recall. But I always had the pleasure of listening to Mother read her letters aloud after dinner."

"A frequent correspondent then?"

"A woman of many words and an almost equal number of complaints," Batrice amended.

"*My Dearest Granddaughter,*" she read aloud, and stopped. "Something is obviously wrong. I've never been her dearest anything."

"I write to beg you to attend me in my hour of direst need. My physician has assured me that I am not long for this world and must put my affairs in order as soon as possible. I wish I could convey to you my regrets, granddaughter, over our estrangement. At a time when I am about to leave behind this life forever, I find that my greatest wish is to bring my family together once more. Please make haste, so that I may

see your face one last time before I die. Perhaps we can forgive one another, and I will be allowed to at last depart from all my sorrows and trials in peace.

If you do come, be sure not to bring too many servants as I cannot be troubled to make arrangements for them in my present state. Also, I must insist that you refrain from wearing strong scents, as it disturbs my delicate senses and may cause me to enter an irremediable decline. There is to be no dancing or frivolity, and I recommend that you come prepared with at least three mourning gowns, one of which ought to be crepe, so that you will not disgrace me amongst my friends and neighbors after I am gone. Black gloves, as well, unless you cannot order them in time, in which case gray can be considered acceptable.

Your nearly departed grandmother,
  Lady Elanza Entwhistle

"Hah," Batrice said, folding the letter and stuffing it into the bottom of her embroidery basket as the carriage headed up the slight incline to the palace gates. "So, what else are we going to do today?"

"My dear," Lizbet said, her forehead creased with concern, "your grandmother is dying. I believe we can put off our activities until a more appropriate time."

"My grandmother has been dying for the past twenty years," Batrice retorted. "It is very nearly the only activity she approves of. Especially now that she has found a physician who doesn't mind diagnosing her with the awfullest things, only to pronounce himself a miracle-worker when she is cured within a sennight."

"Nonetheless," Lizbet replied, "if we are to maintain the fiction that you are under my sponsorship as nothing more than a gently-bred debutante, hoping to rise in society, you must act as society expects."

"Meaning what, exactly?" Batrice regarded her with suspicion.

11

Anything society expected was bound to be maddeningly dull. There would be no one to stab and nothing to set on fire. Or rather, it wouldn't be allowed, no matter how much she might wish to.

"Meaning that you must attend your grandmother with all possible haste," Lady Norelle said briskly. "Even if she is faking, one does not simply ignore the request of a respected elderly relative."

"One does if she's only requesting it so that she can complain about her thankless family, who never pay attention to her unless she's on her deathbed."

"I will be ordering a traveling coach," Lizbet went on serenely. "You will need a driver and a guard, though I don't know whether I will have time to hire a trustworthy maid before you depart. Will tomorrow morning be soon enough?"

"Soon enough..." Batrice spluttered. "Soon enough for what?"

"Soon enough to prepare yourself to say your goodbyes to your grandmother, of course. Perhaps I will also send a selection of gifts, to be accompanied by a note of condolence from the Crown. It might be just the thing to cheer her up and help her decide she prefers to live after all."

"You're making me take a seven-day coach journey?" Batrice demanded incredulously. "To visit my grandmother? Who isn't dying, and probably isn't even ill?"

"Your cover is the most important asset you have," Lady Norelle reminded her, gazing out the window at the view of Evenleigh's rooftops, "and for the moment it depends on society's approval. There will be very few things worth destroying that cover for, and this is certainly not one of them."

When Batrice frowned and opened her mouth to utter further objections, Lady Norelle silenced her by leaning forward and placing a gentle hand on her knee.

"Batrice, this life you have chosen is neither easy nor simple. It is complex, demanding, frequently disappointing, and often lonely. Yes, there are moments of excitement, but far more usual are the weeks of boredom that are vital to the success of our mission—which is neither more nor less than maintaining peace, both with our neighbors and within our borders." She smiled, probably to take the sting out of her words. "Consider this a lesson in judging when is the right time to choose a harder path for the sake of your future. Maintain your cover, so that you can return to hunt down foreign spies another day."

"But how will my visiting my grandmother affect society's perception of me if no one else even knows about this letter?" Batrice understood what Lady Norelle was saying, but it still seemed ridiculous to insist that she go all that way, waste all that time, over a letter no one had read but her. "I'm certainly not going to tell anyone, so how would they even find out there was anything to disapprove of?"

Lizbet offered her an amused glance as the carriage came to a stop at the side entrance to Evenburg. "Exit this carriage, letter in hand, and I promise you, within the hour, at least three people will express their condolences. It is how this world works. Nothing is a secret, so if you wish a thing to remain unknown, you must take care not to hide it."

Batrice pondered that as she reluctantly descended from the carriage and returned to her room to prepare for her unexpected—and unwanted—journey. Lady Norelle had not reached her present position by being foolish, so it was always worth listening to whatever bits of wisdom she let fall in casual conversation. Even if they didn't seem to make much sense at the time.

If you wish to keep a secret, keep it in plain sight. It was worth adding to her journal, along with Lizbet's other pithy sayings.

Such as... *If you are forced to lie, stick as close to the truth as possible.*

If you don't believe your story, no one else will either.

Better to sound ridiculous than hesitate.

Someday, her journal was going to make for very interesting reading.

CHAPTER 2

The next morning, Batrice entered the courtyard at the front of the castle wearing a scowl and her white wool traveling cloak. She was still not entirely resigned to this journey. Seven days there, seven days back, and no way of knowing how long her grandmother would demand she stay before she decided to recover from her "deathbed."

There was also the alarming possibility that her parents would be present as well. They were even more intimately acquainted with her grandmother's eccentricities, but also felt more bound to cater to her whims, lest she leave all of her not-inconsiderable wealth to Batrice's uncle.

An outcome which, in Batrice's opinion, ought not to be lamented. The last thing her family needed was any further temptation to think themselves better than their neighbors.

True to Lady Norelle's promise, a coach awaited her, already packed with the trunk that had been carried down from Batrice's room earlier that morning. The door was open, the matched bays in the traces were shifting their feet restlessly, and a pair of unfamiliar men stood beside Lady Norelle, conversing quietly with one another.

"Ah, finally." Lady Norelle motioned her over, and Batrice did her best to find an expression that wouldn't communicate quite so much of her displeasure all at once. "Miss Reyard, this is your driver for the journey. His name is John." She motioned towards a muscular blond man with a short beard and light blue eyes that he directed rather pointedly at the ground, and whose acknowledgment of the introduction consisted of nothing more than a brief nod. His apparent shyness notwithstanding, Batrice noted that he was actually quite good looking. She thought she might enjoy coaxing him to speak to her as the journey progressed.

"And your guard, Rupert," Lady Norelle continued. Batrice turned from considering John's broad-shouldered appeal to greet the other man, who glowered right before he bowed.

Rupert was at least a head taller than Batrice, but no more than a few years older, with slightly wavy dark hair, broad shoulders, and a face that would make a debutante swoon. He wore a perfectly pressed tunic and a sword at his hip, and Batrice could tell at a glance that he was the sort of person to whom the word "fun" meant "bothersome nuisance."

Also, that he didn't like her very much. Or at least didn't like being asked to guard her, which instantly made Batrice's life more interesting. There was very little she enjoyed more than needling someone who resented her existence. And the fact that he was exceptionally handsome? That only made it better.

"So pleased to meet both of you," she said, smiling with unfeigned delight. "It's going to be so exciting to travel through the northern woods, don't you think? All those miles through dark and forbidding forest, with no one nearby but us?" She shivered in anticipation. "Do you think we'll meet any brigands? Or even wolves?"

Lady Norelle, who probably knew perfectly well what Batrice was thinking, shot her a sharp glance as if to say, "Are you sure this is how you want to begin?"

Oh, she was definitely sure. If she absolutely must endure the trip, not to mention endure her grandmother, she was going to have as much fun as possible, and Lady Norelle did say she wanted Batrice to practice behaving like other young ladies. Which, in her experience, meant insincerity and misplaced enthusiasm.

"The roads are well patrolled, Miss Reyard," Rupert said stiffly, "and it is a well-known fact that there are no wolves in the forests of Andar. I am certain our journey will be uneventful."

"Oh, I do hope not," Batrice responded wistfully, which was not uttered for the sake of pretense. "It really would be a shame if *nothing* interesting happened."

"I suspect interesting follows you wherever you go," Lady Norelle observed, reaching out to embrace her warmly. "Nevertheless, I did promise your parents I would be responsible for your safety, so for the sake of my reputation, please attempt not to insert yourself into the middle of any catastrophes. Which I hope you will interpret as a suggestion that you refrain from creating any as well. Trust Rupert to keep you out of harm's way and return as soon as your grandmother allows."

Batrice hugged her back. She would miss her mentor. It had been a relief, these past months, to discover that there might be a place where she could finally feel like she belonged, and to believe that even her peculiar skill set might end up proving useful in some way.

"I swear I will refrain from creating any catastrophes," she promised. "But if they drop right into my lap..."

Lady Norelle gave her a gentle shove towards the coach. "Your new maid should be here at any moment, and then you must be on your way. I have work to do, and the sooner you leave, the sooner your grandmother can make a miraculous recovery."

Batrice chuckled and set one foot on the step, just as a frantic voice called out from behind her.

"Batrice... I mean, Miss Reyard, wait!"

Batrice couldn't quite imagine who might be hailing her so familiarly. She hadn't managed to make any close friends since she'd arrived, and no one she'd known from before was likely to drop in on the Evenburg bailey unannounced.

"Don't leave without me!"

Batrice looked over her shoulder to see a plainly dressed young woman scurrying in her direction.

"Ah," Lady Norelle said, "this must be the maid. I asked a friend to recommend someone who wouldn't mind a bit of travel, and she offered to send me one of her own staff. Hopefully, the two of you will get on well."

Batrice stifled a groan. The last thing she wanted was one of Lady Norelle's friends' maids following her around, no doubt preparing a report on her every move. But it really wouldn't be entirely appropriate for her to travel such a long distance with only two handsome young men like Rupert and John for company, so she was just going to have to put up with whoever had been found to accompany her.

Despite the poor girl's unusual clothing choices. The early summer sun was warm, but the maid wore a thick cloak that completely covered her dress. She had pulled the hood up over an already hideously large bonnet, which concealed her face completely as she kept her chin tucked and bobbed a hasty—and perilously shaky—curtsey.

"So sorry I'm late, Miss Reyard."

Now that she was standing so close, her voice almost sounded familiar. But when would Batrice have had a conversation with someone else's maid?

"Not to worry," she said breezily. "We were only just now saying our goodbyes. Where are your bags, then?"

The maid produced a bulging carry-all from beneath her cloak and tossed it into the carriage, where it hit the far side with an audible thump.

"I, uh… I suppose we're all set then," Batrice said, offering Lady Norelle one last jaunty wave before ascending the step and taking the rear-facing seat. That was usually reserved for servants, but she'd never been sick while traveling and didn't much care which way she faced. Besides, at least half the seat had been taken up by a large basket, and there was no point in making the maid share space with such a monstrosity when both Batrice and her handbag could very easily fit on the remaining half of the bench.

A quick glance out the window revealed Lady Norelle returning to the castle, and Batrice watched her progress with longing. She would far rather be staying than going, but at least... she glanced out the other side of the carriage and confirmed that Rupert would be riding alongside, on a magnificent gray horse than made Batrice tap her lips with thoughts of "borrowing" it later on. She hadn't gone for a long ride in ages.

The carriage lurched, throwing her forward, and throwing her maid on the opposite seat back. The hood came off, the maid lifted her chin, and Batrice found herself staring into the startled, round-cheeked face of Miss Coralynne Smythe—one of the reluctant embroiderers from the previous afternoon.

Who stared back a little defiantly, with a stubborn set to her jaw that indicated she expected Batrice to argue and was fully prepared to make her case.

Batrice just settled back into her seat with a delighted smile. Perhaps this journey wouldn't be a complete loss after all. "I don't know exactly what this is," she announced, "but at the very least it promises to be a good story. Are you escaping an unwanted marriage? Attempting to elope with someone your parents disapprove of? Or have you fallen madly in love with the driver and wish to convince him that you're perfectly well suited to his itinerant lifestyle? He is quite attractive, and the two of you would make a lovely couple."

Miss Smythe blinked rapidly, then removed her atrocious bonnet and shook out her headful of dark curls. "My story is whatever will convince you to let me stay," she said, but Batrice could see a flush spread across the tawny brown of her cheeks.

"Oh, I have no intention of kicking you out," she reassured her unexpected companion. "Unless you're here to spy on me."

"Well, I am," Coralynne said comfortably.

Batrice narrowed her eyes. "In that case, I should tell you that I'm completely willing to leave you by the side of the road somewhere far from civilization with wolves howling at your heels."

Coralynne proved extremely disappointing—she didn't appear remotely threatened.

"There are no wolves in the forest," she said decidedly. "And anyway, you won't. Which is why I'm coming with you."

"Would you get in a carriage with any near stranger you thought could be counted on not to abandon you in the woods?" Batrice asked, puzzled by this logic.

"Of course not," Coralynne responded, rolling her eyes. "Give me some credit."

"What sort of credit do you think you deserve when you've admitted you're here to spy on me? Who are you spying for? Lady Norelle?"

"Oh, I'm not spying for anyone else." Coralynne laughed as though that was an absurd suggestion. "I'm here for me."

This proclamation did not make her motivations any clearer.

"You're spying on me for yourself. Because...?" Batrice found herself at a loss.

"I'm coming with you because I heard you were going on a journey through the darkest parts of the northern woods. It sounded thrilling, and you needed a maid. I saw no reason that maid shouldn't be me."

"No reason at all?" Batrice inquired. "Beyond perhaps your parents' objections? The fact that it's likely to be uncomfortable and you have no idea how to be a maid? Or even that you weren't exactly invited?"

"No one invites a maid," Coralynne responded, quite truthfully. "If I had been a real maid, would you have asked if I wanted to go or just taken me?"

Batrice was honest enough to stop and consider the question. "I don't know," she replied thoughtfully. "I suppose I would have assumed your consent had been gained by Lady Norelle before she hired you. But that's not exactly my point. How angry are your parents likely to be when they find you missing?"

Coralynne grinned impishly. "They'll be ecstatic."

Batrice had met the Smythes—a somewhat starchy older couple with two daughters and a highly conventional sense of the appropriate—and she was having difficulty imagining their excitement at the prospect of their daughter's disappearance. Her eyes narrowed. "What exactly did you tell them?"

"I left a dramatic, tear-stained note under my pillow proclaiming my intention to elope with the disfigured heir to a northern barony."

This required a lot more thinking than Batrice had planned to do that early in the morning.

"The only northern barony is currently held by a thirty-year-old former sea captain," she said finally. She should know, because Lady Norelle drilled her mercilessly on the details of the peerage. "His heir is two."

"Yes, well, I also told my maid I was eloping with the illegitimate son of a wealthy merchant," Coralynne replied, not noticeably disturbed by these observations.

"And I take it eloping in truth was out of the question?"

Miss Smythe shuddered. "Have you ever met a man you'd care to elope with? Outside the pages of a book, that is."

She had a point, though Batrice hadn't completely given up on eventually finding such a man. Her first proposal had been such a ridiculous, unromantic affair that she'd decided never to consider marrying anyone she wouldn't be willing to elope with if he should ask. And though she'd met any number of attractive men in her travels, none of them had shown the good sense to fall in love with her, or to inspire her to fall in love with them, more's the pity. A tragic love affair might have proven vastly entertaining.

"No," she admitted. "I haven't. And if you haven't either, why will your parents be so very thrilled by your announcement?"

Coralynne settled back in her seat and crossed her ankles neatly. "Because they want to marry off my sister and I'm getting in the way," she said glumly. "Look at me. I'm twenty-four, I would rather travel than pour tea, I haven't much in the way of money, and I can't attract a suitor, so they've despaired of ever getting rid of me. If I elope, they can breathe a sigh of relief and get on with finding a husband for Mariella."

Batrice raised an eyebrow at this. Coralynne Smythe was not exactly hag-ridden—she had a lovely figure, gorgeous dark curls, a smooth, tawny complexion, and expressive dark eyes. She was intelligent enough to dislike embroidery and resourceful enough to have gotten herself into Batrice's carriage without being found out. Perfect wife material for anyone wise enough to notice.

"So what *are* you going to do, if you're not really planning to elope?"

Coralynne brightened. "I'm writing a book!"

"A book?" Batrice was beginning to feel rather lost. This conversation was not going in any direction she would have expected, and she considered herself a reasonably flexible person.

"Yes!" Coralynne confirmed with an enthusiastic nod. "I've secretly been writing novels for years. I've even had one published—*Romelda's Revenge*. Perhaps you've heard of it?"

At Batrice's blank look, Coralynne seemed momentarily crestfallen but recovered before Batrice could come up with a suitably polite response.

"Never mind that then," she said. "You see, the trouble is, I've completely run out of ideas. We always visit the same people and do the same things. I simply had to get away from there and experience something new before I could write my next book."

"I see." Batrice most definitely did not see, but if this little chat was to get anywhere, agreement seemed important. "So you're running away from home and spying on me to get material for your next book."

Her unexpected companion nodded.

"Why me?" This was an important question, as there were any number of ways for a girl to run away from home. It seemed fairly odd that Miss Smythe would have chosen Batrice as her ticket out of town, let alone her literary inspiration. They knew each other, but barely, and had rarely even spoken.

"Because you're interesting," Coralynne said. "And you're not afraid of being different."

Startled, Batrice eyed her companion anew. She'd observed that Coralynne was quiet in company, but it hadn't really occurred to her that Coralynne might be watching her in return. And was it true? Was she really not afraid of being seen as different?

She supposed it was. Being an actress was one thing—as an actress you had to be comfortable with the attention and scrutiny of others, but you could hide quite effectively behind the costumes and the characters you played. As an acrobat, however, she'd grown accustomed to being seen in a different way. She'd found that she actually enjoyed attracting the reluctant admiration of those who might not approve of her lifestyle, but who had no choice but to admire her hard-won skills. The work had tested her limitations and broadened her horizons, and, even more importantly, had taught her to find joy in choosing her own path, without respect to the judgments of the society she'd been born to.

But that hardly seemed like sufficient motivation for Coralynne to pretend she was a maid and tell her family she'd eloped. There was really no going back after that, and Coralynne had always seemed so very sensible.

"I still don't understand," Batrice said finally.

Coralynne reached into her carry-all and produced what was unmistakably a journal. "I intend to learn your secrets," she said firmly.

"My what?" For a moment, Batrice was terribly afraid that someone had found out her real purpose for being at Evenburg.

"In addition to observing your adventures, I'm going to find out how you manage to be so confident all the time," Coralynne continued earnestly. "You're different, but you're not afraid for people to know it. I want to be a novelist, which means I'll be living a very different life as well, and I want to do it with confidence. So I've decided to stay close to you and take notes. Afterwards, I'll return home, confess everything to my parents, and begin work on my next book."

"Yes, but everyone will believe you've eloped," Batrice pointed out.

"I intend to spend the rest of my life writing novels, so it hardly matters."

"But..." Whatever Batrice would have said next was driven clean out of her mind by the tortured groan that emerged from the basket on the seat beside her.

When she first stepped into the coach, Batrice had paid very little attention to the basket. It was large and bore the royal seal, and she assumed it contained whatever gifts Lady Norelle had seen fit to send for her grandmother's enjoyment.

But apparently, she'd been wrong. When the groan was followed by an earsplitting howl, Batrice jumped back, Coralynne shrieked, and the carriage came to an abrupt stop in the middle of the road.

Rupert's dark, disapproving head appeared in the window, and Coralynne hastily pulled her hood back up. "Something wrong, my lady?"

Batrice showed all of her teeth in a bright but probably unconvincing smile. "I don't know," she said, edging back towards the basket warily. "I don't suppose Lady Norelle told you exactly what she was sending to my grandmother?"

His expression didn't change. "I'm here to ensure your safety, Miss Reyard, not be privy to the contents of baskets. Perhaps the sensible thing to do would be to open it?"

Was that sarcasm? Batrice almost laughed in delight at the discovery that her astonishingly attractive guard was capable of such a thing.

"But it howled," she said instead, allowing herself to sound far more plaintive than she was feeling. "Baskets are wonderful things, to be sure, but I'm not entirely comfortable with them howling at me. Do you think you could look? Just to ease my mind?"

With utterly exquisite timing, the basket wobbled on the seat, drawing a squeak from Coralynne and another imploring look from Batrice, directed at her reluctant knight.

Who stared at her a moment longer, until one eyebrow twitched so minutely Batrice wouldn't have noticed if she hadn't been watching for it.

"Of course, my lady."

She thought she heard his teeth grind together as he opened the door, leaned in, and flipped up one side of the basket's lid.

A floppy-eared golden head with a squashed nose and enormous, permanently startled dark eyes popped out of the basket and stared around at its bemused audience.

"Oh, good heavens." Batrice eyed the creature balefully. "It's a dog."

"Yes," Rupert said, carefully and distinctly. "It's a dog. Perhaps we could get underway again now that we've established this fact?"

"But why is there a dog?" Batrice thought it a rather important question.

Rupert cast his eyes heavenward as if imploring some sort of divine assistance. "Because someone put the dog in the basket, my lady. May I instruct John to drive on now?"

Batrice peered out the window past him at the city street, where a curious crowd was beginning to gather.

"Oh," she said. "Of course. And thank you so much for your assistance." She smiled so sweetly no one could ever have mistaken it for sincerity.

Rupert drew back, muttering, mounted his horse, and motioned for John to continue.

Having needled the poor man enough for one moment, Batrice turned her attention back to their unexpected companion and frowned at the furry little intruder.

"He's so sweet," Coralynne exclaimed, leaning forward on the seat and removing her hood again.

"Hah." Batrice folded her arms against the wiles of the revolting little creature. "I promise it's not sweet. It's a lap dog. They're vile little minions of evil who live only to torture you."

"No, they're not," Coralynne said, in the silly, sappy voice people so often used on babies and puppies. "He's just a sweet boy, isn't he?" The dog put its front feet on the edge of the basket and wagged its tail at the sound of Coralynne's endearments, revealing that someone had dressed it in an enormous ruffled collar decorated by a shiny silver ball.

Batrice held back a gag. "I suppose it's possible he's not yet completely corrupted, but every lap dog I ever met eventually became a monster of gargantuan proportions. Give me a proper big dog instead, or better yet, a cat. Besides"—and this was the most alarming part—"my grandmother hates dogs. I don't know why Lady Norelle would have assumed she wanted one. Or what we're going to do once my grandmother finds out we have him."

They'd been on the road for all of three minutes, and somehow this trip was already becoming complicated. There was still an entire week's journey ahead, over bad roads through deep woods with no doubt numerous stops at less-than-reputable inns. With an aspiring novelist, an uptight guard, and a howling puppy.

Batrice settled into her seat, propped up her feet on the opposite cushions and grinned. Unless she was very much mistaken in her companions, the potential for chaos was considerable, and prospects for catastrophe nearly endless. This might just be the best seven days she'd had in ages.

CHAPTER 3

Their first stop was at an inn, perhaps thirty miles outside of Evenleigh. Coralynne's enthusiasm for travel had dimmed somewhat as the roads turned from cobblestone to dirt—even in a well-sprung royal carriage there was a fair bit of jolting, and Batrice resisted the temptation to inform her that their journey would only grow more uncomfortable along the way.

She had personally traveled in far worse, and anyway, she was almost wholly occupied with deciding how she was going to manage their unexpected furry companion. They'd been forced to stop four times for him to relieve himself, and that only after he'd used the floor of the carriage when they'd failed to anticipate his needs. Batrice did not expect to find very many innkeepers who would be thrilled at the idea of a dog in their rooms, let alone an incontinent one that was given to highly excitable barking.

The only thing that seemed to keep him quiet and entertained for any length of time was chewing—as evidenced by the state of her hem and her bootlaces. So when they pulled to a stop for the evening in front of a large, bustling inn, it was out of sheer desperation that Batrice dropped the puppy back into the basket and threw her handkerchief in after him before closing the lid.

When Coralynne raised a scandalized brow, Batrice laid a finger across her lips. "We can't have him howling, can we?" she hissed as the coach door opened.

Coralynne shrugged and followed her out the door, stumbling a little when her feet hit the ground.

Batrice almost felt sorry for her. It was obvious her new "maid" hadn't traveled much and was somewhat unprepared for the rigors of a long coach journey. But really, she probably should have asked more questions before inviting herself along. It was a considerable mercy that neither of them seemed susceptible to traveling-sickness.

Thanks to the royal crest on the carriage doors, the innkeeper showed a gratifying degree of deference from the moment Batrice crossed the threshold.

"And how may I be of service, my lady?" He bobbed a bow and smiled through a red bush of a beard.

"A room, sir, for myself and my maid, plus another for my guard and my driver, if you please." Batrice hoped she'd managed a reasonable imitation of the royal tone—polite and distant, without being condescending. Acting the part of a noblewoman on the stage generally involved more overacting than anything else, and would hardly be appropriate when she was traveling in a Tremontaine coach.

"Of course, my lady, of course. Adjoining rooms on the second floor. And will you be needing supper in your rooms?"

"That would be delightful," Batrice replied, without a shred of conviction as she glanced mournfully around the common room. She would have greatly preferred to eat with the others and enjoy the convivial atmosphere, but she could hardly abandon Coralynne in their room with the dog. "My guard and driver will, of course, make their own preferences known."

Rupert and John would probably choose to eat in company, but one never knew—perhaps they were sullen loners who preferred to eat in silence. Though Batrice strongly suspected not. With their looks, they would no doubt be quite popular with the female guests.

After a grateful smile at the innkeeper, Batrice followed what appeared to be one of his numerous red-headed progeny up the stairs to a spacious room on the second floor. There were two beds, and a cheerful fire already crackled on the hearth.

"Well, this is nice," she observed, setting down her handbag and taking off her cloak as Coralynne collapsed onto one of the beds with a groan. "Why don't you have a bit of a rest while I nip downstairs to ask one of the men to bring up the basket first thing?"

Coralynne waved a hand from the bed but said nothing, so Batrice descended the stairs alone and glanced about her, hoping for a glimpse of her fellow travelers.

When she peeked into the common room, it was about half full, and there were several boisterous conversations in progress. A large elderly man in a wig sat by the fire, waving a cane through the air to punctuate whatever tale he was sharing with the pair of finely dressed young men seated opposite, while a third young man wearing a somewhat old-fashioned coat and muddy boots leaned on the mantle. An older woman in a startling yellow dress held court at the nearest table, complaining loudly about her meal, opposite a handful of unshaven locals wearing rough clothing. They were gathered around another table where they appeared to be engaging in a game of dice, right beside two middle-aged women in plain, dark cloaks, who sat eating their dinner with single-minded focus. Near a pile of baggage in one corner, a demure young blonde sat beside a statuesque older woman still wearing her traveling cloak and gazing balefully about the room as if she expected to be attacked at any moment.

Batrice was taking in the scene with cheerful interest when she was jostled rudely by a man just entering through the front door of the inn. He had dark hair and wore a dark cloak, and instead of apologizing, he sneered down at her and held his cloak a little closer.

"I suggest you stop blocking the passageway unless you're prepared to be trampled," he said icily. "Did your mother never teach you that lurking in doorways is only practiced by ill-mannered children?"

Batrice heard a gasp from someone, probably the blonde girl's chaperone, though she couldn't tell whether it was directed at her or at the man who accosted her.

"Oh, you poor thing," Batrice said, looking up at the dark-haired man with a slight curl to her lip. "Did someone spit in your beer, or are you always this rude?"

The glare she received in return should probably have sent her scurrying in the opposite direction, but she'd never quite learnt the trick of being intimidated by such behavior. "I feel," she observed after a moment, "as though you're expecting me to do something. Do be so kind as to tell me what it is so I can decide whether to laugh or to go on doing as I please without reference to your high-handed whims."

"Perhaps," the man answered in chilling tones, "you should close your mouth until you understand exactly whom you are addressing."

"I'm addressing a total boor," Batrice threw back at him, just as the innkeeper appeared from somewhere—looking pale beneath his beard— and Rupert came across the threshold holding the puppy's basket as far from his body as possible. John followed close behind, carrying her trunk.

"I believe this is yours, my lady," Rupert said, holding out the basket.

"Oh, thank you, Rupert," she said sweetly. "Do be a dear and take it upstairs to my room."

"Do you intend to let these persons stay at your inn?" the dark-haired man snapped at the innkeeper.

"They have been entered in the book, sir, and already paid for a room." There was sweat running into that red beard now.

"I'm sorry, is there a problem?" Batrice murmured demurely.

"No, no problem at all—" the innkeeper began to say.

"The problem is with your abysmal standards," the dark-haired man

29

interrupted. "I shall have to take myself elsewhere if this yapping, inconsiderate schoolgirl is your idea of genteel clientele."

"I'll have to ask you to treat the lady with respect," Rupert interjected with a hint of steel in his voice, managing to look quite threatening despite the basket still dangling from his hand.

Batrice decided he was even more handsome when he was looming dangerously.

"Might we adjourn to the parlor to continue this conversation," the innkeeper pleaded, looking around at his other guests, an expression of panic on his gradually reddening face.

"I refuse to adjourn anywhere, and if this is how you treat a marquess, I will ensure that your pathetic establishment is never again patronized by anyone of rank or importance."

"But..." the innkeeper said, pointing at Batrice.

"Oh, I hardly think..." Batrice added.

"Yes, you hardly think," the dark-haired man snapped, taking a step towards her.

Rupert dropped the basket and reached for his sword. The puppy yelped, the basket opened, and Batrice made a dive for the furry little nuisance while the innkeeper clutched at his beard and let loose a rather rude word. One of the females behind them in the common room shrieked in shock—either at the word or the puppy—loudly enough to set everyone's ears ringing.

"How dare you draw on a peer of the realm!" The marquess was ready to be affronted, but the puppy had escaped, and no one took any further notice.

"Isn't it a darling!" the young blonde woman exclaimed, dropping to her knees on the floor, much to the horror of her chaperone. The puppy ambled up to her, utterly unaware of the commotion he was causing, and planted his paws squarely on the front of her dress.

The screeches of the woman in yellow rose over the din as she pointed at the dog, demanding that it be put "Out! Out! Out!"

"You can't bring that in here," the innkeeper groaned.

"Anetta, get off the floor this instant!" the young woman's chaperone insisted, while the marquess gathered his cloak and turned dramatically towards the door.

"I am finished with this farce," he proclaimed, in a dramatic tone that really required a curling mustache to render it believable.

"Please, your lordship, if you will only wait for a moment, we will sort it all out, I promise you." The poor landlord followed his prized guest toward the door while casting beseeching glances back over his shoulder.

Rupert had replaced his sword and was now looking at Batrice with almost puzzled exasperation.

"I'm not the one who dropped the basket," she pointed out innocently—and truthfully—before hurrying after the dog.

Who was by now frolicking closer to the fire, entranced by the flames and encouraged by the laughter of the two expensively dressed young men, who seemed to be enjoying the whole scene.

But it was the one in the old-fashioned coat who simply reached down, grasped the ruffled collar and plucked the pup from the floor, holding it up to gaze with mock sternness into its panting face. "Very ill-done of you, young one," he said mildly, before tucking it against his chest and turning to Batrice.

"Yours, is it?" he inquired, looking down at her with laughing brown eyes.

Batrice discovered that she had to force herself to pull air into her lungs. The man was young, as she'd thought, perhaps only a few years older than she, with longish light-brown hair tied back from his face in a neat tail. And oh, dear, that face. It was handsome, but not too much so, with warmth and amusement in just the right proportions. And beneath his overlarge and somewhat shabby coat, his shoulders were broad enough to suggest strength, while the hands that held the puppy and toyed with the silver ball on its collar were...

Batrice had always felt the need to observe a man's hands before she decided what to think of him. Were they stained with dirt or ink? Calloused from labor or skill? Or dainty, pale, and soft? The hands of a workman, or the hands of a courtier? Not that there was anything wrong with being either a workman or a courtier, but the observation did help her form an appropriate perspective on any new acquaintance.

This man had perfect hands—strong and slightly tanned, with neatly trimmed nails and work-roughened skin...

And she was staring, which would never, ever do.

"I would be delighted to say that I've never seen the creature before," she replied at last, with a sigh that was midway between admiration and regret. "And it truly isn't mine, but I fear it did, in fact, arrive with me, so I suppose I owe the proprietor an apology for disrupting his business, and the guests an apology for interrupting their evening."

"I suppose you do," the man said, eyes twinkling in a way that suggested he hadn't minded having his evening interrupted. "Had you intended to stay in this charming establishment for the night?"

"Do you think there is any amount of groveling that would induce the innkeeper to allow it?" she responded, looking back over her shoulder at the chaos and wincing.

"Depends," he said, smiling a bit as he held the puppy out for her to take.

"On what?"

"On whether you're a more distinguished guest than the one you offended."

Batrice considered that as she observed the growing crowd of disgruntled guests surrounding the innkeeper. On the one hand, she'd arrived in a royal carriage, but the offended gentleman had been an actual marquess, while she was technically nobody.

Before she could reach a conclusion, Rupert strode across the room and held out his hands for the pup with a dark glance at both her and her bene-factor. "We've been asked to leave as soon as possible," he said grimly. "They've sent someone up to fetch your maid."

"Well, I guess that answers that," Batrice said brightly, as Rupert turned and stalked off towards the door.

"Your husband?"

Batrice felt her mouth drop open for a moment before she was able to recover from her shock.

"Him?" A laugh escaped her. "Most definitely not. He's my guard."

"Ah." Her companion shot her a piercing look that took her little more than an instant to interpret.

"And no, I'm not being a snob about his birth or his occupation. I know nothing about his family, and he's really quite attractive—I'm simply not in the market for a husband who disapproves of everything about me and wishes I would stop making his life difficult."

"Are you?"

"Making his life difficult?" Batrice laughed. "Probably, yes. But, thus far at least, not exactly on purpose."

"Well, I'm happy to have met you, Miss..."

He was obviously finished with the conversation. Batrice forced a smile onto her face. "Reyard," she said, with a perfunctory curtsey.

The gentleman bowed in a manner as old-fashioned as his coat, and yet it seemed to suit him perfectly. "I hope your journey proves less eventful in the future."

He turned and strolled away, leaving Batrice to stare after him, confu-sion furrowing her brow. He'd been friendly up until Rupert's interruption. Perhaps he hadn't wanted to be involved in her troubles with the innkeeper—tainted by association as it were. Or perhaps he'd merely been polite up until that point and now had better places to be.

Looking around her, Batrice supposed she might have wanted to escape the situation too. There were no fewer than three arguments in progress—two featuring hysterical tears—broken dishes in the hall, and at least one guest carrying hastily stuffed bags and declaring his intention to depart that very instant.

Batrice didn't mind a bit of chaos, but she preferred it to be intentional. This time, at least, it hadn't actually been her fault, and yet she sensed she would be the one blamed anyway.

Just then, a blinking Coralynne appeared in the door to the common room, brushing back her tangled curls, her eyes wide and mouth open as she took in the commotion.

"Why didn't you tell me?" she wailed. "All of this perfectly good material and I missed it!"

Batrice groaned and went to patch things up as best she could, while putting off Coralynne's questions and glancing about occasionally to see if she could catch a glimpse of the handsome guest in the old-fashioned coat.

She was so busy bargaining for a cold supper and ensuring they retrieved all their bags, it didn't occur to her until the carriage was rolling away from the inn that the man had deliberately failed to tell her his name.

Dusk was already falling when they took to the road again, and Batrice might have grown sleepy but for Coralynne's insistence that she be told *everything* about the confrontation, only to grow despondent as she realized the full scope of what had occurred.

"It was perfect," the pretend maid said mournfully. "Such a marvelous addition to my book, with a caped villain and a handsome hero, and I wasn't even there to see it."

"Yes, well, I assure you it wasn't quite so pleasant to experience as it is to hear about," Batrice muttered. "The villain didn't even have the decency to have a mustache, and the hero couldn't be bothered to introduce himself properly." After those tantalizing details, she was forced to resign herself to fielding ever more precise questions about the scene, down to the color of the chaperone's dress and the style of the young gentlemen's cravats.

It was full dark before they pulled up in front of a much smaller, less well-kept hostelry in the next town.

When Rupert opened the door, his expression was even more grim than usual.

"The dog stays in the stables with the horses," he said sternly. "There are no decent inns for the next twenty miles, and it's too dangerous for the horses to continue on."

"Couldn't agree more," Batrice said, clutching her handbag and descending the steps with a profound sense of relief. She'd been afraid they might not find anywhere to stay that night.

"Miss Reyard," Rupert added, "I must ask that you consider the damage you could be doing to reputations beyond your own by your ill-considered speech and behavior."

"I beg your pardon?" For a guard, he certainly made himself free with his opinions.

"A little discretion would not have gone amiss in your conversation with the gentleman at our last stop."

"He ran into *me*," she snapped, feeling unjustly accused. "And then had the nerve to be angry with me for being in his way. What would you have had me do?"

"I wasn't talking about the marquess," Rupert replied in chilling tones.

What was he talking about? The man who had returned the puppy? She had done nothing beyond three minutes conversation. She hadn't even flirted.

"I didn't..." she spluttered, but he was already striding off to alert the innkeeper to their arrival.

John climbed down from his perch, glanced her way, then turned to the horses. "Don't mind Rupert, Miss," he said in a low voice, his eyes on the ground. "Being suspicious of strangers... it's his business. His job to protect you. Not fond of the unexpected, that's all."

Batrice blinked at what she was forced to admit was probably wise advice from a most unexpected source.

"Thank you, John. I appreciate your candor."

He didn't turn to acknowledge her, reinforcing her suspicion that he was probably shy. A pity too. With his well-defined jaw and broad shoulders, he could have drawn a great deal of female attention had he been willing to speak up for himself. He was observant though, which Batrice had learned to appreciate in a man.

"And I will consider what you've said," she added thoughtfully, in the general direction of his back.

The driver nodded and moved off to the horses' heads without further comment.

An introspective frown firmly in place, Batrice adjusted her cloak and headed inside, more than ready to be finished traveling for the day so she could think through everything that had occurred since she'd departed Evenburg.

Mercifully, it didn't take long for them to get settled in their rooms, though Batrice thought that was probably because the dark, run-down, out-of-the-way inn had few patrons and even fewer luxuries. As she and Coralynne entered their tiny chamber at the top of the stairs, she mourned the cheerful fire that had already been burning at their last stop. This room was cold and dark but for a single candle, with only one bed, a cracked mirror, and a narrow window that permitted a chill breeze to enter, whistling as it made its way through gaps in the frame.

"Oh, this is perfect," Coralynne said, lowering her hood and beaming as she took in the unwelcoming sight. "Exactly the sort of room I would have imagined."

"Imagined for what?"

"Oh, you can't have much of a story in a perfectly warm, safe room at a busy, popular inn," Coralynne explained. "There has to be some hardship, or no one will care what happens to the heroine. In a dark, creaky inn, there are all manner of dramatic possibilities. There could be secret passages, ghosts, or a thieving innkeeper waiting to steal her purse, so she has to continue on her journey with no money. She might hear someone sneaking towards her room in the dark. Or sense something lurking outside the window."

"But we're on the second floor," Batrice pointed out.

Coralynne fixed her with an imperious stare. "Which can be reached easily by a villain with no scruples about climbing up to the roof."

Batrice shivered a bit in spite of herself. She had no particular fear of staying in less than reputable places—after all, her acting troupe had often been unable to afford even inns as nice as this one—but she'd never really bothered to imagine all of the things that might have happened. Neither dirt nor darkness had ever troubled her much.

But now that Coralynne mentioned it...

No. It was rather ridiculous, really. What purpose could a villain have for pursuing a pair of young women who obviously had nothing to steal?

While John was bringing up Coralynne's bag and Batrice's trunk, a young boy slunk in to start a fire in the tiny grate. He muttered sullenly the entire time, leaving them with a fitful flame that nearly smoked them out of the room before Batrice took over. Fortunately, she had plenty of experience with keeping up a fire.

In the meantime, Coralynne had removed her bonnet, retrieved her journal, and was sitting on the bed scribbling furiously. "I really have to get down all the details of the day," she explained, "before I forget. So much has happened. And I don't want to miss describing this room."

Resigned to her "maid's" peculiarities, Batrice lit a second candle and placed it on the washstand, near Coralynne's side of the bed. Then she went to open her trunk, hoping to still get a decent night's rest in spite of the hour. This inn would no doubt grow too loud for sleep well before the sun peeked over the tops of the trees.

But when she opened her trunk, all thought of sleep disappeared.

Instead of neat piles of folded gowns and carefully placed shoes, there was a jumbled up heap of all her belongings. Her dresses were not only tangled, they were smudged and crumpled, and the box with her combs and pins had been dumped to mingle with the rest of the trunk's contents.

"Coralynne," she said carefully, "did you get into my trunk earlier?"

"Why would I have gotten into your trunk?" The older girl didn't even lift her head from her journal. "My bag was in the carriage, and besides, your trunk was strapped on the roof all day."

That was true. Perhaps it had fallen when John was getting it down at the last stop, and everything had been shaken up by the process of returning it to the roof.

But no. Her gray reticule had been on the bottom of the trunk, next to her silk slippers, and it was now on top. One slipper was still on the bottom of the trunk and the other... Batrice began sorting through her dresses, refolding the majority and setting a few aside to be cleaned.

But the other slipper was missing.

A chill swept over her as she accepted the undeniable truth—someone had searched her things.

But who? And, perhaps more importantly, why?

She acknowledged that it couldn't very well have been Coralynne. The two of them had been together all day, except for the brief period where Batrice had left her in the room at the last inn. That had certainly not been long enough for her to have snuck out and searched a trunk, even if it had been accessible, and during the short time after John had brought the trunk into the inn, there had been too many people about for a thorough search to be feasible.

There had also been a few moments where they'd stopped to allow the puppy to attend to its personal needs, but Batrice had never gone far, and besides, either Rupert or John would have noticed if Coralynne had been rummaging about in the luggage.

Although if they truly believed her to be Batrice's maid, they might have thought it perfectly normal.

Then again, what about Rupert or John? Either of them would have had sufficient opportunity to search the trunk, but why would they have bothered? Batrice was no one important, and it was Rupert who was handling the money for the journey. Perhaps they had believed her to be carrying jewelry, but she really couldn't imagine Lady Norelle entrusting her safety to anyone she suspected of being a thief.

So who else could it have been? Someone at the previous inn, perhaps? Could her trunk have been sitting unwatched for longer than she realized? If it had, that broadened the possibilities a great deal, to once again include Coralynne.

Feeling significantly disturbed, Batrice repacked as best she could, hesitating a bit when she pulled out her nightgown. Did she really want to be caught in a state of undress if the mysterious thief made another attempt while they were sleeping?

After a brief glance at Coralynne, she decided that spending all day with a novelist had made her entirely too jumpy. Thieves did not generally crawl through windows to ransack the belongings of innocent young women, any more than ghosts roamed the narrow hallways hoping to inspire terror.

Grinning sheepishly, Batrice began to get ready for bed. The last thing she saw before she fell asleep was Coralynne, biting her lip and filling up the pages of her journal by the flickering light of the candle.

CHAPTER 4

The night passed without incident, and Batrice slept surprisingly well, awakening only when the innkeeper pounded on the door to announce that their carriage was ready and they'd best hurry if they wanted breakfast before they departed.

She and Coralynne hastened through their morning toilette, put up each other's hair, and prepared their bags to be taken down.

As an extra precaution, Batrice tied a bit of string across the latch of her trunk so she would be able to tell at a glance whether it had been opened. She should be able to check it each time they stopped to determine whether it had been meddled with.

Breakfast was warm but tasteless porridge, eaten in the inn's dark, smoky common room, and Batrice was only too happy to escape, hoping for better things the next night. As soon as she entered the inn yard, Rupert approached, the puppy's basket in hand and a grim expression shadowing his delightful features. It was really too bad, that tendency to frown. Batrice thought she could have become somewhat obsessed with staring at him, had he not insisted on ruining his good looks with such a grim outlook.

"Did you sleep well?" Batrice asked brightly, and received a glare in return. That was probably a no.

"Did the dog have breakfast?"

With another glare, the basket was thrust in her direction. "Take it. And keep it out of my sight."

She flipped up the lid of the basket and was rewarded by a sunny expression on the pup's golden-furred face as it looked up from chewing on a... was that a *pig's foot*? Batrice shut the basket firmly and decided she didn't want to know. It was happy and therefore not yowling, which was all that mattered.

John was checking the horses' harness, so Batrice approached him and tried not to look threatening.

"Did something happen last night?" she asked carefully, quietly enough that Rupert would not be able to overhear.

"Pup didn't sleep well," John reported, with a quick glance in her direction that revealed a tiny smile beneath the beard. "Howled a fair bit. Got out of his basket and chewed up a boot."

Well, that would explain Rupert's mood. Batrice edged closer to where the guard was busy tightening his cinch and eyed his footwear surreptitiously. It didn't take long to determine that the top of one boot was indeed decorated with tiny teeth marks and missing a few bits of leather.

She thought about insisting that he had no reason to be grumpy with *her* about it, but judged it a lost cause. Rupert was already convinced of her perfidy and wasn't likely to care whether the puppy had been her idea or not. It was her fault he was here at all.

Before she could attempt a conciliating gesture, Coralynne emerged from the front door of the inn, looking bright and sunny and cheerful.

"Good morning," she called, before Batrice could head her off or warn her that their traveling companion was not exactly in the mood for pleasantries.

But Rupert looked up from his work, crossed the yard, and took Coralynne's arm with an actual, genuine smile. "Good morning, Miss Smythe. I trust you rested well. Allow me to assist you into the carriage."

Batrice's jaw dropped.

Her eyes narrowed as Rupert escorted Coralynne to the carriage, opened the door, lowered the step, and handed her in with a polite smile and a nod. He looked at Batrice, then returned to his horse with a deliberate stride and utterly ignored her.

So that was how he wanted to proceed. It was obvious the man was trying to make a point, and while she was happy he was treating her "maid" with courtesy, it rankled a bit that he seemed to blame Batrice for everything. Or at least to actively dislike her.

Could he have been the one responsible for upending her trunk? It seemed petty and mean spirited for a man Lizbet Norelle had entrusted with her protégée's safety.

As John ascended the box and Rupert mounted his gray, Batrice helped herself into the carriage and wondered whether the remaining six days would prove to be as eventful as the first.

It didn't take long for her to discover that eventful was not always a good thing. About the time their path split from the main road and headed down a shadowed forest track, the clouds began to lower and darken, and by midday, rain was spattering on the coach windows.

Batrice halted the coach long enough to suggest that Rupert join them inside, where he would at least stay dry, but he shook his head, wrapped himself in an oilskin cloak and continued on. She knew it had to be miserable—she'd traveled in the rain and always hated the feeling of cold, damp clothes and the icy rivulets that found the gap between collar and neck with unerring accuracy.

But he was determined, and it wasn't as if it would help them to stop—the road would only grow more difficult with time.

They slogged on for a few more miles, while the puppy snoozed and Coralynne gazed dreamily out the window at the rain. Batrice found herself growing more and more agitated, and eventually called Rupert over to the window again.

"Are you certain we shouldn't stop?" she asked. "I'm afraid of either miring the coach or injuring a horse if this rain continues."

"Wouldn't dream of stopping, my lady," he said, with a hint of mockery. "Only imagine what might happen if we were unable to continue. You could end up out of doors in the rain, overnight, with no silk sheets or china teacups to comfort you."

"If I had a china teacup, I would throw it at your head," she snapped, causing his eyes to widen. "Believe it or not, I'm concerned with the safety of the horses and the driver."

Rupert shook his head, apparently choosing to ignore her outburst. "We could be stuck for days if we don't keep moving. There's a village in a valley only a few miles ahead. We'll stop there."

Batrice settled back in her seat with a scowl, hoping he knew what he was talking about.

Their pace slowed for a bit as the horses made their way up an incline, then started down into what she assumed was the valley Rupert had mentioned. A glance out the window made it appear they were about halfway down, right before a sudden crack of thunder startled her back into her seat. The coach jerked, the puppy began to whine from his spot on the cushion next to Coralynne, and suddenly the coach was hurtling forward, slewing from side to side in the mud and throwing all three of its occupants violently around the inside.

"Don't worry," Batrice panted from where she'd landed on the floor, bracing her feet against the door and trying not to wince. She'd landed awkwardly on her arm, and while it wasn't broken, it was most certainly bruised. "The horses were probably just startled by the thunder. John will get them back under control."

She could hear him shouting, but the carriage didn't seem to slow. If anything, it gained speed until she heard panicked-sounding shouts followed by a bump and a sickening crack. They rolled on, but roughly, until the coach jerked hard, as though it had collided with something. It slowed abruptly, and tilted dangerously to one side before settling back on its wheels and finally coming to a stop.

Batrice took a deep, shuddering breath and got to her feet, helping Coralynne regain her seat and placing the shivering puppy in the older girl's lap.

"What was that noise?" Coralynne asked, looking pale and shaking visibly.

"Might have broken an axle," Batrice answered, though that didn't explain the collision. "If you're uninjured, I'll get out and see what's going on."

Coralynne settled back in her seat. "All right," she whispered, cuddling the puppy closer and reaching for her bag.

The moment Batrice descended from the step, her cloak wrapped tightly around her, she sank ankle deep in mud. The rain was still falling, and neither Rupert nor John was anywhere in sight until she walked behind the carriage and realized what had made that terrible noise—they'd encountered another vehicle, and violently from the look of things.

Two tall, powerfully built horses stood by the side of the road, their traces cut to separate them from what had probably once been a phaeton but was now little more than a pile of splinters. And lying next to that pile was a...

"Good gracious," Batrice exclaimed, forgetting the mud and running forward until she came to a stop beside John. "Is he going to be all right?"

The driver of the phaeton had not escaped the accident. He'd been thrown clear, but his eyes were closed, and blood covered the side of his head.

"Don't touch that..." Rupert started to say, but it was much too late, and Batrice wouldn't have listened anyway.

She dropped to her knees in the muck and yanked off her cloak. The soft white wool was already liberally bedecked with mud around the hem, but the hood was still clean, so Batrice wadded it tightly and pressed it against the injured man's head.

"Do we have bandages?" she asked.

"I'll check," John said quietly, and squelched off through the mud.

"My lady, you're ruining your clothing, and we don't even know what sort of man this is," Rupert pointed out, until Batrice shot him a glare worthy of her grandmother.

"He's unconscious and injured because we ran into him. Someone needs to stop the bleeding, and there's no one else to help him but us."

"He was the one who stopped in the middle of the road," Rupert said stiffly.

"And if our horses weren't completely out of control, he would have had time to move," she reminded him, wiping the blood from the injured man's forehead with her cloak. "Besides, I do know what sort of man this is."

"How could you possibly?"

"He's the sort of man who would rescue a puppy," she said, with a stab of worry as she gazed down on the face of her acquaintance from the night before.

But, rather than softening, Rupert crossed his arms and managed to look even more forbidding than before.

"And I don't suppose it occurred to you to wonder what he might be doing out here?"

"Perhaps the same thing *we're* doing out here?" Batrice really couldn't help her sarcasm. "If you're suggesting that he's following us, might I point out that he was here first? And it's a bit ridiculous to suspect the poor man of having purposefully caused an accident that nearly killed him."

"I didn't say anything about him getting hurt on purpose." Rupert eyed her grimly. "Only that it's hardly the main road."

"Maybe he has a dying grandmother too," Batrice retorted. "I don't see how it matters why he's here unless we take steps to ensure he doesn't bleed to death."

"No bandages," John reported, slogging through the mud in her direction.

"Is the axle broken?" she asked, almost afraid to hear the answer.

John looked surprised at her question but had no encouragement to offer. "Aye," he said grimly. "The horses spooked badly, and we hit a bit of a tree that had fallen across the road. Probably what stopped the gentleman before us. Just didn't have time to clear before we were on top of him."

Batrice nodded and continued to wipe the blood from the unconscious man's head. She still couldn't find where the blood was coming from, which might be a good sign. If the bleeding had stopped, they could move him out of the rain until he regained consciousness.

"Rupert," she said, "you and John help me, please. We need to get him inside the coach."

"We cannot possibly allow a stranger into the coach with you and your maid," Rupert replied coolly. "And in case you weren't aware, a broken axle means we won't be going anywhere until it's mended."

"Yes," Batrice acknowledged, praying silently for patience, "I am aware. However, none of us are going to be traveling in this much rain, and this man could be badly injured. How can we possibly be heartless enough to leave him out here instead of allowing him to rest and recover inside?"

Rupert's answering expression was unreadable, but at length, he nodded. Together, he and John lifted the unconscious man and carried him none too gently across the muddy ground towards the coach. When

Batrice flung open the door, Coralynne looked up, startled, from the pages of her journal.

"Oh gracious," she said, setting it aside and shifting as far from the door as possible. "What's happened?"

"We collided with another vehicle, and the driver is injured," Batrice informed her.

It took some grunting and mild swearing on the part of Rupert and John, but they were able to deposit their burden on the seat opposite Coralynne, whose eyes were round and nearly as startled-looking as the dog's.

"I'll take his horses and head for the village," Rupert informed them immediately after. "There should be some sort of cart there that I can rent to convey you ladies someplace warm and dry while we see to the repair of the coach and find a doctor for... this other fellow."

Batrice could only glance doubtfully at the thick woods surrounding their position. She wasn't sure what sort of village they might find out here, or how far it would prove to be, let alone whether there would be anyone willing and able to repair the axle of the carriage.

"Thank you," she said, despite her misgivings. "I'm sure we'll be quite safe here."

"John will be nearby, so you need only shout if he wakes up and tries anything."

Batrice almost chuckled, but didn't think Rupert would appreciate any humor she might find in the situation.

"We'll be sure to do so," she replied solemnly, drawing a suspicious stare from the guard, but as she was, apparently, agreeing with him, there was little he could do but stalk off, muttering under his breath.

Batrice shut the door of the coach and settled gingerly onto the cushion next to Coralynn, who had picked up her journal and appeared to be preparing to write in it again, her inkwell balanced one corner of the page.

"How can you possibly write anything at a time like this?" Batrice wanted to know, eyeing the puppy, who had approached the stranger's boots and was sniffing curiously at the mud on the bottom of them.

"How could I possibly *not* write at a time like this?" Coralynne returned calmly. "We're in a storm, in the middle of a dark and forbidding forest, and have suffered a mysterious accident. Abandoned to our fate by our sole protector, we must wait in trepidation, with no company but a sinister stranger who may only be feigning unconsciousness in order to learn our secrets."

"Or," Batrice said, "we're just cold, wet, and muddy, our carriage is broken, and we may have accidentally killed an innocent man."

"Have you no romance in your soul?" Coralynne protested. "Can't you imagine the possibilities?"

Yes, she could. Only too well. But that didn't mean she had to allow her imagination to dictate any of her actions.

"I'm quite romantic enough, thank you very much," she said lightly. "For example, I've noticed that our driver and our guard are both very handsome and that you blush quite perfectly any time one of them is in the vicinity."

"Hah," Coralynne said, her cheeks turning pink as she returned her gaze to the pages of her journal. "I suppose it's no good denying that they're handsome, but it's no use. I believe Rupert is quite besotted with you."

Batrice couldn't help a peal of laughter. "Rupert? Besotted? He loathes me, and is five times more polite to you."

"Ahah," Coralynne said, stabbing her pen at Batrice. "It's all a ruse, you know. He's pretending not to be interested because he knows there's too great a difference in your station, and doesn't believe you could ever return his feelings."

"His feelings?" Batrice scoffed. "We've known one another barely more than a day."

"Sometimes, that's all love requires," Coralynne responded serenely.

"And who's to say he hasn't seen you around the palace? Glimpsed your beauty from afar and wished for a chance to know you?"

"*I'm* to say," Batrice argued. "I mean, look at me—my hair is plain, straight, and brown, my eyes are brown, and my face is hardly beautiful enough to inspire such irrational behavior. Besides, he's been nothing but disagreeable since our journey began."

"Oh no," Coralynne corrected. "Your hair is the rich hue of a newly turned field in the spring, and your eyes shine like polished acorns in autumn. Your skin glows with the innocent blush of youth, while your manner is that of a confident and accomplished woman. In a word, irresistible."

Batrice's mouth dropped open. "So my hair looks like dirt and my eyes remind you of squirrel fodder?"

Coralynne grinned and returned to her writing.

Not sure whether it would be more appropriate to laugh or be offended, Batrice deliberately shifted the conversation away from herself. "If Rupert is in love with *me*," she inquired, unable to resist finding out what other ideas might be running amok on the pages of that journal, "what of John? He's quite handsome too, and very strong. A bit reticent, but that's not always a bad thing."

"Oh, no." Coralynne didn't even lift her head. "He's quietly devoted to your safety. He knows you'll never see him as anything but a driver, but prefers it that way, as his heart was broken long ago, and he's sworn never to love again."

This time, Batrice did laugh. "I can't help but admire your imagination," she said, "even if I am forced to disagree with your assertions. And what of our strange companion here? What sort of romantic tragedy would you imagine for him?"

"Why, he's the villain of the piece, of course."

Batrice looked at the man's face, free now from blood, and wondered. Could Coralynne and Rupert be right? Could there be something sinister about his perfect hands and his gorgeous brown eyes? She hoped not. "He doesn't look all that villainous to me," she remarked casually.

"Oh, but it would never do if we could tell he was the villain right away. A story requires some mystery. Perhaps he's a spy, well-practiced in deceiving others and convincing them of his innocence. The reader must be captivated by wondering whether the innocent maidens will be devoured by the wolf, or whether they will be rescued in time by their dashing cavaliers."

Batrice couldn't help laughing again at the idea of John the Coachman as a dashing anything.

"I really can't wait to read this story of yours," she said. "Though I hope I have more to do in it than play the innocent maiden, waiting around to be rescued."

"I'm sure you will," Coralynne assured her. "After all, the heroine must encounter grave danger if there's to be a dramatic climax to the tale."

"You mean, such as being stranded in a wrecked carriage, alone but for a dangerously attractive spy?" she asked.

But it wasn't Coralynne who answered.

"As gratifying as it is to know that you find me attractive, perhaps you'd be good enough to tell me exactly how I came to be in your carriage?"

CHAPTER 5

*B*atrice supposed she should be grateful for proof that she was still quite capable of blushing, thank you very much, despite her family's conviction otherwise.

"You waylaid us," she replied promptly, to cover her embarrassment. "On your great black horse, while wearing a ridiculous mask. I believe you said something silly like 'your money or your life,' before my guard heroically leaped from the top of the coach and pulled you from your steed. When you hit the ground, you struck your head on a rock and were stricken unconscious. My companion and I, being vapid young maidens, found your occupation romantic and took pity on you. We begged that you be allowed to await your fate in the comfort of the coach, rather than lying in the mud while we consider how best to hang you. Which would, of course, be a fittingly romantic way to die, so I hope you won't ruin everything by objecting."

Coralynne ruined it by giggling. "You know, you're really quite good at this," she said in a loud whisper, and commenced scribbling in her journal again.

"Are you sure?" the man said, creases of amusement forming at the corners of his eyes. "I feel certain I would have remembered doing something so utterly nonsensical."

"You did hit your head *very* hard." Batrice smiled serenely and reached down to pick up the puppy, who had begun to lick the mud off the man's boots.

"So there was no downed tree, and I was not very nearly run down by a speeding coach and four?"

"Apparently you didn't hit it quite hard enough," Batrice answered, wondering whether she ought to smile to show that she was kidding. Mostly. "Yes, actually, all of that is true. We're terribly sorry. The horses were spooked by the storm, and our driver didn't see the tree until it was too late."

"Well, neither did I, so it isn't like I'm going to blame your coachman," the man replied, closing his eyes again. "Where are your escorts?"

Batrice's eyes narrowed. "Perhaps Coralynne was right, and you were feigning unconsciousness in order to learn our secrets. Be warned—if you attempt anything untoward, this innocent-looking dog has been trained to lick you to death on command."

"You forget, I've met that dog, my lady. I believe its only talent is creating mayhem."

She held the dog up to her face and peered into its eyes with an exaggerated frown. "Is it true? In that case, I shall temporarily christen you Mayhem. If my grandmother doesn't like it, she can pick out something fluffy and silly-sounding after I'm gone."

At a quickly muffled protest from Coralynne, she added, "Though perhaps I shouldn't have said that. Miss Smythe here believes you are a dastardly villain and a spy, who will only use such confidences against me."

"How exactly could I misuse the information that you have a grandmother?" His eyes were open again, and Batrice found that she couldn't resist the temptation to laugh. Spy or not, at least he had a sense of humor.

"Perhaps," Coralynne interjected, "you could allay our fears by sharing your name."

"I suppose I'm willing to trust you that far," he replied, his lips quirking with amusement, "considering that you were kind enough to allow me to await my hanging out of the rain."

"A lady must always be generous," Batrice informed him piously. "Even to highwaymen."

"As it happens, I'm nothing more interesting than a scholar," he announced, "and my name is Jamie."

Batrice eyed him sharply, then exchanged a skeptical glance with Coralynne. The cut of his coat—which was the same one he'd been wearing the day before—could certainly be explained by a devotion to scholarship rather than fashion, but neither his build nor his hands suggested such a sedentary lifestyle.

"Oh?" Coralynne probably thought she was expressing polite interest, but her face revealed her suspicion. "What do you study?"

Their enigmatic guest smiled. "The unexpected," he said.

"It's quite all right," Batrice said, in an overloud aside to Coralynne. "I'm certain Rupert can find a reason to hang a scholar just as easily as a highwayman."

Then she nodded politely to their guest. "As I mentioned before, my name is Miss Reyard. And Miss Smythe and I are not alone—our coachman is waiting outside with the horses while our guard rides towards the nearest town in search of help. We seem to have a broken axle, and will be unable to continue on until it's repaired."

Jamie, if that was really his name, shifted to look out the window. "From what I recall of the collision, I imagine my conveyance is in need of rather more than a new axle."

"Ah. Yes." Batrice offered him a sympathetic look. "I'm afraid it might not be worth rescuing. Was it yours or was it a hire?"

"Mine," he said with a shrug. "I bought it recently to make my journey easier, but it was never in very good shape. The fellow who sold it to me warned that it might just fall apart on me one day."

"I am so very sorry," Batrice said earnestly. "I'll ensure that you're recompensed for the loss of your phaeton. And if there is any other way we can be of help, we'll be happy to aid you. Perhaps we can convey you to your destination if it happens to be nearby?"

"I have no desire to inconvenience you," he replied casually. "And my destination is rather out of the way."

"Well, we're on our way to Peridale," Batrice offered, at the same time Coralynne said, "Our journey takes us to Lansbridge."

Their guest looked from one of them to the other before unleashing a devastating smile. "Would it help if I assure you that I harbor no nefarious intent? Following you to either of those destinations seems like a great deal of effort for no discernible gain."

"No gain? As a scholar, then, do you take no interest in schools or libraries?" Batrice inquired. "The university at Lansbridge is generally considered one of the finest in the country, and their collection of works from other kingdoms is quite extensive." Lansbridge lay in an entirely different direction, but she saw no reason to embarrass Coralynne by pointing it out. Besides, it seemed as reasonable a tactic as any for discovering what their new acquaintance was really doing this far from civilization.

"University?" the self-proclaimed scholar echoed. "A rather grandiose word for an unimaginative school for boys, don't you think?"

So he wasn't a complete fraud.

"Well, you must at least admit that the library is a fine one," Batrice went on. "And not at all a waste of effort for a serious student like yourself."

"Oh, but I never said I was serious." On that note, the man closed his eyes again, leaving Batrice with a puzzled frown.

"Are you in any pain?" she asked, choosing to abandon the question of his veracity on the topic of his profession.

"It pains me to think of the time I've added to my journey," he said, without opening his eyes. "And I believe there is a terrible lump on my head. But otherwise, all I require is sufficient quiet in which to rest."

Coralynne's pen momentarily ceased scritching across the page of her journal.

"Your writing will not, I assure you, prevent me from sleeping."

An assertion which proved quite demonstrably true, as he commenced a light, irritating snore that, while not exactly resonant, made it difficult for Batrice to focus on anything else.

To make matters worse, the puppy decided it was perfectly content to curl up next to her and make tiny snoring sounds of its own. Which might not have bothered her, had she not been feeling embarrassed, fidgety, and unable to focus on the most pressing issues at hand.

Someone had searched her trunk. And she still had no idea who it might have been, so this was hardly the time to be distracted by a handsome face. Or a pair of strong, masculine hands. Or an escaped strand of his light brown hair that now fell alongside his sculpted, clean-shaven jaw...

"Batrice!" Coralynne whispered loudly. "Stop ogling the highwayman."

Batrice kicked her lightly in the ankle. "You know perfectly well he's not a highwayman," she hissed. "And I wasn't."

"Were too. Think of how disappointed Rupert would be if he found out you were making eyes at someone else."

Batrice was forced to make a significant effort to prevent her eyes from rolling back in her head. "Rupert is always disappointed in me, and it has nothing to do with his imaginary affection, Coralynne."

"Hmm," was all Coralynne would say, as she returned to her writing.

Suddenly Batrice wanted very badly to open the carriage door, run out into the rain, and allow the cold droplets to wash away what felt very much like frustration—with Lady Norelle for forcing her to go on this journey, with her grandmother for feigning illness, with Rupert for disapproving of her for no apparent reason, and with whoever had rummaged through her trunk for failing to leave behind sufficient clues as to their identity or motivation.

But she couldn't. Shouldn't. Didn't.

Instead, she forced her mind away from the breathy little snuffles of Mayhem, the scraping of Coralynne's pen, and the light rasp of Scholar Jamie's snore and compelled herself to focus on the question of what someone might have been looking for amongst her things. Had it been personal? Or a chance theft resulting from a momentary opportunity?

Despite her preoccupation, it seemed an eternity before their rather damp interlude was interrupted by the squelch of footsteps in the mud outside.

The carriage door opened and she was greeted by the grim and scowling face of an extremely wet Rupert, whose mood had obviously not been improved by a ride through the rain.

"Miss Reyard," he said stiffly, "I regret to report that there were no carriages for hire at our destination, only a pony cart that might be sufficient for the most important of our bags. The innkeeper there is expecting us, but we will have to make our way on horseback. I was able to acquire extra mounts, but..."

"Excellent," Batrice said, and almost meant it. Anything to get out of the stifling carriage, though she wasn't exactly thrilled about riding in the rain.

The puppy opened its eyes and yawned, drawing an annoyed glance from Rupert. "Fortunately, the innkeeper is well-disposed towards dogs and agreed to house this one for the night for only a small extra fee."

"Wonderful!" Coralynne exclaimed. "I am so looking forward to a room and a hot bath after such an eventful day." The moment she said the word "bath" a blush spread across her cheeks, but Rupert smiled. Actually smiled! And an extremely attractive smile it was too.

"I apologize for the wait, Miss Smythe, and for being unable to provide you with a more comfortable mode of travel. I hope the accommodations will prove adequate."

"I'm sure they'll be a vast improvement on spending the night in these woods," she declared emphatically.

"Hah," Batrice muttered under her breath. "You say that now. Wait until you've spent the next hour with rainwater dripping down your neck."

When Rupert shot her a disapproving look, she smiled sweetly and handed him the puppy. "Do be a dear and hold Mayhem while Coralynne and I mount up, would you?"

But he didn't scowl as she expected, only looked back at her with an odd challenge in his eyes. "Before you make the attempt, perhaps I should mention that there is only one saddle."

Batrice regarded him coolly, trying to decipher the nature of his challenge. Did he expect her to commandeer the saddle for herself? To demand that she be allowed to ride double with her guard and ignore the needs of her "maid" and everyone else in the party? Or simply to protest that she couldn't possibly go on under such trying circumstances?

The man was impossible to read, and as much as she might have enjoyed continuing to needle him, this wasn't the appropriate time or place. Irreverent she might be, but did he think she was stupid? Or did he simply lump her in with the other blindly entitled members of her class?

Probably, she admitted to herself, and forced a mental shrug at the idea. What did it matter that he'd misjudged and underestimated her?

"Coralynne," she said, turning away from Rupert's hard stare, "are you able to ride alone?"

"I... don't know." The other girl turned pink and looked down. "I've never ridden before."

"Then it's simple," Batrice said lightly. "Rupert, perhaps you would be good enough to take Miss Smythe up with you. I am more than capable of riding bareback, and I'm sure John is as well. As for our guest..."

She turned to the sleeping scholar to discover him watching her with an amused expression.

"I, also, am well able to ride," he said, sitting up, yawning, and straightening his coat.

"Is your head feeling all right?" Batrice couldn't help but glance at the dried blood staining the hair on his temple.

"I'm sufficiently recovered, Miss Reyard." His manner might be drowsy but his gaze was sharp, a fact Batrice noted for later. Had he actually been sleeping at all?

"There, you see?" She turned to Rupert and nodded briskly, allowing no hint of her real feelings to emerge. "All sorted."

The guard's stare grew, if anything, more pointed, until he nodded in return and stepped away from the carriage door to permit them to descend.

While Rupert helped Coralynne into the saddle and Jamie accepted the reins of what appeared to be a retired farm horse, Batrice observed carefully as John handed the luggage down from the roof to be stowed on a rickety pony cart by a stranger. She couldn't quite tell from that distance, but it appeared as though the thread remained tied across her trunk's latch, meaning that it hadn't been tampered with during the day's journey.

Sadly, it would be impossible to keep her eye on it while they made their way to the inn.

So instead, she hiked up her skirts with one hand, grasped her horse's mane with the other, and vaulted onto its broad back with a sigh of satisfaction. She'd always preferred riding bareback—had even experimented with acrobatics a few times—but she'd had no opportunities to indulge since moving to Evenleigh. Such activities were hardly considered proper for Miss Batrice Reyard... a fact of which she was reminded by Coralynne's slightly scandalized but mostly admiring expression.

She chose not to look around to gauge anyone else's reactions, accepting the puppy from Rupert without a word, then waiting as patiently as possible while John collected the carriage horses and mounted the off leader.

"I'll return later to help collect the carriage," Rupert said, as much to the group as a whole as to her. "And to assess whether there's anything of the phaeton worth salvaging."

She nodded. "Then let's be going. The sooner we leave, the sooner we can be out of this rain."

Rupert approached Coralynne, who was blushing furiously, and mounted up behind her, but without his usual grace. Instead, he appeared stiff and uncomfortable, as though he was making every effort in his power not to touch the woman in front of him.

Batrice found herself tempted to smile and ended up looking over at Jamie as an excuse to look anywhere but at the awkward pair. Most inexplicably, she discovered that he was looking straight back at her. For some reason, his gaze gave her a strange, unsettled feeling somewhere in the region of her stomach, a sensation she didn't really care to analyze too closely, so she tucked the puppy close to her chest, pulled her ruined hood up over her hair, and urged her horse into a shambling jog down the muddy road.

It was a strange parade—eight horses, six humans, and a cart—that straggled through the dusk, growing steadily wetter as it went. The squelch of hooves and the creak of wheels became a chorus Batrice was more than ready to be done with by the time they arrived, weary and dripping, in the lamplight on the edges of the inn yard.

The innkeeper came bustling out along with a pair of hostlers to take their horses, unload their bags, and hustle the ladies inside as quickly as possible. Batrice responded to their welcome with a smile, despite dismounting into ankle-deep mud, and followed Coralynne through the wide front door into a space as warm and inviting as it was blessedly dry.

A tall, thin woman with sharp, angular features directed the staff to take their cloaks—not without a horrified glance at the mud and blood caking Batrice's—bring hot tea, and settle them in front of the fire while their bags were taken up and their rooms prepared for the night. The puppy was removed by one of the maids, who promised to feed and wash him until he was clean enough to be brought back inside.

Batrice was so busy enjoying her tea that it took her a few minutes to begin looking around her at the other guests in the common room, and thus was surprised to realize that there was more than one familiar face present.

The large old gentleman wearing a wig had also been staying at the first inn, as had the imposing older woman, who was now wearing a violently purple traveling dress in place of the yellow she'd sported previously. As before, the man was engaged in chatting eagerly with his fellow travelers, while the woman appeared to be entirely focused on her dinner, though she did throw Batrice and her party a sharp, disapproving glance when they came in. And the two middle-aged women in nondescript clothing—were they familiar as well? She thought they might be, but couldn't recall their faces clearly enough to be sure.

Was it normal to encounter the same travelers each night on a journey such as this one? Batrice had no idea. Her travels as an actress had not exactly included regular stops at reputable inns.

What she did realize suddenly was that there was at least one face that should have been present that was quite conspicuously missing—Jamie had dismounted in the inn yard at the same time she had, but was now nowhere to be seen.

CHAPTER 6

*B*atrice's first thought was to wonder whether Jamie's injury had been worse than he'd pretended, and he'd finally collapsed.

Her second was to wonder whether his intentions had perhaps been more nefarious than he'd admitted...

But that was absurd. Next, she'd be wondering whether Coralynne was correct in her assumptions about Rupert's romantic inclinations, which was obviously not the case. If anything, he was besotted with Coralynne herself, and wouldn't *that* make an interesting addition to the novel she claimed to be writing.

Perhaps Jamie was helping with the horses. Inquiring about hiring a new conveyance for his journey. Or seeking out a doctor to examine his head injury. Come to think of it, there were any number of reasons why he might choose to avoid the people who had nearly killed him.

With that uncomfortable thought, Batrice returned her attention to her tea, and eventually dinner, attempting to bolster Coralynne's suddenly flagging spirits with conversation.

It was little use. The older girl stared into her soup and showed no interest in writing anything down, which, in Batrice's admittedly limited experience, meant there was something terribly wrong.

Eventually, a tap on her shoulder dragged her attention away from her attempts to sound jovial and upbeat in spite of their rather traumatic experiences.

"Your bags are in your room, Miss Reyard," Rupert told her. "Perhaps you and Miss Smythe should consider retiring for the evening. It's been a difficult day, and I'm sure we could all use the rest."

But his eyes were on Coralynne as he said it, and when Coralynne turned bright pink from her neckline to her forehead, Batrice thought perhaps she knew what had tied the other girl's tongue—and pen—in knots.

"Yes," she said agreeably, "I think you're right," which drew a suspicious stare from Rupert and a grateful smile from Coralynne. "We will retire directly. Please inform me tomorrow as soon you have news on repairs to the coach, and do look after Jamie."

"Jamie?" Rupert's confusion almost immediately gave way to disapproval. "That man is hardly our concern."

"We are responsible for his condition," Batrice said sternly, "and his lack of transportation. I expect you'll wish to offer him reimbursement for his vehicle, or render some other form of aid."

When he hesitated, she pressed her point. "Our carriage bears the royal crest, sir, as you only recently pointed out to me yourself. Can we do any less as representatives of our king?"

He didn't like it, but he also didn't argue, because in this case, at least, she was right. As little as he trusted Jamie, the circumstances didn't leave Rupert much choice.

So he nodded, lips pinched together in frustration, and Batrice—quite commendably, in her own estimation—was mature enough not to rub it in. She merely took the still mute Coralynne's arm and led her inexorably away, following one of the maids up the stairs and into the room that had been prepared for them.

It was small, but warm, with one large bed and a cozy fireplace that Coralynne stretched out her hands towards with a sigh that seemed to carry the weight of a thousand worlds and everything in them.

"Really," Batrice said, keeping her tone light as she turned down the bed covers to ensure that it was clean. "One would think you've never been in love before."

A soft gasp was her answer, followed by a stiffening of shoulders and a determined folding of arms across the chest.

"I am not in love," Coralynne said. "And I write about people falling in love, so I should think I would know the signs."

"Oh, but I used to pretend to be in love on a regular basis, so I'm quite certain you're well on your way," Batrice responded calmly.

"Pretend to be in love? Whyever would you do that?"

Oops. Somehow she'd forgotten that Coralynne didn't know about her dramatic career. She'd also forgotten that certain aspects of her own past were supposed to remain safely buried.

"I don't suppose you'd agree to forget I said that?"

Coralynne's glare made it clear that amnesia was out of the question.

"It's a secret, but as long as you promise to keep it, I will admit that I used to be an actress."

Apparently, she'd hit on exactly the right topic to distract her companion from a bad case of the doldrums.

"Oh! Were you really?" Coralynne's eyes shone as she scurried across the room and sat on the bed next to Batrice, leaning forward eagerly. "You *must* tell me what it was like. Dashing? Exciting? Dull? Dangerous? Or simply awful? Why did you quit? Are you even a gentleman's daughter, or are you still pretending? Does anyone else know?"

Oh good heavens. Lady Norelle was going to kill her.

"I'll make you a deal," Batrice said sternly. "I will tell you more—*after* we're in bed."

Coralynne sighed again, but capitulated, and bounced up to retrieve her bag. It was only after she'd been rummaging in it for a few moments that she lifted her head with a frown.

"Someone has been in my things," she announced. "My pounce pot is missing."

Batrice jumped to her feet, frustration over her slip forgotten. "Are you certain?"

Coralynne must have heard something strange in her voice. "You don't seem surprised so much as resigned," she pointed out. "Did you expect this to happen?"

"No," Batrice hastened to say. "But yesterday..." She paused, hoping to explain in a way that wouldn't make it sound as though she didn't trust Coralynne. "I thought someone had rifled through my trunk, but it was difficult to be sure. There was a chance it had merely been overturned or shaken more violently than usual, and I didn't want to jump to conclusions."

"And you didn't tell me, because..." Coralynne sounded rather offended.

"I didn't want to worry you."

"Hmmm." That wasn't exactly exoneration.

Batrice crossed the room to look at her own trunk and was dismayed to discover that the thread she had placed across the latch was nowhere to be seen. "They've been into my trunk again, as well," she said, moderating her voice just in time as she realized how thin these inn walls probably were. The thief must have seized his (or her) opportunity after they'd arrived this evening, and could very well still be nearby.

He could also very easily be named Jamie.

The thought bothered her more than she cared to admit, but her frustrations were interrupted by a knock at the door. It was a maid, carrying a clean and enthusiastic Mayhem.

"I'm sorry, Miss," the maid said as she handed over his furry, wriggling body. "I didn't want to take his collar off to wash it, for fear of losing that pretty bauble there. But he's had his bath and his dinner right enough."

"Thank you ever so much." Batrice swiftly rummaged in her handbag and pressed a few small coins into the maid's hand. The girl's eyes brightened, and she curtsied before trotting back downstairs.

Sure enough, the pup's fur was clean and smelled of lilacs, which made Batrice smile a little. His ruffled collar seemed to have collected more than its fair share of grime, but the silver ball was still shining brightly beneath it, so she set the little miscreant free to roam about the room as she returned to her trunk.

This time, she very carefully took out each item and set them in a pile to one side, trying as she did so to remember precisely what she'd packed. "My face powder," she said at last. "They've taken my face powder."

She'd rarely used it since leaving the stage but still carried it around for reasons she wasn't sure she could have voiced aloud.

"And left your jewelry?" Coralynne pointed out from behind her.

"I don't exactly have jewelry," Batrice admitted. "Just a few hair combs and pins that look like they might be valuable. Though they aren't. Just stage frippery, really."

"But what use could someone have for pounce and face powder?" Coralynne voiced the unspoken understanding that the same person must have committed both thefts. But what motive could there possibly be?

Both stolen items were relatively inexpensive. Easily obtained. Who would go to the trouble of going through a stranger's luggage and risk being caught merely to remove such commonplace substances?

Suddenly Coralynne's eyes lit up. "A mystery!" she declared. "This is so exciting."

"A moment ago you were looking like someone ate your favorite pastries and absconded with all of your pens," Batrice complained. "How can this possibly make it better?"

"I was just tired," Coralynne said meekly. "And I'd much rather think about a mysterious thief than…" She abruptly closed her mouth.

"Than devastatingly handsome guards?" Batrice wasn't willing to let her off the hook that easily.

"Never mind that," Coralynne scolded. "Don't you want to find out who the thief is?"

"Very much so," Batrice replied firmly. "Which is why you're going to have to agree to proceed as if we have no idea anything is amiss. We're going to have to set a trap."

"Ooh, that sounds perfect. But how? Haven't they searched everything already?"

"Everything," Batrice pointed out, "but my handbag. That's been with me ever since we got in the carriage. I think I ought to leave it in my room tomorrow to give our thief ample opportunity to strike again."

"Do you think..." Coralynne paused, looked around as though someone might be listening, then leaned forward.

"What?"

"It's only just occurred to me that your trunk was first tampered with after we met Jamie," Coralynne whispered loudly. "What if he really *is* a villain? Or a spy? Or even just a thief? What if he was following us?"

Batrice groaned. "You too? Even if he is a villain, as I have already explained to Rupert, how could he have been following us if *we* ran into *him*? And what sort of thief endangers his very life for the sake of pounce and face powder? It doesn't make the least bit of sense, Coralynne."

"If he's a villain, it doesn't have to make sense," Coralynne said, her tone growing stern. "You really must be careful, Batrice. What if he's plotting something much worse than theft? You're traveling in a royal coach! What if he intends to kidnap you and use you in a plot against the Crown?"

Batrice burst out laughing. "Surely if he were the sort of person to plot against the Crown, he would also be the sort of person to know that I'm not a very worthwhile target for abduction. No one would ransom me, and he'd be stuck feeding me and putting up with my exuberant personality forever."

Batrice suddenly thought it might be nice to find someone who wouldn't mind putting up with her forever. But villainous foreign spies were probably not the best candidates, though she could imagine it wouldn't take much for Coralynne to paint such a situation in the most romantic light possible.

"Whoever it is," she said, attempting to return their conversation to reality, "perhaps they will be tempted to enter our room for a search if I appear very publicly without my handbag tomorrow."

"But won't we be leaving tomorrow?"

"It will take some time for the coach to be repaired," Batrice assured her. "At least a day I should think. Plenty of opportunity for us to deal with this thief before we go any further."

The following morning, Batrice rose early. She hadn't had much luck sleeping, and as she tossed and turned had given much thought to what she ought to do next. What would Lady Norelle expect of her? When she gave an account of this journey, she wanted to be able to say that she'd acted in a mature and responsible way, so that she might be entrusted with more than pretending to be a debutante.

So before the fire was lit or the maid brought water for washing, Batrice eased herself out of bed, dressed hastily, and slipped out to look for Rupert, taking care not to wake the puppy who was snoozing in his basket by the hearth.

According to the innkeeper, Rupert had breakfasted early and left, so she continued her search in the stable, where she found him looking over the horses, running his hands down their legs and checking their hooves for injury.

"Will they be all right?" she asked quietly.

Clearly, she'd managed to startle him, because he whirled and fixed her with an annoyed glare. "What are you doing out here? It's hardly a proper place for you, especially without your maid."

"What, alone with you in a stable? Would that be a more proper place for Miss Smythe, then?" she inquired sweetly.

"How could you be so insulting to someone whose life is dedicated to serving you?" he snapped, startling her with his vehemence.

Sometimes she still forgot how very rigid society could be about things she no longer considered to be important. Such as the idea that two adults holding a perfectly normal conversation while standing on opposite sides of a horse could somehow be viewed as scandalous simply because they were the only persons present.

Perhaps Lady Norelle was right—she did need to spend more time remembering how to behave as the person she claimed to be. Because much of it now struck her as somewhat ridiculous, and it would be disastrous if she forgot such commonplace conventions under more dangerous circumstances.

But in the meantime, it was rather telling that Rupert defended Miss Smythe's supposedly maligned virtue so fiercely. Poor Coralynne was going to have to adjust her romantic theories in the very near future.

"I wasn't being insulting," she said, resisting the urge to sigh. "I was merely attempting to point out... Oh, never mind." Rupert's frown made it clear he wouldn't care for any attempts to justify herself, and it wasn't like she could explain. Not fully. *Oh, by the way, I didn't mean to offend your fair lady, but my ideas are a bit outlandish because I used to be an actress, and did you know you've fallen in love with a gentleman's daughter pretending to be a maid?*

"Look, I only slipped out to inform you that I believe someone has been going through our bags and stealing small items."

Rupert stood straighter and moved away from the horse. "What sort of small items?"

"Er. Well, Coralynne is missing her pounce pot, and my face powder has disappeared."

It sounded ridiculous when she said it out loud.

For the briefest instant, Rupert's eyes glittered oddly, but his expression almost immediately turned incredulous. "Pounce and face powder? And you imagine they were stolen?"

"I know they were," Batrice insisted.

"How?"

She wasn't quite ready to admit that she'd failed to tell him about the problem for an entire day and tied string across her trunk latch instead.

When she didn't answer, he shook his head. "So you've invented a thief for what purpose? To malign my ability to do my job? Or because you were careless and misplaced a few paltry personal items?"

Her eyes narrowed. "You don't believe me."

"You should have come up with a more convincing story. At least tell me your jewelry is missing."

It probably wouldn't do any good to explain that she didn't have any. Maybe she should have sent Coralynne to plead their case instead.

"Very well," she said pleasantly, lifting her chin and smiling. "Do return to your duties. I wouldn't wish to distract you with my paltry complaints."

She turned on her heel and left, ignoring his call of "Miss Reyard!" as she stalked back across the inn yard with the fire of determination in every stride. Fine. So much for her good intentions. She'd tried to do the right thing, but if he was going to belittle her, she would just have to prove him wrong. She and Coralynne would catch the thief on their own.

Now that she thought about it, Coralynne's involvement might make the whole matter a bit more complicated. Miss Smythe was lovely and enthusiastic and genuine, but Batrice wasn't sure she was at all capable of subterfuge. She would be staring at everyone they met, whispering about whatever story she imagined for them and making it difficult to trap even the worst thief into making another attempt.

No, she would need to do this alone. She would also need a plan, and Batrice had always done her best thinking while in motion. Plus it was too early for breakfast, and Coralynne would be asleep for some time yet.

Looking behind her to ensure that no one was watching, Batrice slipped out of the inn yard and set off down the road towards the rest of the village with a brisk step and the beginnings of a smile on her face.

It felt wonderful to be out and about, and early morning walks had always been her favorite. Everything seemed possible when the sun was newly up, and no one was disappointed with her yet. And with no one to see her, she could let herself go, swing her arms, lengthen her stride, even splash in the puddles if she wished.

With a delighted laugh, Batrice broke into a run and flew down the margin of the road, holding her skirts out of the wet but not being particularly careful where she stepped. She really missed her old boots at moments like this. They'd gone all the way to her knees, and been both worn and comfortable from miles and miles of tramping through every imaginable weather. She'd learned sword-fighting in those boots, ridden bareback and astride in those boots, and it had been a sad day when she'd been forced to pack them up again to become—

"Miss Reyard!" The call came from behind her. A man's voice.

Ugh. Rupert must have followed her.

Dropping her skirts, Batrice turned, expecting to see her guard's disapproving scowl, but he was nowhere to be seen.

Instead, Jamie strode towards her, hands in his pockets, with the early morning sun gleaming on his golden-brown hair.

Drat the man for being so decidedly handsome.

"Are you typically an early riser, Miss Reyard," he asked as he came closer, "or are you on some particular errand this morning?"

"I probably shouldn't admit to it," she allowed, "but I do love mornings. And the country air is so crisp and fresh after a rain. But what of you? Are you feeling somewhat recovered? Were you able to find a doctor last evening?"

He shook his head as he came to a stop beside her. "No doctor to be found in this out-of-the-way hamlet, but I am feeling much better today, thank you. Might I accompany you into the village? I'm sure your guard would feel better if you were not alone."

Batrice couldn't help a bit of a grin. "Given my present company, I'm not certain that's true. I doubt he would approve of any guardian other than himself, and he seems particularly suspicious of you."

Jamie looked down at her, eyes gleaming. "Does he object to scholars in general, or is there something about me in particular?"

"He thinks you're following us."

One of his eyebrows shot up. "As a scholar, I'm afraid I must protest his illogic."

"Or perhaps he dislikes your looks." She shrugged and began walking again. "It's difficult to tell with Rupert. But given that he is disdainful of me as well, I wouldn't suggest becoming too pleased with yourself—his distrust is far more common than his approval."

"An admirable quality in a guard, I should think."

As they continued down the road together, Batrice did her best not to admire him openly, but it was something of a challenge. His hair was neatly tied back, as usual, giving her a chance to observe his firm, angular jaw, and bright, intelligent gaze. Again she noted the breadth of his shoulders, and the evident strength in his hands, which suggested he hadn't always been a scholar.

The best way to learn something was to ask, she'd decided long ago. "Have you always been a scholar?"

He glanced down at her. "I confess, I have not. I've been informed that in my infancy, I was more given to chewing on my fingers."

Batrice tried to look annoyed, but only succeeding in bursting into laughter.

"Apparently I also had a preference for getting dirty and eating a great deal."

Batrice shot him a mock glare. "If you've quite finished enjoying your own cleverness, I believe I was asking whether it has been your only career?"

"No," he said, "but it is my primary pursuit at present."

"And did you make that change because you enjoy scholarship or because you had no choice?"

"You're very straightforward," he said, his lips curving as though that amused him. "And perhaps more perceptive than is strictly comfortable."

"Is that your way of telling me to mind my own business?" Batrice inquired. "I would apologize for being nosy, but I've always found that in the end, it is better to simply ask and be told no than to pretend I don't have questions."

He watched her steadily. "Then do you not believe there are some things better left unasked? Even for the sake of the feelings or safety of others?"

"Give me credit for more nuance than that," she protested, beginning to feel a trifle defensive. "Do I look like a silly young debutante who says whatever comes into her head without a moment's thought?"

He grinned. "Yes."

Batrice couldn't help laughing. "I suppose I asked for that. And as I am young, and a debutante of sorts, perhaps I should simply curtsey and say thank you."

"Why 'of sorts?'"

Drat. She shouldn't have said that. Pretending to be someone she wasn't was proving far more difficult in reality than it had ever been on the stage. Oddly, it seemed that learning lines was a great deal simpler than improvising on the spot.

"I suppose because I haven't much interest in catching a husband." She covered her mistake with a half-truth. "I am staying at court at present, in hopes that I will acquire some polish, and perhaps because my parents believe it possible that I will catch the eye of someone above my circumstances. But in truth, I have no such ambitions for myself."

"Then what ambitions *do* you have?"

The question seemed to be in earnest, but Batrice stopped and turned to her companion with a bit of annoyance. "You are far better at asking questions than answering them," she accused him, "so don't bother thinking you've been so clever that I haven't noticed. If I answer that, I will demand that you answer a question in return."

He folded his arms and regarded her thoughtfully, eyes fixed warmly on hers.

Batrice focused on remembering to breathe. He really had no business being quite that good-looking.

"I suppose I could agree to that, but there are some questions I may not be able to answer. My family..." he paused.

"Doesn't know where you are?" she guessed.

"Something like that."

"There you go being annoyingly vague again," she complained. "If we do this, I will refuse to accept any answer with less-than-satisfactory details."

"As will I," he countered.

Batrice looked up at him, wondering whether she was a fool for having this conversation at all. But she was enjoying herself immensely. Jamie was handsome, intelligent, and didn't treat her like a child. She got the feeling he had led an interesting life—nothing like the strange stilted existence led by most gentlemen's sons—and she wanted to know more about it. About him.

Rupert would most certainly not approve. Her mother would very likely faint. And Lady Norelle? She probably wouldn't approve either. But on this beautiful morning, Batrice was ready for some adventure, and it had been a long time since she'd found someone she could really talk to.

"Sir, you have a deal," she said.

Some impish impulse prompted her to hold out her hand. Jamie looked at it for a moment, then smiled and accepted it in the firm, warm clasp of a gentlemen's agreement.

"Shall we?" he said, gesturing down the road.

CHAPTER 7

*T*hey began to walk again, this time a companionable side-by-side amble, not in any particular hurry to reach the village now coming into view around a gentle bend in the road.

"Shall I begin?" Batrice asked. "Or ought I defer because I am a thoughtful young lady of delicate sensibilities?"

"Even a scholar knows that a gentleman must always allow a lady to precede him, except where there may be danger lurking. Do you intend for this conversation to grow hazardous?"

"Of course. A boring conversation is nothing less than a blight on society."

He chuckled, a deep, warm sound that Batrice decided she liked a little too well for her peace of mind.

"Then I will begin, and remind you as I do so that I've graciously allowed you to duck my previous question. But tell me, Miss Reyard, do you prefer a rapier or a saber?"

"A saber, by far," Batrice responded without thinking, then felt her jaw drop. "Did you honestly just ask me that?"

"Did you honestly just answer that?" her companion replied with a devilish grin. "And without having to think about it, too."

"I was expecting you to ask about my family or my favorite activity. Do I prefer a coach to a barouche, that sort of thing. Who begins a conversation with rapiers and sabers?" She was beginning to feel flustered and didn't care for it at all.

"What good is there in questions you've probably been asked a thousand times? You would have practiced, polished, polite answers that really don't mean anything. To really get to know a person, it's important to ask something surprising. You're far more likely to get an honest answer."

And far more likely to learn something the other person might prefer to hide. It wasn't as if she hadn't employed the same technique to good effect in the past. But how could she possibly explain having a preference for the saber over the rapier without admitting to her life on the stage?

Time to go on the offensive.

"What is your parents' profession?"

He cocked his head curiously. "Now there's a fascinating question for the daughter of a gentleman to be asking. Who says my parents have any profession at all?"

"I don't require your analysis of my choice, just an answer, if you please," Batrice reminded him sternly.

"Well then, my mother dabbles in the sciences, and my father in politics. And to prove my goodwill, I will offer as a bonus that my three older brothers are all terrifyingly large and enamored of sharp, metallic objects."

"And you're not?" she asked skeptically.

"I already gave you a bonus answer, so you'll have to use that question later if you truly wish to know."

Oh, but this was fun. Batrice tried to look disappointed and couldn't.

"Very well, sir. But I maintain that I was simply interested and not attempting to cheat."

"Being a gentleman, I will choose to believe you," Jamie said, his eyes twinkling. "Tell me, Miss Reyard, have you embarked on your present course due to your own inclination or more out of a sense of obligation?"

"My present course?" Batrice echoed. "Do you refer to my course in life, or to my presence on the eaves of the inhospitable northern woods?"

"I'll let you choose." His enigmatic expression gave nothing away.

"Then I suppose I must offer the rather vague response that it's a bit of both. I am not particularly inclined to traipse through the woods to visit my grandmother at this present time, but I am obliged to do so by my present course, which is very much of my own choosing." She began to laugh at herself. "Was that answer oblique enough to draw protests?"

"It was a masterpiece of obfuscation," Jamie declared, "and as such, entirely unsatisfactory."

"I suspected as much." Batrice sidestepped a particularly large puddle. "Then you will have to be satisfied with the truth that, given a choice, I would not be visiting my grandmother. She is composed almost entirely of prejudices and disapproval, and regularly pretends to be dying in order to compel her family to attend her."

"I must assume there is an inheritance to be fought over."

Batrice shot her companion a sideways glance. "If that is your attempt to determine whether my family is rich, and therefore whether I am an acquaintance worth your time and effort, the answer is no." It was probably irrational to feel disappointed, but she did, a little. "My grandmother does have a fortune to bestow, but it's quite paltry in comparison to those you would find attached to most Evenleigh heiresses."

Jamie stopped walking and fixed her with a keen gaze. "Seems a sensitive subject."

Batrice shrugged and looked away. "Perhaps, perhaps not, but either way, you'll have to wait to find out." She pointed ahead at the neat gathering of homes and business around the cobbled village square. "We've reached our destination. Whatever your business here, I should leave you to it." She turned and began to walk back the way she'd come.

"Miss Reyard."

She stopped but didn't look over her shoulder.

"Forgive me. I intended no offense."

She nodded briefly. "None taken. But I should return to the inn. My maid will be upset if she wakes up and I am not there."

Not quite the truth perhaps, but she was too confused by her own feelings to linger. Without so much as a backwards glance, Batrice hastened back towards the inn, determined to master her wayward emotions before she encountered Jamie again.

She entered the common room a short time later, a bit out of breath and ready to think of anything but a pair of warm brown eyes that seemed to make her forget whatever sense she ought to have possessed. Really, it was ridiculous of her to be upset that Jamie seemed interested in her financial prospects. He was a scholar, after all, and a fourth son, without much to hope for in the way of an inheritance.

And there was no way to know whether his questions had arisen from any mercenary inclination. He might have just been curious. It was possible he had never entertained the slightest romantic thought about her, which might actually be more depressing than supposing him to be attracted primarily to her appearance of wealth.

Not to mention, he was a chance companion of the road, and she had no business obsessing over him. He could still, after all, be their thief. Or something worse, if she was willing to entertain any of Coralynne's theories. She knew nothing about him except that he was gorgeous, kind to puppies, fascinating to talk to, and had perfect hands...

"Ah, I believe I've seen you before, Miss," a jovial tenor voice announced behind her. "Perhaps at an inn two nights ago? Were you not the young lady with the dog?"

Batrice turned and encountered the smiling, squint-eyed face of the large, bewigged, older gentleman she'd seen the night before.

"I suppose I am guilty, sir," she admitted, with a small curtsey. "I hope you were not too offended."

"Not at all, not at all," he protested, and pointed at a seat opposite him. "In fact, I would be delighted if you would join me for breakfast. I'm old and crotchety enough that traveling is more of a chore than an adventure, but I do enjoy getting to know my fellow travelers."

"You can't possibly be old enough for crotchets, sir," Batrice said with a smile. "If it were not unladylike to wager, I'd lay odds you're not a day over sixty-five." Actually, she'd have wagered quite differently. She'd seen enough stage makeup to know when a man was using it to alter his age, and this one wore a great deal.

He chuckled and leaned back in his chair, which creaked in protest. "More than a day, I'm afraid. But come, do sit and have some of this delicious egg and potato pie."

Suddenly, Batrice found she was incredibly hungry. "If you will grant me your name, sir, I could possibly be prevailed upon to accept."

"Sir Abner Loringale, at your service, Miss."

"Miss Batrice Reyard," she said, with another curtsey.

"I'd pull out your chair like a gentleman," the old man declared, tapping a cane on the floor, "but it takes me an age to get up and down these days, and you'd find yourself turning gray waiting for your breakfast."

"My hands are quite functional, I assure you," Batrice said gravely, pulling out her own chair and seating herself, just as a maid bustled up with a cup and a steaming pot that smelled quite deliciously of fresh tea.

"The young lady will be having pie as well," the man said, "and perhaps you could provide us with some pastries?"

"Of course, sir."

The maid hastened away as Batrice poured her tea, held it to her nose, and sighed with delight. One cup, then she would dash upstairs to see if Coralynne or the puppy were awake yet.

"Are you setting out early today, then?" the gentleman asked.

"Oh, I doubt that," Batrice said comfortably. "Our carriage was damaged during the storm yesterday, so we'll be staying here until it's repaired. And what of you, sir? On your way after breakfast?"

"Sadly, my gout is paining me after so much travel," he said mournfully. "I'm thinking of resting here for a day or two before continuing on. And perhaps we should consider it fate that we are forced to remain here together—I hear that another of our fellow travelers became ill during the night. A gentlewoman, of about my age. There was even a doctor summoned, according to what I hear from the maids."

Egad, Batrice thought, the fellow was a thoroughly unashamed gossip.

"Do you mean the dignified-looking lady in the purple dress?"

"Why, yes," he said, looking surprised. "Are you acquainted with the lady in question?"

"Gracious no," Batrice replied, taking a sip of her tea. "Another chance meeting, much like yourself. I remember seeing her that first night as well, though she wore yellow at the time. Odd coincidence that we happen to all be going the same direction at the same time, I suppose. Where exactly is it you are headed, if it's not impolite of me to ask?"

"I've a friend near Tavisham," the old gentleman said. "But perhaps you've never heard of it."

"I'm afraid not," Batrice said. "But I'm not really that familiar with this area of the country."

"Not visiting family then?"

"My grandmother, actually. She has an estate near Peridale."

Sir Abner drew back in surprise. "But that is very near Tavisham. Perhaps we shall be seeing more of each other along the way."

"I hope so, sir." She took another sip of her tea, just as she remembered a similar conversation with Jamie, who had never actually revealed his true destination. Had he deliberately avoided it, or had the conversation moved on so quickly he hadn't had the opportunity? And why was it she seemed to return to thoughts of him so frequently?

Perhaps it would be better if she followed Coralynne's example and thought of him as a villain.

"There you are!" As if summoned by Batrice's thoughts, Coralynne appeared next to her, the puppy in her arms. "When I woke up and you weren't there, I feared something had happened to you during the night," she scolded.

"I'm very sorry," Batrice said, feeling genuinely contrite until she remembered that a real debutante would never act this way towards her maid. She probably needed to have a conversation with Coralynne about the best way to behave if she intended to maintain the fiction of being a servant. "Please do take Mayhem outside for his walk, and then ask Rupert to take charge of him for the remainder of the day. Afterwards, you may return and have breakfast."

Looking puzzled and hurt, Coralynne turned to do as she said, just as Rupert loomed in the doorway. His expression was grim until he caught sight of Miss Smythe, at which point he actually smiled.

"Allow me, Miss Smythe," he said, holding out his arms for the puppy. "I'll take him outside so you can sit and enjoy a proper breakfast."

"Oh, thank you!" Coralynne's smile—and attendant blush—lit up her face. She handed him over, her eyes never leaving the guard's, and watched as he turned to take the dog outside, biting her lip in a distracted manner.

"You'd best come and eat then," Batrice called, feeling amused.

Coralynne started, then nearly tripped as she approached the table. "I'm sorry," she said, a little breathlessly. "I wouldn't wish to intrude, but…"

"Do be seated," Sir Abner said jovially. "I'm not one to stand on ceremony, I assure you. There are few seats left, and I wouldn't wish to separate you from your mistress."

"Oh, perhaps I should go back to our room," she protested, but to no avail.

Batrice thought this was as good a time as any for the room to be left empty, and her breakfast companion seemed unwilling to contemplate the idea of losing a second pair of ears. In fact, he proved as good as his word and addressed numerous comments to Coralynne herself, which made Batrice like him all the more.

They discussed the roughness of the roads, the reason Batrice traveled in a royal coach, and the difficulties of bringing along a canine companion, which led Sir Abner to recall Mayhem's soulful eyes and excessively ruffled collar in an admiring fashion. Batrice chose to humor him and wondered evilly whether it might be possible to sneak the pup into Sir Abner's carriage rather than her own when it was time to depart.

They finished their breakfast in a leisurely manner, in part to allow any enterprising thief ample opportunity to investigate their room, and in part because... well, because Jamie had yet to return, and Batrice wasn't quite ready to give up hope of seeing him again.

It was possible that he'd found another vehicle to convey him to his destination, and he owed her no debt that would demand he take his leave. If anything, the opposite. He could very well depart without a word, and she would never see him again, which, she acknowledged, was probably for the best, but that didn't mean she had to be happy about it.

"Are you waiting for someone?" Coralynne asked under her breath after they'd taken leave of Sir Abner and walked away from the table. "Or are you always this distracted at breakfast?"

Batrice groaned. "Was I that obvious?"

"Worse," Coralynne said, a bit shortly. She was probably still upset over Batrice's earlier dismissal. "If even *I* noticed, I'm sure everyone else did, too."

Batrice remained silent until they reached the top of the stairs and held her finger to her lips as they approached their room. Coralynne's forehead creased, but she said nothing as they crept towards the door.

With a hasty twist and shove, Batrice opened it, hoping to surprise their thief in the act, but much to her disappointment, the room was empty.

"Drat," she said, dropping onto the bed.

Coralynne shut the door behind her with rather more force than necessary.

"Are you going to explain?" she said, her expression making it clear that she'd been hurt.

"What was I supposed to do?" Batrice asked in exasperation. "I'm supposed to be traveling with a maid. Everyone thinks she's you! In public at least, we have to maintain that fiction, for the sake of both our reputations. However much I may dislike the unfairness of such conventions, my real maid would never have just approached the table and sat down to eat breakfast with me."

"Oh." Coralynne's face fell. She sat next to Batrice. "I'm sorry. I guess I wasn't thinking. I'll try harder, I promise. Do you want me to fetch you anything? Fix your hair? I'm really terrible with hair, but I can make an effort to get better."

Batrice nudged her with an elbow. "Don't be silly. When we're alone, we're just..." What were they? They were well past acquaintance stage, and even if Coralynne didn't see it the same way... "We're friends," she said firmly. "But even with Rupert and John, we should be careful if we don't want to be asked any awkward questions."

The other girl nodded. "I'll remember. So what are we going to do today? Do you think the coach will be ready?"

"I doubt they'll be able to repair the axle so quickly," Batrice assured her while eyeing her handbag, which she'd left lying so temptingly on the dresser. Had it been moved? She couldn't be sure. So she got up, retrieved it, and sat back on the bed, rummaging through it to catalog its contents. Everything seemed in order...

But just to be sure, she dumped it out on the bed. There was her mirror, her comb, and her tiny pouch of coins. A handful of hairpins, an old pair of gloves and...

A scrap of paper?

She had no memory of placing such a thing in her reticule, so she picked it up and felt a brief chill as she read the words printed in plain, block letters.

"I think," she said, "we are going to have to be more careful." There was no hiding this from Coralynne, even if she wished to. Not any more.

"Why?"

She held out the note for Coralynne to read.

"*Expect even greater catastrophes if you remain on your present course,*" she read aloud, then met Batrice's eyes with a startled gasp. "It's a threat! Someone doesn't want us to reach your grandmother's house. But why? And how did it get into your purse?"

"It wasn't there last evening," Batrice said. "So I assume it was placed there this morning." Unless of course someone had come into their room during the night and slipped it into her handbag then.

She shivered at the thought. Surely no one would have dared. And if there had been an intruder, either she or Coralynne would have awakened. Wouldn't they?

"What are we going to do?" Coralynne sounded as though she couldn't decide whether to be thrilled or terrified.

"We're going to figure out who's responsible, of course," Batrice said briskly. "It's someone here in this inn with us, but it may not be a guest. It could be a person who can disguise themselves as a servant, a guard, or even a groom."

"We should tell Rupert," Coralynne declared earnestly. "It's important for him to know about any potential threats to our safety."

"I tried to tell..." Batrice stopped before she said something either unwise or unkind. In most cases, she said what she thought without much concern for consequences, but she preferred to think she could learn. Disparaging Rupert would only alienate Coralynne, which was the last thing she wanted to do. In this case, perhaps it would be better to use the tools at hand to accomplish what was needed.

"You're right," she said instead. "He really ought to know, but it wouldn't be quite the thing for me to go to the stable myself. Would you mind taking him the news? Perhaps he will have an idea of how we ought to proceed from here. And perhaps he will also have news of when our coach will be ready to travel."

Coralynne blushed, protested, and proclaimed that she couldn't possibly, all while getting up and putting on her wrap. Batrice eventually simply opened the door and pushed her through it, grinning as her "maid" descended the stairs with trembling fingers and a tiny smile.

Even if Rupert continued in his insistence that they had merely invented the thefts, at least it would give him and Coralynne a chance to spend some time together. And it would provide Batrice with an opportunity to do a bit of investigating without worrying about who might be watching, or whether they would be judging her methods.

Because if they saw her, they would most definitely judge.

CHAPTER 8

Batrice looked both ways. The hallway was empty, so she eased out of her room and was just shutting the door when someone spoke directly behind her.

"I have the strangest feeling there's a story here."

She jumped and whirled, her back slamming against the door, while the doorknob dug painfully into her hip.

"You!" she hissed.

"Me," Jamie said complacently, eyeing her oddly. "Is there a reason you're dressed like that?"

Stifling a growl of annoyance, Batrice could only manage one thought —she had to get them out of sight. Opening the door again with one hand, she reached out impulsively with the other, grabbed his sleeve, and yanked him into her room.

"What are you doing lurking in the hallway?" she muttered defensively, after the door was safely shut behind him.

"I'm not the one dressed as if I were on my way to a mop fair," he said, a gleam of amusement lurking in his eyes.

"Do you see a mop?" she retorted.

"No, but I see a dress and a cap that wouldn't be out of place on a chambermaid twice your age."

Batrice removed the cap and tossed it onto the bed with a huff. "It's not that bad," she muttered. "And you still didn't answer the question. That seems to be a terrible habit with you, one that ought to be addressed immediately."

"If you must know," he said, leaning back against the closed door and crossing his arms, "my room is just down the hall."

Oh. Well, that was awkward.

"You still shouldn't sneak up on people," she insisted. "Why couldn't you have walked down the hall like a normal person? A person who makes noise?"

"I'm afraid I must point out the irony of you accusing *me* of sneaking while you're dressed like that. Unless you're going to claim you've actually been a servant all along and you and your maid switched places?"

Her pause was a little too long.

"It wouldn't actually work," Jamie pointed out, "unless you have more appropriate clothing than that ill-fitting sack you're wearing. You'd also have to try to act a little more like someone who cares about the opinions of others."

"Drat." It should probably bother her more that there was a man in her room and he'd caught her engaging in attempted espionage. There was no way for him to know that was what she'd been doing, but it was still embarrassing. She should have been more careful. Especially considering that he was one of the people she'd been hoping to investigate.

"If it helps, I promise not to tell anyone," he offered. "Unless, of course, you're using this disguise in order to rob the guests of their valuables at every inn along the road, in which case I will have no choice but to report you."

"That's absurd—" she started to say, and then stopped because she'd had exactly the same thought. The thief could have been someone disguised as a maid or a groom.

Did Jamie's frank acknowledgment of the possibility make him more or less of a suspect? And how could she turn this situation around, now that he'd ruined her initial plans?

"Actually," she said, deciding to take the leap, "I'm afraid that is exactly what someone has been doing. But that someone isn't me. My maid and I are missing some personal belongings, and my trunk has been rummaged through. I was hoping to make some headway in finding the person responsible until you interrupted me just now."

"Find them how?" he asked, one brow raised. "By breaking into all of the guest's rooms and hoping to find your missing possessions?"

"If necessary." She fixed him with a hard stare. "You see, whoever is doing this has been following us. They've struck three times now, at separate locations. So it isn't so much that I'm hoping to find our things as I'm hoping to discover exactly which people were present in both places."

Jamie met her eyes, still looking amused. "I feel as though there's more you're wanting to ask. Would it help if I answered now, or would you like an opportunity to phrase the question delicately?"

"I can't see how delicate phrasing will help," Batrice said, seating herself on the bed facing him. "Was it you?"

"I wouldn't exactly go around admitting to it if it was," he replied calmly. "And what kind of thief returns to the same victims three times? Either he's a terrible thief, or he's asking to get caught, and frankly, I think I'm a bit insulted that you would consider me a candidate for either."

"Why would that make him a terrible thief?" She had her own ideas, but she wanted to know what he would say.

"If he doesn't know what he's after, he should have simply taken the valuables the first time and moved on. If he's after something specific, he's clearly both desperate and bad at searching. Or he's inappropriately identified his mark. Either way, he's endangering his mission by continuing to single you out after he's revealed his presence by stealing something other than his true target."

"Your insightful explanation doesn't make me less likely to suspect you," Batrice pointed out, a little impressed that he'd thought it through that thoroughly.

"Perhaps I simply don't care whether you suspect me or not," he countered.

For several long moments, they stared at each other. She probably ought to be worried. Scandalized even. She was alone in her room with a man who might be a thief, and who certainly had no respect for propriety. He refused to claim that he was innocent, and was less than forthcoming about himself and his motivations.

But for some reason, even if he were the thief, she would have sworn she was safe with him. During the months she'd lived on the road, it hadn't taken long to develop a decent sense for which men would respect her and which would take advantage in whatever ways they could get away with. And Jamie, while he might be maddeningly handsome and irritatingly mysterious, didn't frighten her.

"I really didn't think you would," she finally admitted, "but I decided I might as well ask, given that you're the most logical person to suspect."

"Which would make me a very poor thief indeed, if I made myself so glaringly obvious."

"But you could have been making yourself obvious for exactly that reason," she argued.

He chuckled, a low, rich sound of amusement that sent shivers down her spine. "How about instead you tell me who else you suspect and perhaps I can be of assistance. Or I could accompany you to the village to report the theft to the nearest magister." When she didn't answer, he added, "Even better, you could explain why you're investigating this yourself when you have a vigilant and suspicion-prone guard as a member of your party."

"Hah," Batrice said, throwing him a disgusted glance. "You'd like that, wouldn't you? For me to explain everything so you can avoid getting caught the next time. Or to insinuate yourself into my good graces so I'll stop suspecting you altogether. I'm not entirely stupid, you know. I might occasionally act more quickly than I think, and I often don't think through the potential consequences of my actions as thoroughly as I should, but I won't be blinkered by your solicitude."

"All right," he said, surprising her. "Should I simply admit my guilt?"

"That would be helpful, yes," she replied sarcastically. "It would at least save me from creeping about in this ridiculous outfit. It might even allow me to sleep better at night knowing that if someone were to attempt to rob me again, at least it's someone I know."

"All right," he said, in a more serious tone. "I confess. It was me."

"Of course it was." Batrice narrowed her eyes at him. This was turning into a bit of a farce, and she really didn't have time for it. Coralynne could return at any moment. "Tell me, then, if you really were the thief, exactly how you intend to dispose of what you stole."

"I don't," he said with a shrug.

"You're just going to keep them?" she asked, allowing her eyes to widen. "Whatever for?"

"For my own amusement, of course."

"Well, I must say, I'm a bit shocked," she said primly, wondering what he could possibly be thinking had been stolen. He obviously didn't know the truth. Or was he only pretending not to know? This entire situation was making her head spin.

"Shocked that I know what to do with them, or shocked that I find them amusing?"

"There is nothing amusing, sir, about a lady's private belongings," she said with mock outrage.

"Perhaps not," he said, shrugging. "But I intend to keep them all the same. I hope you don't mind."

"Oh, but I do," she replied archly. "I need them. So now that you've been found out, you should return my possessions immediately."

He took two steps closer and looked down at her with suddenly serious eyes.

"No, I really don't think I should," he said softly. "But you should assuredly be more careful. What if I really am the thief? You're alone here, and if I wanted to harm you, there would be no one to stop me."

"No one?" she retorted, feeling a bit irritated by his assumption. "What am I, then? I don't know why you think I require a man to defend me, but if you insist on accosting me or attempting to damage my person, I am perfectly capable of doing something about it without flailing helplessly or calling for Rupert."

"And if I was too fast for you?"

"Yes, I'm very scared," she said calmly. "But you're not going to hurt me. There's nothing in it for you but risk, and, while I'm speaking plainly, you're simply not the type."

"You seem very certain of that."

"I am," she said frankly.

"You're very sure of your instincts for a debutante."

"You're suddenly very threatening for a scholar," she shot back.

His lips quirked with a sudden flash of humor. "If only I thought you took me seriously, as a scholar or otherwise."

She couldn't help herself. She leaned in and let herself smile back, just a little. "What sort of otherwise?"

Suddenly he was only a handsbreadth away. She'd barely seen him move, but then his hands were braced on either side of her on the bed. He leaned closer, and Batrice somehow lost the ability to breathe. There was a strange ache in her chest and a tingling in her fingertips where they rested on the coverlet.

"As a man, Miss Reyard," he said softly, his gaze roaming her face until it seemed to rest on her lips. "As a man who is accustomed to seeing the world pass him by, and thought little of it until he met you."

Dear heavens, he was flirting with her.

And she liked it. She liked it a great deal more than she should, considering that he wouldn't answer questions and was probably a thief. And for perhaps the first time in her life, she wanted very badly to flirt back but couldn't manage so much as a single word.

Where was her stage presence when she needed it the most?

The stage. Yes. Maybe she could find something to say if she pretended she were someone else.

"Are you going to kiss me or what?" she blurted out.

Well, it wasn't the practiced response she'd had in mind, but she supposed it would do. It was, after all, the only significant thing on her mind at the moment.

But much to her dismay—and embarrassment—he only sighed and retreated. Without kissing her first.

She'd been kissed before, of course. One was kissed often on the stage, but never by anyone she'd actually *wanted* to kiss her. And she did want Jamie to kiss her.

Why though? She barely knew him. Yes, he was beautiful and had gorgeous hair, intelligent eyes, a nice set of shoulders and perfect hands, but... that was hardly sufficient recommendation for kissing.

At least, that's what she ought to have been telling herself. What a proper debutante would have been thinking. Batrice was obviously not a proper debutante, because she was still dreaming about his lips.

"I might be only a scholar," he said, and she thought he sounded just a tiny bit hoarse, "but even I know that I shouldn't kiss you. Not here, and not now."

"Then when and where?"

"Nowhere and never, I expect," he returned, with what sounded like regret.

At least, she hoped it was regret. If she couldn't even inspire regret, what use was her career as an actress? And a little regret would go a long way towards softening the sting of what felt very much like rejection.

"Now you're going to give me some rot about being only a scholar and not good enough for the likes of me, aren't you?" she groused, trying to conceal her disappointment.

"Actually, I was going to say that it just isn't done to kiss someone right after you've admitted to stealing from them."

Her eyes narrowed. "You're ridiculous. You've had little opportunity, and no motive. I don't know what use a scholar could possibly have for those items unless..." She pondered it a bit. Could she get him to reveal whether or not he actually knew what was missing? "Even if you needed money, I can't imagine you would even know where to sell such things."

He only grinned. "Very good, Miss Reyard. But not good enough. You'll have to keep trying if you're hoping I'll admit to anything else."

"Don't think I won't," she said darkly. "This isn't over, you know."

"That," he said softly, "is exactly what I'm hoping."

And then he left her, with no sound but the click of the latch behind him.

Despite her regret, despite her annoyance, despite everything... Batrice discovered that she wasn't quite able to stop smiling.

Whatever he was—an admirer, an adversary, or simply an enigma—he was exactly the sort of adventure she'd hoped to find on this trip. And whether he was the thief or merely an opportunistic flirt, she was going to have a great deal of fun finding out.

The door opened again, so suddenly Batrice was startled out of her reverie. She had no time to even alter her expression before Coralynne tripped into the room with a beatific smile, sobering only when she saw Batrice.

"What *are* you wearing? And why do you look like you have a delicious secret that you're simply bursting to share?"

"What? Oh." Belatedly, Batrice realized she was still in her maid's costume. "I was... practicing," she said, not having to try too hard to sound embarrassed.

"Oh." Coralynne looked decidedly uncomfortable. "You mean... regarding what you said last night."

"Yes." Batrice drew up her knees and patted the bed, inviting Coralynne to sit down. "I'm sorry I didn't say anything sooner. It wasn't that I meant to hide my past from you, but it's become a habit to conceal it because of what it might do to my reputation."

"But surely you didn't think I would judge you for being an actress," Coralynne protested, sitting down and tucking her curls behind her ear.

"No. But my own family disowned me when they found out. So now that I've been sponsored by Lady Norelle, I'm doing my best to be respectable, and wouldn't want to create any sort of scandal by linking her name with my past behavior."

Coralynne nodded. "I do understand." She leaned forward eagerly. "And now that I know, will you tell me more about it? I promise not to breathe a word to anyone else, and it would be such a marvelous source of inspiration for my book."

Batrice held back a groan. People seemed to harbor many misapprehensions about life on the stage, but most prevalent was their assumption that it was a freewheeling, romantic existence. It wasn't. She'd enjoyed it, certainly, but it was a lot of work. Free of her parents' expectations? Yes. But those who chose such a life were also constrained by the need to feed, clothe, and house themselves by their own efforts.

"Of course," she said, hoping her smile looked more real than it felt. Maybe if she told Coralynne the pure, unvarnished truth, it would dispel her illusions about what it would be like to leave society behind to be a novelist. Not that she hoped to persuade her friend to abandon her dreams. But a woman should know more clearly what the implications would be before she took any irrevocable actions. And that was assuming they could gloss over the small matter of her already having pretended to elope.

"But first, what did Rupert say?"

Coralynne blushed again. "About what?"

Batrice hastily concealed the urge to grin. "About the thefts. You were going to tell him about our things being stolen."

"Oh. Right. Um..." Coralynne glanced down and began to pluck at the coverlet with her fingers. "I suppose I... well, I think I might have forgotten to mention it."

This time Batrice had no luck at all holding back laughter. "My dear, when are you going to admit that you are hopelessly in love?"

"What?" The other girl tried and utterly failed to look shocked. "That's ridiculous. I am not in love. I might find Rupert... distractingly attractive, but I couldn't possibly be in love. Besides, as I've told you before, Rupert is in love with you, and I would simply never have a chance with him."

"Why not?" Batrice asked fiercely. "Why are you so content to imagine love stories for other people and yet so firmly reject your own when it's right under your nose?"

Coralynne's mouth opened, and her eyes flew wide, but for once, she really didn't seem to have an answer. Until she hung her head and began toying with a loose string on the bed again.

"Don't think I haven't imagined a romance for myself, Miss Reyard," she said softly. "I've imagined ever so many. Ever since I was, oh, fourteen or fifteen, I've wondered what it would be like to fall in love, and painted myself a picture of the handsome gentleman who would sweep me away and dedicate himself to my happiness."

"But?"

"But he never came," she said simply. "Not one single man of my acquaintance ever inspired half the feelings those imagined ones did. And after spending years dreaming of love, I simply wasn't willing to accept less."

"Then what about now?" Batrice insisted. "Don't tell me you've given up."

"After hoping for so long, eventually I had to stop." Her eyes pleaded with Batrice to understand. "It's exhausting, continually looking around the corner, believing in something that may never appear. I knew I needed to find my joys and my satisfaction in other things, and I have. I love my work. I'm looking forward to being free to write and live as I choose, without the pressure of being expected to find a husband."

"And I'm glad for you," Batrice said sincerely. "I really am. But is this truly enough reason to ignore something that's right in front of you? Can you not hope, just a little? Enough to give it a chance?"

"And have all those hopes dashed when I realize it was all in my imagination yet again?" Coralynne said. "No. I can't, Miss Reyard. If romance is ever going to find me, it will have to sweep me off my feet and carry me away, because I'm done being in love alone."

It was humbling to be entrusted with such a deeply personal truth, and Batrice felt her eyes prick with tears at the pain and loneliness in her friend's voice. Scooting closer, she wrapped her arms around Coralynne's shoulders and hugged her fiercely.

"I understand," she said, and strangely, she did. "I promise not to tease you about it anymore. Now, what is it you want to know about being an actress?"

Coralynne hugged her back. "Everything," she announced, in a slightly shaky voice.

"Everything it is."

CHAPTER 9

They were both laughing over one of Batrice's more amusing stage mishaps when they heard a knock at the door. Batrice jumped off the bed to open it and found a maid standing in the hall, wearing a worried expression while holding out a folded garment.

"I'm ever so sorry, Miss. We washed your cloak, but the stains just wouldn't come out."

Batrice accepted the folds of formerly white wool and shook them out so she could see just how bad the damage was.

"Oh my," she said, unable to suppress a chuckle. The hood was now a rusty, reddish color from the quantities of blood she'd mopped up, and the rest was mottled with irregular patches of brown. "Perhaps I should go roll in the mud a bit longer, so it can all be the same color."

Once she realized Batrice was not going to berate her, the maid let out a relieved sigh. "Also, begging your pardon, but the other members of your party are wishing to speak with you below, Miss."

"Thank you." Batrice nodded and smiled before closing the door and turning to Coralynne. "Hopefully they'll have news about the carriage!"

But it was nothing so cheerful. Instead, once Batrice changed out of her maid's outfit, and they descended the stairs, they found Rupert waiting for them with an expression oddly caught between nervous and angry.

"It is my duty to inform you"—he addressed his icy comments to Batrice —"that your dog has escaped."

Escaped?

"*My* dog?" she inquired coolly, unwilling to allow herself to be verbally trampled on when she'd done nothing to deserve it. "Might I remind you that the dog has nothing to do with me? I didn't even know it was in the carriage until we were underway."

"It is in your charge," he replied stubbornly, almost urgently. "And as it is a blight and a pestilence and completely impossible to contain, I must ask that you be responsible for its behavior."

"Actually," she reminded him, "the dog was in *your* charge when it escaped."

"From a completely enclosed area." He almost snarled the words. "It was sleeping in a stall when I left to determine how the work on the coach was progressing, and when I returned from the wheelwright, it had disappeared."

"And you automatically assumed it was due to inherent evil on the part of a dog, rather than human agency?"

His face went oddly pale at her suggestion. Perhaps he had, indeed, assumed such depths of depravity on the part of an admittedly annoying but not exactly malevolent animal. Or, he was only now realizing that if the dog had been stolen, he would be the one held primarily responsible.

"We will simply have to split up to look for it," Batrice announced.

"Neither of you is wandering around the countryside alone," Rupert growled.

"Of course not," she said sweetly. "We will, of course, go in pairs. Cora-lynne can go with me to protect my virtue, and you can go with John."

He looked startled for a moment but recovered quickly. "John is aiding the wheelwright in hopes of finishing the work by tomorrow morning."

"Well, we can hardly go traipsing around the countryside in a group of three," Batrice argued. "We wouldn't get much searching done."

"Perhaps I could be of help?"

Jamie. Batrice very deliberately did not turn around. She was too busy concealing the myriad emotions provoked by the sound of his voice.

"Thank you," Rupert said stiffly, "but I'm sure we will not require your assistance, so don't put yourself to any trouble on our account."

"But I'm happy to assist. Did I hear correctly that Mayhem has gone missing?"

"You gave it a name?" Rupert groused.

"Yes, he's disappeared." Coralynne answered Jamie's question when it became clear no one else was going to. "And we would very much appreciate any help in finding him. The poor thing is probably terrified being out there on his own."

In Batrice's experience, puppies liked being out on their own—getting dirty, digging holes, chewing on everything, and rolling in whatever putrid substances they could find.

"Then we should begin searching without delay." Jamie was sounding suspiciously polite.

"I do wish I could be of service." The mournful voice of Sir Abner intruded from a chair by the fire. "If only I were younger, more spry, I would be delighted to go tramping about the countryside with you young folks."

"Thank you," Batrice said, wishing her grandmother was a bit more like the kindly old man. But Lady Entwhistle was neither jovial nor helpful, and would have frowned excessively on Sir Abner's relaxed approach to social standing. "But I'm sure we'll be able to find him without much trouble. He can't have gotten far."

It didn't take long to realize that the furry little beast had proven her wrong. No one around the inn yard could recall seeing him, although one of the hostlers presented them with a harness strap that had been completely chewed through. Rupert grudgingly promised to pay for it, his teeth clenched tightly together against what would probably have been a series of epithets unsuitable for the ladies' ears.

While he discussed the matter with the hostler and grew visibly more agitated, Coralynne stood nearby watching his every move, so Batrice took the opportunity to slip out and away, glancing around her before choosing a path into the trees that surrounded the back of the inn. A forest like that probably looked like a giant playground to a pup that had been raised in the city, so he had likely wandered off in pursuit of some fascinating smell.

"Where are you, you miserable little hairball?" she called into the depths of the wood. "You'd best come back, or I swear I'll find an even uglier collar for you."

The chuckle behind her might have startled her had she not been very well aware by that time of Jamie's sneaking abilities.

"You know, it's entirely possible that his collar is at fault in this whole business," Jamie observed.

"I suppose he could have gotten it caught on something," she acknowledged, trying to appear unaffected by his presence. "I assure you, it wasn't my idea to inflict something that ridiculous on him, despicable minion of evil or not."

"I didn't mean it in that way," Jamie said soberly. "Perhaps you've been among the gentry too long to realize it, but that bauble he's wearing appears to be real silver. Well worth stealing for anyone in financial straits."

It was true. Now that he'd pointed it out, Batrice wondered why she hadn't considered that before.

"But why steal the whole dog? The collar would be easy enough to remove, and no one would bother to look for it."

Jamie shrugged.

"Come now," she said, with a hint of sarcasm, "as an admitted thief, shouldn't you have some insight into the way a fellow thief's mind might work?"

"I suppose I should," he said, with a wry quirk to his lips, "but in this case, I'm afraid I have nothing to offer. Perhaps I prefer rather less obvious forms of theft."

Sensing the conversation turning in a less humorous direction, Batrice set off into the trees again, pretending to be wholly occupied with peering around her for any sign of the wayward pup. In reality, she was sneaking occasional glances at Jamie, wondering whether she ought to be worried that he'd followed her into the woods.

"Why exactly are you following me?" she asked. Her tone was supposed to sound innocent, but the words came out a little snappish.

"You did suggest we search in pairs."

"To make Rupert feel more comfortable," she argued. "I should probably not be out here in company with a man who steals from ladies' trunks, leaves threatening notes, and seems to appear in my vicinity with alarming frequency."

Now that she thought about it, the note didn't really seem to fit. It was one thing to steal small items, but to threaten random travelers with misfortune unless they abandoned their journey? Perhaps that had been nothing more than an incredibly strange prank dreamed up by someone in her party.

"You've received a note?" The suddenly sharp tone in Jamie's voice made her stop and turn to face him. "What did it say?"

"So you aren't going to claim responsibility?" she asked lightly. "I have a difficult time imagining myself the target of *two* criminals bent on some mysterious course of action."

"No." He sounded almost harsh. "It wasn't me. Did the note threaten your safety?"

She placed her hands on her hips and took a moment to observe him. Oddly, his denial of being the one to leave the note made her wonder whether he might not have been telling the truth about the theft. If he was willing to deny the note, why not deny both?

"No," she said, after a long pause. "At least, not directly. It threatened further catastrophes if we continue on our present course. By 'catastrophes,' I suppose it was referring to the carriage accident and the thefts. But I really don't have any way of knowing. It was rather cryptic."

His brow knitted as she spoke, and she decided he was still incredibly handsome even when he was angry.

"And before you ask, it was in block print, so there's no use trying to figure out whose handwriting it could have been."

"I expected as much," he said, sounding distracted.

"You expected it?" she echoed. "Then you have prior experience with threatening notes? Do you receive them often? From other scholars jealous of your work, perhaps?" She meant it as a joke, but he remained serious.

"Scholars are as prone to devious behavior as anyone, Miss Reyard."

"Noted." After Rupert's dismissal of her worries, Jamie's reaction was perhaps even more unnerving than it might have been otherwise. He seemed to genuinely believe there was some form of danger. "Given your experience, then, what would you suggest we do?"

"Inform every member of your party, to begin with."

"I tried." She failed to conceal her irritation. "Rupert believes I've lost my mind. Or at least that Coralynne and I have lost our possessions and are blaming it on a thief in order to be dramatic."

She'd hoped he would immediately denounce Rupert, but he only grunted under his breath.

"Have you considered halting your journey? Surely it isn't worth anyone's life."

"I would like nothing better than to simply return home," she admitted. "At least, that was the case until..."

Batrice could see his eyes crease with the beginnings of a smile. "Until you were threatened. Then you immediately became determined to see it through because you couldn't allow this unknown villain to best you."

She hadn't really examined her feelings until he pointed it out, but...

"You're right," she said, a bit horrified by how easily he'd seen through her. Understood her. "I want to know who it is and why they've chosen to threaten me. I'm no one, really, and there's no apparent explanation for any of this. So I can't walk away now, not with the mystery left unsolved."

He nodded. "I couldn't either. But I hope you'll agree to be cautious. This note might seem little more than odd to you, but whoever left it could be more serious than you imagine. And..." His eyes locked with hers. "I have no desire to see you hurt."

"I thank you for your concern," she said primly, choosing to look at the ground rather than continue to bear the intensity of his gaze. "But for the moment, I believe my primary focus must be finding that wretched dog. It isn't even mine, and I suppose I would feel a bit bad if I lost it somewhere along the road."

"How did you end up transporting someone else's dog?"

She shrugged. "It was meant as a present from my court sponsor to my ailing grandmother, or so I assume. No one asked me whether my grandmother liked dogs or whether I wanted to be stuck with one on a long carriage journey. Just left it in my coach in a basket, and by the time I realized what had happened, it was too late to protest."

"In a basket?" His expression grew odd for a moment but soon became more amused than anything. "And I assume by the vehemence of your protests that you really don't care for dogs yourself?"

"Loathe them," she announced. "At least, the small, whiny variety. I am rather fond of the large floppy sort that lays around the fire and stares up at you adoringly without needing constant reassurance or attention."

He appeared to consider that for a moment. "If your dog is of the variety that requires frequent attention, I doubt that it would have wandered far into these woods where there are no people at all. Have you considered that it might have followed someone to the village?"

"No," she said frankly, "but I should have. Can you find your way there without needing to go back through the inn yard?"

"Avoiding someone, Miss Reyard?" he asked, one eyebrow raised.

"Yes." She didn't bother to elaborate, because somehow, she knew he would already understand.

He laughed. "Then follow me."

Jamie appeared utterly certain of his course through the trees, so Batrice focused on finding her footing on the uneven ground. Once again she wished for her boots, rather than the flimsy buttoned affairs ladies were expected to wear with their dresses. These sank into the soft, mossy ground, and gave no purchase at all when clambering over a downed tree or crossing a rocky patch.

But she wasn't about to complain or give Jamie any other reason to believe her incapable of keeping up. Not even when she realized that the ground ahead fell away due to a small, rocky drop-off, and that Jamie had simply leaped down and continued on.

Batrice sized up the drop and considered her chances of jumping off and landing on her feet without her skirts flying up and displaying far more of her undergarments than would be regarded as strictly respectable. Or, she could sit on the edge, and lower herself down slowly, but it would leave her dress filthy and probably torn, which wouldn't exactly look respectable either, especially not when she emerged from the woods in company with a strange man.

When she looked up from her musings, Jamie stood only a few feet away, regarding her with a devilish grin.

"You came this way on purpose," she accused.

"I might have," he acknowledged, strolling up to the base of the rock. "If I were familiar with the area and looking for a way to flirt with a young lady by helping her out of a precarious situation."

"Which would make you a cad," she announced.

"Only if I planned it," he countered. "In this case, I'm as new to these woods as you are, and can only be considered a gentleman for offering to help you."

"*Have* you offered to help me?" she asked, folding her arms. "Because I seem to have missed that part."

"Miss Reyard, I would consider it an honor if you would allow me to assist you in your hour of need," he replied, with a deeply exaggerated bow.

She couldn't resist answering in kind. "Why, my good sir"—she fluttered an imaginary fan—"it is quite chivalrous of you to offer. I declare, I am overcome with gratitude for your magnanimity."

"You should probably know," he said, holding her gaze as she reached down to place her hands on his shoulders, "that magnanimity is not in my nature."

The moment she jumped, his hands—his perfect hands—caught her waist and swung her around until she landed gently and smoothly on the ground. But they didn't let go, and Batrice somehow failed to step away.

Instead, they stood, toe to toe, with her hands now, inexplicably, resting on his chest, where she could feel his heart beating somewhat faster than she thought their little stroll through the woods could explain. There was a strange, breathless sort of flutter in the vicinity of her own heart, so perhaps he felt it too...

"What *is* in your nature?" she asked, close enough now to see flecks of amber and gold in his brown eyes, which still hadn't left her face.

One of his hands abandoned her waist and crept up slowly until his thumb brushed ever so gently across her cheek, leaving a trail of fire in its wake.

Batrice's heart thundered in her chest, and her breath stuttered. Was he really going to kiss her this time?

He leaned in a little closer and whispered, "You had dirt on your face."

She jerked away from him, disappointment turning her stomach to lead. "Thank you," she said, as emotionlessly as possible, and stalked off without really bothering about direction.

This might have proven embarrassing if she'd managed to get herself lost, but by that time they were close enough to the village that she could make out the sounds of human habitation—the clang of a hammer, and the shouts of children at play. After only a short distance, she stumbled onto the road that led west out of the village.

Not stopping to see whether Jamie was behind her, she turned towards the main square, shaking out her skirts and straightening her hair as she went. It seemed likely that Mayhem would be causing some sort of trouble wherever he went, so she didn't even bother to approach any of the villagers, just walked through the center of town listening for a commotion. And sure enough, she found one when she heard children shouting behind what appeared to be a butcher shop.

Batrice dashed around the side, vaguely aware of Jamie at her heels, and found a small crowd gathered around something on the ground. Some of them were cheering, and the shouts of "get 'im" caused a surge of anxiety until she shoved her way through and discovered that they were, in fact, cheering *for* Mayhem. He was filthy, and the ruffles on his collar were torn, but he appeared entirely pleased with himself at having cornered some sort of small, rat-like creature. Ferocious puppy growls rolled from his throat as he tried to find a way into its hiding place under an abandoned wooden crate.

"You, sir, are in a great deal of trouble," Batrice said sternly, grabbing him by the scruff of his neck and holding him up. Somehow, the ridiculous silver ball was still dangling from his collar.

"Aw, can't you leave 'im, Miss?" one of the boys begged. "He was only going after the goblin."

The *what?*

Shoving the puppy at Jamie, who took it without protest, she crouched down to peer into the shadows inside the broken crate. A tiny, wrinkled, hairless creature with enormous ears stared back at her out of round blue eyes. As she shuffled forward, it shrank even further back and hissed malevolently.

"There is no such thing as goblins," she said firmly, and reached into the crate as a chorus of gasps sounded around her.

There was a brief scuffle, but it took only a few moments for her to withdraw her hand, bringing with it what proved to be nothing more than a cat—a small, terrified, completely hairless cat.

Batrice burst out laughing and cradled it to her chest, where, after a moment or two, it stopped struggling and began to relax, as if realizing it might actually have found a safe haven.

"It's only a kitten," she announced, shooting a stern look at the boy who'd called it a goblin. "And it's completely terrified. How could you let it be attacked like that?"

"It's unnatural, Miss," the boy said solemnly. "Nobody wants a thing like that lurking around."

All right, so it was odd-looking. Maybe even ugly. But in a strangely endearing sort of way. Batrice cuddled the kitten closer. "Who does it belong to?"

"Nobody knows," the boy said with a shrug. "Been trying to get rid of it in case it's bad luck."

Suddenly outraged on the kitten's behalf, Batrice stared down at the boy and took a threatening step closer. "I suppose we should also get rid of *you* if all your hair should happen to fall out."

His eyes widened. "Can't do that, Miss! My mum would be ever so upset."

"Well, how do you think the kitten's mum feels?" she snapped. "But in any case, I'm taking the cat, so you won't need to worry about seeing it around here anymore."

She whirled and made a credible attempt to stalk away, but nearly collided with Jamie. He still held Mayhem and was watching her with laughter creasing the corners of his eyes.

"Terrorizing children, Miss Reyard?"

"He deserved it," she replied defensively.

"And I don't suppose you've considered what you're going to do with the cat now that you've saved it."

"I'm taking it with me, of course," she said loftily, unwilling to let him see her chagrin. Confining herself and Coralynne to the inside of a carriage with two animals already ill-disposed towards one another did not, at that moment, seem like one of her best ideas.

"Do you always collect strays, then?"

"Only when necessary." And really, what else could she have done? Anyone could have seen that the kitten needed someone to take its side.

"You've the start of an impressive collection, Miss Reyard. First a puppy, then a scholar, and now a kitten."

"You forgot the would-be-novelist, the nearly mute coachman, and the disapproving guard," she muttered, moving around him to head back down the street in the direction of the inn.

Really, it was growing a bit ridiculous. But she couldn't have left the poor creature behind to be tormented just because it happened to be born without hair. And the longer she looked at it, the cuter she found it—wrinkled face, enormous ears and all.

"And do you have a plan for explaining how you disappeared in search of one animal and came back with two?" Jamie inquired innocently.

"Of course," she said, lowering her lashes and glancing up at him from the side. "I plan to tell them everything was your fault."

CHAPTER 10

*T*he remainder of the day might have been described as tense. Rupert had at first exhibited a rather shocking degree of relief when Batrice and Jamie reappeared with the puppy, but had since grown increasingly ill-humored, no doubt over being forced to pay for the ruined harness. He immediately acquired a leash and spent the entire afternoon at the wheelwright's, most likely to avoid saying anything he might regret to Batrice.

And he hadn't even seen the cat. She'd smuggled it into the inn beneath her coat and hidden it in her room.

Coralynne had gaped and exclaimed in horror at first, but soon fell under the spell of the adorably wrinkled creature and agreed to keep it secret until they were underway the following day.

Which dawned bright and hopeful, at least for Coralynne and Batrice. The puppy had spent the night in the stable howling pitifully, a piercing sound that had been audible even from inside the inn, which meant that Rupert and John likely hadn't slept more than a few uneasy hours.

Sure enough, as the girls were enjoying a leisurely breakfast in the inn's common room, Rupert stalked in with shadows under his eyes and the beginnings of a beard gracing his jaw. Coralynne, from the look on her face, rather liked the effect but fixed her gaze firmly on her plate as he approached the table.

"We'll be ready to depart by midmorning, Miss Reyard," he said stiffly. "If you and Miss Smythe would be so good as to ensure that your baggage is ready to be brought down after breakfast."

"Of course." Batrice smiled brightly, feeling only slightly guilty for the difficult night he'd had. The puppy wasn't exactly her fault after all. "Oh, and Rupert?" He paused in mid-retreat. "Have you been able to discover whether our friend the scholar has been able to replace his phaeton?"

"It's hardly my business, Miss Reyard."

"Oh, but I believe it is," she said. "The circumstances have not changed. The accident was our fault, and we ought to take responsibility. If he has not yet secured another way to continue his journey, I believe we must offer to convey him to his destination, or at least insofar as we are able without too great of a detour from our present course."

She'd thought it over at length the previous day, and decided that she wasn't quite ready to let Jamie out of her sight. And not only because she rather liked looking at him, though it was certainly a worthwhile consideration. No, she still hadn't quite reconciled his behavior with his claims to be the thief that had stolen her face powder and Coralynne's pounce.

Until she'd resolved that matter to her satisfaction, she would rather have him where she could keep an eye on him.

That way, if there were any further disturbances—whether searches of their bags or sinister notes—she would be able to confirm either his guilt or his innocence.

"It would not be appropriate, Miss Reyard," Rupert said between clenched teeth. "While you are traveling under the aegis of the royal crest, you must adhere to certain standards of decorum. Taking up random strangers along the road is not the sort of behavior Lady Norelle expects of you."

"Nor is abandoning someone when we have been the cause of their injury," she replied, for once entirely confident she was in the right. "It would be a stain on the king's reputation, and I could not face Lady Norelle after perpetrating such a grave injustice."

"And his apparent fascination with you has nothing to do with your determination to aid him?"

Batrice could feel herself flushing slightly under his cold-eyed scrutiny, but refused to budge. "I'm sure you're wrong, but in any case, I cannot allow his behavior to be the guide of mine. He has offered me no insult, nor has he behaved inappropriately towards any member of our party." Well, mostly he hadn't. She wasn't sure about that moment in the woods. Or that moment in her room...

But the most inappropriate thing about that, in her opinion, had been his failure to kiss her. Not that she intended to share that information with her guard.

"I'm sorry," she said firmly, "but I will not be changing my mind. It is the right thing to do, and cannot truly be considered inappropriate when I am attended at all times by my maid. Please make the necessary inquiries, and should Lady Norelle disapprove, I will take full responsibility for overriding your wishes and advice."

Rupert's face turned hard and expressionless as he snapped his heels together and offered her a precise, straight-backed bow. He could not have signaled his frustration more strongly had he slapped her in the face.

She sighed as he left and returned her attention to her breakfast, but her appetite was gone.

"He really does mean well, you know," Coralynne said in a small voice, her eyes on her plate.

"I know," Batrice said wearily. "And he is a good man with only our well-being in mind. But that does not make it easier to fight him for what I know is right when I am already fighting my own instincts in search of a way forward."

"What do you fear?"

"I still have no idea who stole from us, Coralynne. I cannot decipher who might have written that note, nor what they might hope to accomplish. Are there more disasters in store along the road? Or was it a meaningless threat to throw us off the scent of the real culprit?"

"I have given it some thought," Coralynne announced, "and have a few ideas for you to consider."

"Then please share, but if you're only planning to accuse Jamie of being a highwayman again, perhaps we might devote ourselves to a new theory."

"If this were a novel..." Coralynne began, and Batrice only just managed not to slap her palm to her forehead.

This was not a novel or a play. It was real life. It was never easy or predictable—it was messy and filled with pitfalls. People were never exactly one thing or another.

"...our friend, the scholar, would most definitely be the villain. He's handsome and disarming and mysterious, exactly the sort of person to seem trustworthy while plotting to rob us of everything."

Batrice opened her mouth, but Coralynne wasn't done.

"Of course, this is not a novel. But I still think we must consider the unexpected. If this story were a mystery, we might suspect the butler or the aging governess. We simply need to determine a motive."

"Who is the butler?" Batrice asked, feeling a bit confused.

"Anyone who may have disappeared into the background of our perception," Coralynne explained patiently. "Someone we would never think to consider a danger or a threat."

Hmmm. She might be onto something there. But who? When Batrice considered those who had been present on all occasions where thefts had taken place, and whom she would initially hesitate to suspect, she first came up with Rupert and John. Should she be wary of them? Consider their potential motives for villainy?

And what of the woman in the purple dress? She might seem elderly and dignified, but what if it was a ruse? What if she were not actually sick at all, but feigning illness in order to remain close to Batrice and her party?

Perhaps the only way to know for sure was to continue on while remaining alert for any further thefts or suspicious behavior. From anyone. Anyone at all.

When they finally stepped into the yard in preparation for departure, Batrice tried not to hold her breath, but it was impossible not to feel at least a degree of anticipation. Would Jamie be coming with them?

Fortunately, she wasn't kept in suspense for long. He strode from the inn, a bag over one shoulder, and offered a quick bow to her and Coralynne.

"Miss Reyard, Miss Smythe. I suspect that I have you ladies to thank for my inclusion in your party this morning."

"Without a doubt," Batrice said brightly. "On occasion, I can be trusted to do the right thing. Your accident was our fault, so I intend to do whatever we can to set things right. Have you spoken with John or Rupert about your destination?"

"No need, Miss Reyard," he assured her. "You mentioned Peridale, and I am traveling on even beyond there. I am content to ride with you as far as you go and then find my own way afterwards."

"Excellent." Batrice very carefully did not permit her exultation to show on her face, but she felt a distinct sense of satisfaction at realizing that she wouldn't be forced to say goodbye to the mysterious scholar just yet. She also felt a deliberate nudge from Coralynne's elbow, but whether it was by way of warning or congratulations, she wasn't sure and didn't care to ask.

Once they were all seated, and Mayhem had been handed in by a silent and inscrutable John, Batrice opened her handbag and withdrew the sleepy and somewhat annoyed kitten.

It peered up at her and yawned, showing its mouthful of needle teeth, then promptly curled up in her lap, giving every indication that it intended to go back to sleep.

Mayhem, however, had other ideas.

The moment he caught sight of his erstwhile enemy, he set up a ferocious barking, with the occasional howl of outrage mixed in for good measure.

Jamie managed to restrain him, while Batrice was poised to grab the kitten, should it seem inclined to join the fray, but it merely lifted its head, shot the pup a dirty look, and curled up again.

Batrice burst out laughing. "And that is why I prefer cats," she said. "Perhaps if we put Mayhem in his basket it will help him feel comfortable enough to nap. I know he barely slept at all last night."

Jamie managed the feat, and the coach rumbled out of the inn yard only a brief time later. Sure enough, only a short distance down the uneven road, the jolting lulled the puppy to sleep, whereafter they were all granted a blessed respite from his bloodthirsty yowls.

A respite that seemed to set the tone for the remainder of the day's journey. Both animals slept for the majority of the time, and other than brief stops out of necessity, their drive proved smooth and uneventful. They rolled past miles and miles of unbroken forest, with only the occasional small village to break the monotony, and what inhabitants Batrice glimpsed appeared to regard the travelers with more suspicion than curiosity.

Coralynne was unable to write due to the motion of the carriage, so she spent most of the time staring out the window. Jamie appeared to be asleep during the remainder of the morning hours and disinclined to conversation for the majority of the afternoon, so Batrice occupied herself with stroking the kitten's velvety skin and wondering what her grandmother was going to say when she saw it.

Never mind her grandmother... Rupert was going to have a fit.

They stopped for the night at a tiny inn built of dark timbers. Batrice thought it looked particularly unwelcoming, but it wasn't as though they were overwhelmed with choices in the middle of the forest.

As she descended from the carriage, Rupert stood nearby, waiting impatiently to escort her and Coralynne inside, but Batrice balked.

"Actually," she said, "I would prefer to wait until our trunks are unloaded. Coralynne, you may go inside and inquire about the room, and I will stay here with John."

"A common inn yard is hardly an appropriate place for you, Miss Reyard," Rupert said sternly. "You can wait for your bags inside."

"No, I think not." She wasn't going to be swayed. Not this time. "Whether you believe me or not, both Coralynne and I have been subjected to the indignity of having our belongings rifled through by some stranger, and I will not risk having it happen again. I intend to keep a close eye on my trunk from now on."

"I don't understand why you insist on maligning my ability to see to the safety of your bags," Rupert snapped, running a frustrated hand through his hair.

"Perhaps because you chose not to believe me when I reported that their safety had been compromised," Batrice said. "Now please, Rupert, you are making a bit of a scene."

Perhaps she derived a bit too much satisfaction from the shocked stare that answered her, but he did rather deserve it, for treating her as he had.

"I am sorry if you don't like it, but I will not be swayed," she continued firmly. "You may report my behavior to Lady Norelle if you choose, but there is no danger involved, and there is no impropriety when we are standing in the open. If a highwayman should descend on the inn and make off with me in your absence, you have my permission to disapprove of me as much as you like, but until then, I am choosing to involve myself in the protection of my possessions and those of my maid."

A brief staredown ensued, but it was over quickly. To Batrice's surprise, Rupert's expression changed to something far more neutral, and he nodded.

"Very well, Miss Reyard."

After he, Coralynne, and Jamie had disappeared inside the inn, John came around the front of the horses and approached her, though he still didn't quite meet her eyes.

"Thieves, Miss Reyard?"

So Rupert hadn't told him.

"We believe so, as ridiculous as it sounds," she admitted. "Our bags were very clearly disordered, and each of us was missing an insignificant personal item afterwards. I realize that it's difficult to believe anyone would go to the trouble for so little gain, but it was distressing to realize someone had been pawing through my dresses."

"I've not seen anyone," John said, "but I'll keep a better eye out."

"Thank you," Batrice said sincerely. "That's very comforting. I'm sure you'll be in the best position to watch over our things whenever they are out of our sight."

John nodded and disappeared again, as seemed to be his habit.

The remainder of the evening, fortunately, seemed to go more smoothly. The rooms were more comfortable than the outside of the inn suggested, and Batrice was able to smuggle her new friend upstairs with no difficulty.

Once she and Coralynne were settled for the night, and they'd determined that nothing further was missing from their belongings, Batrice started wondering once more what the thief might have been after.

They obviously hadn't found it, but why they'd expected to find it might be a better question. There was really nothing remarkable about either her or Coralynne. Neither of them was particularly well-dressed, nor did they wear any jewelry. Her trunk was a bit worn, and she didn't carry a great deal of baggage. With only one driver and one guard, they also didn't give the impression of being particularly wealthy or worried about safety.

But there was one thing about them that might stand out to a casual observer—they were traveling in a royal coach. Rupert had alluded to this in a failed attempt to convince her to behave differently, assuming that others would notice her connection to the royal family and make unflattering assumptions.

What if the reverse were true? What if someone was making assumptions about her wealth or influence based on that crest on the carriage door?

Worrying over the problem kept her up much of the night, so she was not exactly at her best when she appeared in the inn's common room for breakfast the next morning. She was also far too tired to employ much tact when she approached Rupert over his eggs and potatoes.

"What if we're being targeted because we're traveling in a royal coach?" she challenged without preamble. "The thief may expect we're carrying something expensive or important, and if that's the case, he may not rest until he finds it. What if we were to switch vehicles?"

Rupert simply shoveled another forkful of eggs into his mouth.

"Perhaps then whoever is following us would leave us alone."

"Miss Reyard," he said, after he swallowed the eggs, "we are not going to the trouble of finding another adequate vehicle in the middle of nowhere simply because you have imagined yourself the target of a thief. Thieves do not follow young ladies through miles of forest to steal face powder. Perhaps you should try to get more sleep instead of troubling the rest of us with your wild theories."

Perhaps it was for the best that Coralynne was refusing to be in love with the utterly infuriating man. He might be handsome and adept with a sword, but it would be difficult indeed to reconcile herself to allowing a friend to marry someone with neither heart nor intelligence.

None of the responses that came to mind were reasonable or fit for polite company, so Batrice turned to go. She was halfway out of the room when it struck her, and she almost tripped with the force of the thought.

What if it had been Rupert all along?

As before, it was difficult to believe anyone Lady Norelle had entrusted with her safety to be capable of villainy, but what choice did she have? As her guard, he ought to be taking her concerns seriously. Or at least pretending to. What motive could he possibly have for disbelieving her claims? Unless he simply didn't like her and was behaving out of a strongly-held grudge, but why would Lady Norelle have sent her on such a long journey with someone who was capable of putting pettiness over the safety of those entrusted to his care?

Neither theory made sense. But if one of them was to be thought more likely than the other, Batrice was tempted to choose the first. After all, even a generally honorable person might be tempted to moral indiscretion under the right circumstances.

And if it could be true of Rupert, what of John? Could they be in it together, one dismissing her and the other offering a sympathetic ear to allay her concerns?

But how would she ever know? And even if she could find proof, did she want to expose them? Should she accuse them and be wrong, it would make the remainder of their journey unspeakably awkward. And if she were right, they might well simply abandon her and Coralynne on the road, rather than risk being caught in their transgressions.

No. Better to wait. Watch. And never reveal her suspicions to Coralynne until she obtained incontrovertible proof of their wrongdoing. No reason to spoil a perfectly good romance if the object of her friend's affections was nothing worse than a bit of a grump.

CHAPTER 11

*I*t was another uneventful day of travel, and well before the end of it, Batrice had grown heartily bored of the entire journey. Jamie seemed curiously reluctant to be drawn into conversation while Coralynne was present, perhaps sensing her suspicion and distrust.

Their stops grew longer and more difficult to explain, as it took the kitten considerable time to find appropriate places for its personal business, and Batrice still hadn't revealed its presence to Rupert or John. She'd grown quite fond of it, however, and laughingly decided to christen it Goblin, as its strange looks didn't distress her in the slightest. She rather liked that it was different than other cats, and couldn't resist smiling at its playful attacks on her skirts, or the surprised look in its round blue eyes when it pounced at shadows in the woods and completely failed to catch anything.

After each stop, she would march back to the carriage with her head held high, trying to suppress laughter as she imagined what the men must be thinking had kept her in the woods for such an inordinate amount of time.

Jamie more than justified his inclusion in the party by spending his time occupying the puppy with games. He allowed Mayhem to chew on his boots, or sent him chasing from one side of the carriage to the other after the silver ball, which he'd found a way to detach from the ruffled collar. While the puppy slept, he would sit staring out the window, rolling the ball distractedly between his fingers, tracing the etchings in an absent-minded way.

"No, Miss Reyard, I do not intend to steal it," he said, when he caught her watching him. His lips quirked in amusement. "I prefer to have something to do with my hands, and it was a convenient distraction. Would it make you feel better if I solemnly swear to return it before the end of the day?"

"Yes." Coralynne spoke up, a little defiantly, as if fearing that Batrice would contradict her. "After all, we don't really know you. And scholars are well known to be lacking in resources. Perhaps you might be thinking of financing your journey by selling it, reasoning that no one would miss such a pointless object."

"By such logic, oughtn't we also suspect you?" he returned mildly. "After all, novelists are, if anything, more famously impecunious than scholars."

Batrice drew in a quick breath, fearing that the two were about to come to blows, but instead of taking offense, Coralynne beamed at the "highway-man" as though he'd offered her the highest of compliments.

"You're right!" she said brightly. "But how did you know I'm a novelist?"

"It seemed obvious," he said, with a quick glance at Batrice. Apparently, he'd heard what she'd muttered under her breath shortly after they'd rescued Goblin, but wasn't sure she wanted him to reveal the source of his information.

"I'm actually Miss Reyard's maid," Coralynne said, blushing slightly, "but it is my highest aspiration to eventually make my own way through writing."

"And I admire you for it," Jamie replied. "I can say without hesitation that it's a difficult road, but a rewarding one if you have the gift and the ambition to pursue it."

Obviously, it was remarkably easy to win Coralynne's trust, Batrice thought a little sourly, as her friend began to smile, her eyes shining with what looked like hope.

"Oh, thank you," she said fervently. "That's a very kind thing to say. Even if you are a highwayman, you're a very thoughtful one."

Jamie laughed. "I almost wish I could accept such an accolade, but I'm afraid 'sincere scholar' is the best, and possibly the worst, that can be said of me."

"The worst?" Batrice couldn't help quizzing him softly from her corner, while raising an eyebrow at the contradiction. "That's a peculiar view of scholarship, given what else you've done."

"Scholars are as prone to mistakes and miscalculations as anyone else."

"Then you're saying it was a mistake?"

"Only if it makes you think badly of me."

"How could it not?"

"Perhaps if you considered the possibility that my motives were good."

As their eyes locked, and Coralynne stared from one of them to the other, Batrice began to wonder whether they were even talking about the same thing. Was it possible... could he be talking about that almost-kiss? The fact that he'd nearly kissed her, or the fact that he hadn't?

If nearly kissing her was the first thing that came to his mind as a mistake, did that mean he wasn't the thief after all? She wanted to confront him, but it wasn't as if she could do so in front of Coralynne.

They arrived a bit later than usual at their inn that night, an inconvenience which Rupert heroically prevented himself from blaming on Batrice and her rather prolonged forays into the woods. Instead, he assumed an air of stoic martyrdom and refused to speak to her, though he did help Coralynne out of the carriage and escort her inside. At least he didn't offer to take her arm, as that might have led to his discovery of the kitten, which Coralynne smuggled inside beneath her coat.

As Batrice oversaw the unloading of her trunk and accepted a mug of hot tea from the innkeeper, she counted the days and began to wonder wearily whether they would ever reach her grandmother's house. It might have been easier to face the remainder of the journey had she been looking forward to a respite at the end of it, but her grandmother was anything but restful.

No, her visit was likely to consist of days even more endless than those of travel, marked only by tiptoeing and whispers and mutterings of disapproval. It was almost enough to dim her normally sunny personality, at least until Jamie stepped around the corner of the carriage carrying Mayhem, the silver ball now securely reattached to the pup's collar.

At least Coralynne would have no opportunity to accuse him of thievery.

When he caught her eye, he smiled, and Batrice suddenly remembered that being on the road wasn't as bad as all that. There were still uptight guards to annoy, thieves to catch, and a scholar who could make her feel weak-kneed with nothing more than a smile.

"I'll keep the pup with me," John offered suddenly, from where he stood beside the near wheeler. "Time Rupert had a bit of a break."

"I don't mind taking him for a night," Jamie replied mildly. "It's the least I can do to repay you for hauling my miserable self halfway across Andar."

"It's the least *we* can do," John said stubbornly, his eyes on the ground as usual, but a mulish set to his jaw nonetheless. He held out his arms and, after a moment's hesitation, Jamie set the pup in them.

"As you wish," he said comfortably. "I'll just see about a room, then."

Batrice watched him go, wondering how she seemed to keep forgetting that the man claimed to be a thief. Perhaps because he was kind, gentle, courteous, funny, and looked at her in a way that made her stomach feel like a ball of hot wax.

But a thief could be all of those things. She was an actress, and she knew very well how simple it was to feign personality traits one didn't possess. But everything in her insisted that he wasn't acting—neither in his interest nor his claim to thievery.

And there was the problem—a contradiction that threw her usual trust in her own instincts into complete disarray. Not all that long ago, she'd confidently believed that her experience on a stage made her an excellent candidate for a career in spying. What better recommendation than years spent perfecting the ability to lie to a crowd?

But how much use was such experience if she'd come up against someone who simply did it better?

The next morning, Batrice sent Coralynne down first for breakfast and waited until her "maid" returned with scraps for the kitten before she descended the stairs herself.

It was late enough that the inn's dark, low-ceilinged common room was relatively empty, with only three other travelers working their way through a morning meal before departure. Two were men about John's age, both of whom were dressed in workman's clothing and seemed oddly familiar, but Batrice chalked it up to coincidence and an overabundance of suspicion. Now that she was on the lookout for familiar faces, every person she encountered was likely to remind her of someone. She really couldn't imagine where she might have met such men before.

The third was Sir Abner Loringale.

"Hello again, my dear," the old man said with a beaming smile. His face was as heavily made up as before, and Batrice wondered whether he might perhaps be attempting to conceal some disfigurement. It really was too bad that such a kind man felt the need to hide from the world.

"Sir Abner, it's a pleasure to meet with you once more," she replied, bobbing a quick curtsey. "We seem destined to cross paths frequently along our way. I hope your journey has been pleasant since we saw you last?"

"Oh, about as pleasant as can be expected for a fellow whose best years are but a memory," he said with a chuckle. "Won't you join me for a spot of breakfast while I await my carriage?"

Batrice seated herself with a smile and thanked the innkeeper, a tall, gaunt, sad-looking man who served her a plate of hotcakes in complete silence. He followed it with tea, and a small dish of fruit, but no expression other than mournful ever crossed his face. Batrice waited in awkward silence until he'd finished before turning to engage her companion in polite conversation.

"You mentioned a friend near Tavisham, sir. I hope your visit is of a happy nature?"

"I hope so too," Sir Abner said complacently. "The old fellow has always kept a good table, and an excellent wine cellar, so if his overindulgence hasn't finished him off yet, I imagine we shall have a very good time indeed." He winked. "You might think I'm a fine one to speak of overindulgence, but, when you're my age, I feel you ought to enjoy yourself with whatever time you have left."

"But why wait?" Batrice asked, forgetting her manners for a moment.

"What's that again?" Sir Abner seemed rather confused by her question.

"Why wait until you're old to enjoy life? Shouldn't we enjoy fine food, fine weather, and good company wherever we find it, and most especially when we're young?"

The old man adjusted his wig, sat back in his chair, and began to laugh. "Well now, that's told me, hasn't it? I suppose you're right after all. And is that where you find yourself on this trip of yours? Enjoying fine food, fine weather, and good company?"

It was Batrice's turn to laugh. "In my experience, there is something to be said for any food, a place to be out of the rain, and someone you don't mind sharing that place with. I suppose by those standards, my journey is a success."

Her companion regarded her shrewdly. "Then you have not always been as you are now. The privileged among us rarely understand these things before they've attained more years than yours, if they ever grasp it at all."

Batrice paused with a forkful of hotcakes halfway to her mouth.

Drat and drat again. When would she learn to watch what she said?

"My parents are minor gentry," she clarified carefully. "Far from the capital and its wealth. I have seen more of poverty than what one might expect of a young lady in my position, but I can hardly claim to have suffered."

"And you are wise enough to know it," Sir Abner said, nodding. "I commend you."

She forced a chuckle. "Now you'll be expecting me to possess all manner of unlikely virtues, but I assure you, I am as tiresome and preoccupied with my wardrobe and my suitors as any other girl."

Her companion winked. "Which is as it should be."

Rupert strode into the room, ducking slightly to pass under the lintel, and for perhaps the first time since they met, Batrice was genuinely glad to see him. She'd been desperately afraid the kindly old man had been about to start asking embarrassing questions about the nonexistent suitors she'd mentioned.

"Miss Reyard, I'm afraid I must interrupt your meal. Your presence is urgently required outside."

Urgently needed? Her? Coming from a man who insisted on maintaining the fiction that she was helpless, that sounded ominous.

"Of course." Batrice placed her napkin on the table and excused herself, with murmured apologies to Sir Abner.

"What is it?" she hissed under her breath as she followed Rupert out of the room. "Are you going to accuse me of being indiscreet again? With a man of Sir Abner's age?"

Rupert said nothing, only led the way outside, where the morning had dawned cool and cloudy.

Batrice followed him to their carriage, which was parked near the stables where John appeared to be midway through harnessing the horses. Mayhem rolled in the dirt at his feet, growling and chewing on a rein.

Given Mayhem's apparent fondness for leather, perhaps she ought to leave him with John more often.

"Here," Rupert said impatiently, throwing open the carriage door.

Unsure what he expected of her, Batrice moved closer, half expecting him to grab her and throw her in. But he only stood back while she peered into the open door and let out an involuntary gasp of shock.

The interior of the coach had been utterly destroyed.

The curtains hung in shreds, and every cushion was ripped. Stuffing was strewn across the floor, and even the tops of the benches beneath the seats had been pried up.

"Well?" he said.

"Well, what?" she snapped, turning to face him and crossing her arms tightly across her chest. "Are you going to ask me if I'm responsible, because if you do, I swear I'll..." She paused.

"You'll what?" he asked contemptuously. "Feign tears until I promise to believe you?"

That was going a bit too far. "Give me more credit than that," she said, with a falsely sweet smile. "I'll tell Coralynne you are hopelessly in love with her and only waiting for her to give you the smallest encouragement to declare yourself."

The blood instantly drained from his face.

"Interesting," Batrice said casually. "I thought so, but it's good to have confirmation."

Rupert reached out and grabbed her arm. "Do *not* interfere between

Miss Smythe and myself," Rupert hissed softly. "I realize you are immature and thoughtless, but could you at least pretend to consider someone besides yourself?"

She yanked her arm out of his grip and glared up at him, realizing only afterward that she'd adopted a defensive position. Towards her own guard. As if he'd meant to attack her. It was probably absurd, but she was blazingly angry, and wouldn't have minded throwing a punch or two.

"I wish you would tell me what you have against me," she hissed back. "You have done nothing but judge me without evidence and accuse me of misconduct since the moment we started out. Believe it or not, I care very much for Coralynne and regard her as a friend. I also know her heart, and would never intentionally do anything to break it. And considering the way you've behaved towards me, I cannot imagine entrusting you with any heart that I genuinely value."

He sobered and opened his mouth, but Batrice was far from finished.

"And who exactly do you think you are, to pretend that you know what I have considered and what I haven't? Who are you to proclaim my thoughts are selfish? Do you know my concerns? Do you know my hopes and dreams? Until you're willing to ask, go examine your own considerations and leave me to mine. And stop calling me a liar when you haven't a shred of evidence."

She turned on her heel, but Rupert stepped in front of her before she could take more than a single step.

"I..." That was all he got out.

"You what?" Batrice snapped.

"I apologize," he said stiffly. "I shouldn't have insinuated that you destroyed the carriage."

"No, you shouldn't have." She wasn't ready to let him off that easily.

"I should have asked rather than accused."

"Yes, you should have."

He began to look exasperated. "Do you have any idea who might have been responsible?"

"Who, me?" She pointed to her own chest. "The woman who lied about having her belongings stolen because she was desperate to be dramatic?"

Rupert didn't even have the grace to wince. Apparently, one apology was all she was going to get. "Even if you are right and there was a thief, the destruction of Crown property is far more serious than the disappearance of a few personal items," he insisted. "This is a grave matter, and one we will need to address with caution."

Batrice took a deep breath and tried to contain her frustrated rage. He was right, in the end. This was more serious. And now that she wasn't focused on her anger and hurt at being treated with suspicion, it was also incredibly worrying.

This had been an act of violence—far more terrifying than simply searching a trunk. And it indicated that whoever had rummaged through their things had not yet given up. They were still close, and they were still after something.

Had they found it?

And if they hadn't, what lengths would they go to in the future?

She shivered in the cool air. "No," she said finally. "I don't know who might have done this. But it wasn't me, and it wasn't Coralynne. Neither of us would have been capable of prying apart those benches. And as we are Jamie's only hope of reaching his destination, I believe we can absolve him as well." Though she wasn't fool enough to say so, this development also cleared Rupert and John of suspicion. This sort of destruction was on an entirely different level, and she could not imagine it of anyone Lady Norelle trusted.

Bracing herself for argument, Batrice continued. "And I think you must also admit that I might very well have been telling the truth about the thefts. If our possessions were indeed stolen, it puts an entirely different face on the whole matter. It means someone is searching for something, and their methods are growing increasingly violent. They may not stop at threatening our coach, but may progress to threatening the safety of our party members."

Rupert remained stubbornly silent, but the tension in his jaw suggested he was listening and didn't care for her conclusions.

"At least consider it."

His nod was brief, but at least it was a nod.

"Thank you." A tiny, frustrated voice insisted that she shouldn't have to thank her own guard for agreeing to be mindful of their safety, but that was no longer the point. She didn't have to be right. She needed to find a way to work with the man who had the best chance of protecting them should anyone present a physical threat.

Batrice was not helpless. But neither could she bear the weight of protecting anyone beyond herself. And if Rupert was willing to accept the reality of the threat and be on guard against it, Batrice could focus on their other pressing concerns—determining the identity of their mysterious antagonist, and figuring out what exactly that person or persons might be after.

"You will inform Miss Smythe?" The worry in Rupert's voice was real, and Batrice reminded herself that if she wanted him to work with her, rather than against her, she could not continue to antagonize him.

"I will inform her of these most recent developments," she promised. "And encourage her to be wary."

"Thank you."

It was reluctant, but it was a start.

"You're welcome."

CHAPTER 12

Their departure was understandably delayed by the need to put the coach to rights, at least sufficiently enough for them to ride in it comfortably. After the benches were nailed back together, Cora-lynne took charge of mending the rents in the curtains, leaving Batrice to puzzle out the mess that had been made of the seats.

As she crouched on the floor of the carriage, hastily sewing up the rips in the cushions and re-stuffing them as best she could, Batrice was forced to grudgingly admit that perhaps her years of embroidery had not been entirely useless after all. She knew what to do with a needle, having been forced to make her own cushions as a part of her training in "accomplishments." It was certainly not her favorite task, and few young ladies of rank or fortune would ever have need of the skill, but clearly, it did have its practical applications.

Perhaps she would owe Lady Norelle a bit of an apology when she returned to Evenleigh.

By the time repairs had been finished, it was near luncheon. Rupert eyed the coach with an expression between horror and distaste—whether for the embarrassment of being seen in its vicinity or the damage its appearance might do to the royal family's reputation Batrice wasn't sure—but he insisted they get on the road as quickly as possible.

"Perhaps," he suggested, with a glance at Batrice, "we might minimize our stops today in an effort to make better time."

She only shrugged and smiled mysteriously as she stepped into the coach. There wasn't a lot she could do about it, but she would try.

Coralynne was following close behind her, and Rupert held out a hand to help the older girl up. She reached for it, smiling, but missed and tripped over the step. With a tiny yelp, she put out both hands to catch herself, and in the process, Goblin fell from where he'd been concealed under her coat. Startled, he scampered towards Batrice, climbed up her skirts, and perched on her lap where he turned to glare back at the person who'd dropped him.

Who had gotten to her feet and dusted off her hands, without the aid of a certain handsome guard.

Both Rupert and John were fully preoccupied with staring in horror at the thing on Batrice's lap.

Oh dear.

Batrice hadn't meant for them to find out about Goblin just yet, but she couldn't help bursting into laughter at the looks on their faces.

"Gods forfend," John whispered, looking more shocked than she'd ever seen him. "What is it?"

"Hold still, Miss Reyard," Rupert ordered, beginning to draw his weapon. "And don't be afraid. I should be able to kill it before it escapes or injures anyone."

"No, stop!" It was Coralynne who threw herself between Rupert and the carriage door, arms outstretched to prevent him from entering. "It's only Goblin!"

"Goblins aren't real," Rupert growled, almost as though reassuring himself of that comfortable fact.

"Then what else could it be?" John insisted. "What sort of monsters live in these woods?"

"For the love of Andar, it's a *cat*," Batice informed them, barely resisting the urge to roll her eyes. "Which you'd be able to see if you took a moment to observe before you decided that violence was your only option."

"Then why did she call it a goblin?" Rupert still hadn't fully sheathed his sword.

"That's his *name*," Coralynne snapped, quite clearly frustrated. "And he's completely harmless. It's perfectly ridiculous that a pair of grown men are being so absurd over a tiny little kitten."

Which, of course, was the moment Jamie chose to come strolling out of the inn with his single large bag slung over his shoulder.

"Ah," he said. "I see everyone has met Goblin."

Rupert's face froze. Coralynne audibly groaned, and Batrice put a hand to her forehead in resignation.

Of all the wretchedly rotten timing.

"Yes," she said wearily. "Everyone has met Goblin. He's a cat, and he's been traveling with us since Jamie and I rescued him on the day Mayhem disappeared. I'm sorry I failed to tell everyone, but he didn't seem like a threat to our security, and I didn't want there to be a scene. It now seems obvious that I made the right decision."

"What do you intend to do with it?" Rupert asked, stiff-necked and tight-lipped, as though their brief truce had never been.

"I intend to keep it," Batrice said, exasperated. "The children were going to kill it, it hasn't bothered anyone yet, and I like it a lot more than I like the dog I was saddled with against my will."

Rupert was wearing his "we'll discuss this later" face but said nothing more as he handed Coralynne into the carriage, followed by the puppy's basket.

He proceeded to refuse to speak to Batrice for the remainder of the day, though the three of their party who remained inside the coach spent the hours far more congenially, despite their patched and lumpy seats.

They'd been sharing uncomfortable travel stories—Batrice left out most of hers—when Coralynne shifted the conversation in a more personal direction.

"I'm not sure why I haven't asked before, but where are you from?" She aimed the question at Jamie, who looked up from stroking Mayhem's furry belly.

"Here and there," he said, with a smile. "A scholar doesn't always have the luxury of calling anyplace a permanent home."

"Then where does your family live?"

"Near the mountains," he answered. "I grew up traveling on much rockier roads than this one."

Coralynne seemed happy to accept this answer, but Batrice heard only an evasion.

"Is your father a local squire, then? Or perhaps a magister?" She dangled a bit of thread in front of Goblin as though the answer didn't matter to her one way or another.

"No."

"I only wondered because you mentioned he was involved in politics."

"Ah." Jamie shrugged. "Perhaps I should have said he tries to remain involved. He doesn't have much of an audience." Stretching out his legs into one corner of the carriage, he turned a friendly gaze on Coralynne. "And what of you, Miss Smythe? Were you born in Evenleigh, or did you travel there seeking opportunity?"

She blushed, and mumbled an equally evasive answer, while Batrice's brows knit themselves into a frown. He'd ducked the question again. There were probably any number of reasons why a man might not want to share the details of his life, but few of them were innocent. And Jamie, as handsome and helpful and kind as he seemed, was probably not as innocent as she'd hoped.

Could it be that Coralynne had been right all along?

The day crossed into evening and night began to press in on all sides.

The moon was a bright sliver overhead when the coach finally rolled to a stop, but the view outside the window still showed nothing but trees.

"Where's the inn?" Coralynne asked sleepily, just waking up from where she'd been curled against the side of the coach. Mayhem emerged from the crumpled folds of Jamie's coat, yawned, and wagged his tail. Goblin hissed.

"We can't go on," Rupert said abruptly as he emerged out of the dark. "It's too dangerous, and we're risking the horses as it is."

"Have you found a likely spot to camp?" Batrice shook out her skirts and looked up just in time to catch an incredulous expression cross Rupert's face.

"There's a bend in the path ahead where we can pull off the road. Not much natural shelter, but the ground is level, and there's a stream nearby for water."

Batrice shrugged. "Seems adequate. Do we have anything to use for bedding?"

Rupert nodded, but cautiously, as though he expected something to blow up in his face at any moment. "Given the scarcity of towns along this road, we brought sufficient supplies for a night or two out of doors. There won't be any luxuries," he warned, "but we won't freeze."

"Then we'd best get to making camp." Her smile seemed to unnerve him even further.

It was probably a mistake to be quite so obvious about the fact that she wasn't exactly the debutante she pretended to be in public, but she was growing weary of the pretense. Why shouldn't a lady know how to survive a night in the woods? Perhaps she'd been wrong about the usefulness of certain ladylike accomplishments, but she didn't think she was wrong about everything. Her skills, though hardly traditional, were nothing to be ashamed of.

And besides, whining about the lack of accommodations would only further widen the rift between herself and Rupert, which she remained determined to mend, despite his unfortunate response to her new pet.

The question of how to soothe his sensibilities continued to plague her as they set up camp, shivering a little in the cool night air, though it turned out that whoever had packed for potential emergencies had done an adequate job. There was a tent for herself and Coralynne, and plenty of bedding for four.

When Jamie insisted he had no desire to deprive anyone of a blanket and would do very well sleeping by a fire, Batrice shot him a withering glare and redistributed the blankets anyway.

That was when she turned and saw a terrified-looking Coralynne holding a pouch in her trembling hands.

"What is it?" Batrice whispered.

"John just asked me to start the fire!" Coralynne hissed. "What do I do?"

Well, of course he'd asked her. Because a real maid would know perfectly well how to do so. Even though most household fires were started from banked coals, it was still a necessary skill.

"Don't worry," she murmured, removing the pouch from Coralynne's nervous grasp. "I'll take care of it. You can arrange our bedding in the tent."

She walked over to where John had pulled together a rough circle of rocks and crouched down beside it.

"I haven't started a fire in ages," she announced loudly, while removing the flint, firesteel, and tinderbox from the pouch, "so I believe I'll take this opportunity to practice. Does anyone know whether we actually have anything to cook?"

"We'd like to get warm before we die of old age," Rupert said under his breath, as he walked by on his way to tether a protesting Mayhem to a tree.

"If we do, at least you'll be the first to go," Batrice called after him, then remembered she was supposed to be conciliating. Sarcasm was a terribly difficult habit to break.

In reality, it took only a few minutes to get the fire going once John produced an armload of dead branches from a brief foray into the trees. Some were slightly damp and smoked heavily, but there were enough dry ones to burn until the others caught.

Little by little, the camp took shape around her. Jamie helped John unharness the horses and rub them down, while Rupert scouted the area around their camp to ensure it was safe.

The few travel rations they'd been provided with were composed mostly of dried meat and flour, so Batrice dropped the meat in a pot of boiling water while mixing up a coarse dough that baked into rough cakes on the flattest of the rocks near the fire.

"How do you know how to do all this?" Coralynne whispered, sitting next to her on the ground.

"My second family," she replied in a soft voice, hoping Coralynne would understand her meaning. "We all had to help with the chores, and we camped out far more often than we slept indoors."

"I wish you would teach me," Coralynne said wistfully. "I would feel so much better about my plans for the future if I knew more about such things."

"Then I will," Batrice promised. "I'll find a way after we're home. There's no reason why you shouldn't know how to take care of yourself." There really wasn't. No reason beyond tradition and the censure of a society that had probably forgotten why it disapproved of such things.

Their meal was tasteless, but no one went hungry, and Rupert offered her grudging thanks along with numerous puzzled glances. She merely smiled sweetly and said she was happy to have been helpful, without the smallest intention of satisfying his burning curiosity.

After they'd finished eating, Coralynne stayed up quite late, writing by the fire. She said it had been impossible to write on the road, and there was so much she needed to record. Making camp was, she insisted to Batrice in a low voice, a rare and remarkable experience that may prove useful later.

Batrice, of course, stayed up with her. It would seem highly irregular for a gently raised young woman to make ready for bed without her "maid," so instead she played with Goblin, distracting the kitten from the leaping flames by allowing him to play with her fingers.

She pretended not to be disappointed when Jamie turned in early and was finding it difficult to keep her eyes open long before Coralynne indicated she was ready to retire to their tent. Even the prospect of sleeping on the ground seemed to fill the older girl with excitement rather than dread, though Batrice thought she might have a somewhat different perspective by the time she awakened in the morning.

Soon enough, though, they'd settled into their blankets, and it was no more than a minute or two before Coralynne began to snore softly, with Goblin curled up at her feet. The fire still crackled, and Mayhem whined occasionally while John and Rupert exchanged quiet words, all small sounds that nonetheless conspired to prevent Batrice from sleeping, despite her exhaustion. And before too long, Batrice began to hear other noises—the usual rustlings and sighings one might expect to hear at night in a forest.

But rather than lulling her to sleep as they usually did, the sounds began to seem sinister. What if the thief had followed them? What if he was lurking in the dark woods, waiting for them all to fall asleep?

After that, it was impossible to even close her eyes.

The glow of the fire died down, along with the conversation, and still, she couldn't seem to sleep.

Restless and frustrated, Batrice put on her shoes and grabbed her cloak. Perhaps the mottled brown color, unattractive as it was, would help hide her in the dark, provided she could escape camp unseen.

Wriggling out beneath the loose fabric at the rear of the tent, she stepped softly past it until she could slip into the trees, careful not to alert Rupert. His silhouette was still visible by the fire, straight-backed and alert despite the late hour. He probably intended to share watches with John—at least, she hoped he did—but it wasn't beyond reason to wonder whether he might attempt to stay up all night and then ride all the next day. Batrice had to give her guard that at least—he was painstakingly responsible at his duties.

But she was able to move quietly enough that he never noticed as she slipped slowly away from camp, allowing her eyes time to adjust to the dappled moonlight beneath the trees. It was a perfect night for a walk. She could stroll around for a bit, see for herself that there was nothing out there and they were perfectly safe. Then maybe she'd be able to close her eyes.

Once she was well away from the light of the fire, it was difficult to remember what had frightened her. There was only the rustling of leaves and the sounds of night birds, calling to one another through the forest.

Until she heard the unmistakable sound of a twig, breaking, off to her left.

An animal? Or something worse?

Batrice remained still, wrapped in her cloak, deep in the shadows beneath an enormous oak, waiting for it to move again...

And barely stifled a shriek when something brushed against the back of her arm.

She struck backward with her elbow, hard, and heard a grunt of pain before she whirled to face whatever had approached her out of the darkness.

"Do you always hit first?" Jamie asked softly, rubbing his ribs with one hand and leaning on the trunk of the oak with the other.

"I only hit thieves," she whispered back. "And only when they deliberately attempt to frighten me."

"Then I believe you owe me an apology. I was attempting to alert you to my presence, not scare you."

"Then you shouldn't have been lurking behind me in the dark," she retorted.

"So noted."

"What are you doing out here, anyway?" She could hear the accusing note in her voice but didn't care enough to moderate it. Her heart was still pounding.

"Contemplating the meaning of life?"

"That sounded like a question. Don't you know?"

"Actually," he admitted, "I hate sleeping on the ground. It's hard and cold, and I'm not terribly fond of waking up with rocks in my back. So I decided to take a walk instead of lying there, wishing I were somewhere else."

"And where else would that be?" she asked baldly. "Don't think I didn't notice you've ducked every question that might give a clue as to where you're from or who your family is."

"You've not been the source of many revelations yourself," he countered. "Young ladies of the gentry don't typically hit first and ask questions later, nor can they start fires, or make camp fare over an open flame without being taught how."

There was no deciphering his expression in the moonlight, so Batrice had no way of discerning whether he was amused or annoyed. Innocent victim, or conniving villain? She desperately wished she knew.

"Wish you knew what?" he asked, and then she realized she'd accidentally spoken aloud.

"I wish I knew whether I could trust you," she said simply. "My instincts tell me that you mean us no harm, but all evidence is against you. Even your own words. I don't know what to believe, I only know that…"

She stopped before she completely humiliated herself.

"What do you know?" He took a step closer.

Batrice was not shy, and it had never been her style to fake reticence. She tended, if anything, to be overbold. Brash, even. But something about him tied her tongue in knots and stole the flippant words she typically used to cover her confusion or dismay.

"I know that…" She almost tripped over a simple sentence, so she

139

paused to gather herself for another try. "I guess what I'm trying to say is that this would be easier if you were truly nothing more than a scholar," she said finally. "Maybe I could get to know you, without these evasions and pretense. Even dance partners at a ball learn more about each other than I've managed with you, and we've been together almost constantly for days."

"Why do you want to know me?"

She could hear emotion in his words, but it was impossible to identify. It could have been amusement, condescension, curiosity, or suspicion…

"Because I like you," she said, exasperated and uncharacteristically embarrassed. "Do I have to explain everything?" She started to step away, but he reached out swiftly and caught her fingers, wrapping his own around them so tightly that she couldn't pull away.

"Batrice."

He'd said nothing but her name, but she heard more than that. Unfortunately, most of what she heard this time was regret.

"Don't say you wish things could be different," she told him fiercely. "Just don't. I know you feel something, unless you've been lying with your eyes as well as your words, so your excuses would only mean that you don't care enough to make an effort. I'd rather you say you don't like me, or that you're betrothed, even if it's not true."

"I'm not betrothed," he said, and she could hear the smile, even if she couldn't see it. "But Batrice…"

There was a sudden rustling in the bushes to her left. A scurrying, then stillness. Soft, stealthy footfalls.

Batrice took a quick, unconscious step towards Jamie, at the same time he stepped towards her. Her face collided with his chest, and she stopped, heart pounding, unwilling to breathe for fear he would back away again.

But he didn't. Instead, he placed one careful arm around her shoulders and pulled her closer, as gently as if she were a creature of the woods, prone to flee at any moment. His other hand brushed against her hair, feather-light and fleeting, and though a tiny corner of her attention was listening for movement from the forest, every other part of her was focused on memorizing the hard planes of his chest, the sound of his breathing, the smell of his coat, and the pressure of his arm, warm and secure around her.

If only she could have fallen for someone else. Anyone else. Even Rupert. He was absurdly handsome, and probably far more capable of understanding the life she'd chosen than any secretive scholar would be.

But her heart knew what it wanted, knew what it had been waiting for since her first youthful infatuation had ended in heartache.

She'd been waiting for someone who made her feel alive, someone who accepted her for exactly who she was and understood her sense of humor. Someone she could talk to without having to censor half her words for fear that person might judge her, and it wouldn't hurt at all if that someone also had a gorgeous face and perfect hands.

And she'd finally found him, but despite his warmth, humor, and understanding, despite the fact that she felt she could be herself with him, he was somehow still as distant as the moon.

He didn't feel the same for her. Oh, he felt something she was sure. But not enough.

Perhaps heartache was all she would ever know.

She was still pressed close to his chest when the brush rustled again, closer. Glowing eyes winked into existence, glaring balefully at them from the shadows, creeping ever nearer...

"Goblin," Batrice whispered, pulling regretfully away from Jamie and retrieving the kitten from where he crouched under the branches of a young pine. "You scared me half to death."

The kitten meowed and kneaded her arms with its front paws before settling in with a satisfied purr.

"I suppose we ought to return to camp," Batrice started to say, when

Jamie moved, sudden and swift, pulling her back against his chest and pressing one hand to her mouth so no sound could escape.

Furious with herself for allowing him to trap her so easily, Batrice tried to stomp on his foot, then to smash his face with the back of her head, but he evaded her efforts before hissing into her ear.

"Shh! We're not alone."

Oh. She flushed hot beneath the pressure of his hand, then nodded to show that she understood.

He released her, squeezed her shoulder as if to say "trust me, I'm on your side," then stepped quietly off into the trees in the direction of camp.

Unwilling to stay in the woods alone, especially if someone was lurking nearby, Batrice followed, choosing her steps carefully and gathering her skirts with one hand to prevent them from disturbing the brush and giving away their position.

When they were close enough to see the firelight flickering through the trees, Jamie stopped and held up a hand to signal her to do the same. There was no visible change to their camp, but something…

"The horses!" Jamie muttered, and took off through the trees.

But it was too late. One of the horses whinnied shrilly, then two others sounded the alarm, and only a few moments later Batrice could hear the sound of hooves stampeding down the road, accompanied by shrill, frantic barks from Mayhem.

She could do no good where she was—calming frightened horses was not a part of her skill set—so she made her way back into camp just as Rupert was charging out of it, shooting her a wild-eyed glare as he ran. John had just rolled out of his blankets and was pulling on his boots, half stumbling as he tried to get to the horses faster.

Perhaps she should have told them Jamie was already in pursuit, but it wouldn't have reassured them in the slightest, and her time would be better spent comforting Coralynne.

Or so she thought. When she poked her head into the tent, the gentle sounds of snoring emerged from Coralynne's blankets.

Pulling her head back out again, Batrice strode to the fire, threw on several more pieces of wood, and tried not to think about the fact that she was now alone, but for one frantic pup and a sleepy kitten.

And whatever was out there probably hadn't followed the horses.

Setting Goblin beside the fire, she picked up one of the sticks that lay nearby, ready to burn, and stripped off the protruding branches. Breaking off the narrower end until it was about the right length, she swung her impromptu club through a series of sword drills. Perhaps it wouldn't look very intimidating to a mercenary or a true swordsman, but it might be enough to fool an inexperienced thief into believing she knew what she was about.

Thankful for her loose skirts, she slashed, whirled, and blocked, feeling a strange sense of freedom and relief as she settled into the forms she'd once practiced daily. True, they'd been meant for no more than convincing a rapt audience that they watched a real battle, but they required focus and exertion, something she'd missed since she'd confined herself to drawing rooms and embroidery hoops.

She didn't want to lose her skills. Didn't want to forget the person she'd become by virtue of her experiences. No matter what Lady Norelle said, once she returned, she would take up practicing again. In public, she would be whoever she needed to be, but no one could stop her from holding onto this part of herself. It was real, and she valued it for the freedom and confidence it had given her.

Batrice whirled again, into an overhand strike, and her heart leaped suddenly to her throat as her stick was blocked by the shining edge of a naked blade.

CHAPTER 13

The man who held the blade was heavily cloaked and hooded, the lower portion of his face swathed in a scarf or mask of some sort. Gloves covered his hands, and in the flickering firelight, Batrice could make out no details that might betray his identity.

Gripping her stick in suddenly sweaty hands, she held her ground and focused on showing neither fear nor curiosity.

"What do you want?" she demanded fiercely.

The cloaked man didn't answer but shifted his blade, and it was only her hours of unrelenting practice that swung her arms to meet his second strike. It was not meant to defeat her, she realized with surprise—his strike was the next move in the partner version of the sword form she'd been practicing.

Almost without thought, she flowed into the next block, then a low, darting strike aimed at his legs. He avoided it, leaping agilely over her weapon before aiming a downward-angled blow at the side of her neck. She leaned easily out of the way and flowed into the remainder of the drill, focusing on maintaining her feet and adjusting her grips to compensate for her less-than-perfectly balanced weapon. Her breath was ragged and her palms raw from the abrasion of the bark, but for a moment, she felt a surge of joy. It was easy to pretend she was back on the stage, performing before a rapt audience—a daring and desperate heroine fighting for her life against a sinister villain determined to bring about her defeat. Almost out of breath, she paused only for an instant before committing to the final move, a lunge that was intended to skewer her opponent directly beneath the breastbone.

He parried at the last possible second, sliding the flat of his blade down the length of her stick as it flashed forward, forcing it down and away from his body.

Her lunge carried her forward, and might have carried her directly into the edge of his sword had he not simply curled his other arm around her waist, caught her and pulled her against him.

Batrice froze, unmoving but for the heaving of her chest as she tried to regain her breath. If her attacker chose to take advantage of her, she would have a difficult time resisting, but he merely lowered his weapon and released her.

She almost stumbled, but regained her feet and drew back until the fire was between them.

"I don't know why you're following us," she said, the sound of her pulse roaring in her ears. He could have killed her, or simply disarmed her and left her helpless in the dirt, but he hadn't, so perhaps he meant to negotiate. "If you would simply tell me what you want, and why you destroyed the coach, maybe I would understand, but I can promise you we have nothing worth stealing."

He remained stubbornly silent, and for a moment there was no sound but the fire crackling between them.

"But if you continue to follow us," she said sternly, "or threaten our safety in any way, we will do everything in our power to ensure that you face justice. You've stolen from persons under the protection of the Crown and destroyed Crown property, so your punishment will prove harsh unless you stand down and throw yourself on the king's mercy." She thought she sounded both firm and decisive, but an answering chuckle emerged from beneath the concealing hood of her opponent's cloak.

Somewhere behind her, faint but recognizable, Batrice heard the sound of hoofbeats. The loose horses, she thought with relief. They must have been caught, and she darted a glance over her shoulder for Jamie, Rupert, or John. It was only a reflex, and she realized her mistake only a moment later, but by the time she returned her attention to the other side of the fire it was far too late—the hooded man was gone.

She was still standing with her mouth slightly open when Rupert galloped into camp, bareback, and slid off his horse, sword already in hand. At almost the same moment, Coralynne poked her head out of the tent, looking adorably sleepy.

"Batr... I mean, Miss Reyard, why aren't you in bed? Oh..." Obviously, she'd caught sight of Rupert, because her mouth dropped open in what Batrice decided was probably appreciation.

And there was plenty to appreciate. His shirt was open at the top, his sleeves rolled up, and his dark hair was perfectly tousled. Add in his grim expression and his unsheathed blade and even Batrice could appreciate the picture he made standing next to his still-prancing horse.

"What happened?" he demanded. "Were you attacked? Where were you when the horses were released? Where is the scholar?"

"I..." Batrice had to think about each of his questions carefully for a moment. What exactly *had* happened? Had she been attacked? And where was Jamie?

"I couldn't sleep," was what came out of her mouth first, and from Rupert's dark frown, it wasn't going to be enough to satisfy him. "I went for a walk in the woods."

"Alone? Without telling anyone?" His frustration was evident in the glitter of his narrowed eyes and the rise in his volume. "Do you want to die? Or are you just determined to get me fired?"

"Neither," she snapped back, anger and adrenaline flaring bright and hot. "But I've spent too much of my life without requiring a babysitter for it to be my first instinct to ask permission to go for a walk. I'm not some pampered princess who has never so much as crossed a street without an escort, Rupert! I've been responsible for myself, and I like it that way. So I'm sorry about your wounded sensibilities, and I'm sorry I didn't talk to you first, but we both know you would have said no. If you want more apologies later, I will be happy to offer them, but don't you think we have more to worry about right now than what *might* have happened?"

Their eyes met across the fire, challenging one another, and despite her determination to be conciliating, Batrice was far too keyed up to back down.

"You're right," he said finally. "We'll discuss this later. What did happen?"

"A man in a dark cloak entered camp and..." How to explain the next part in a way that wouldn't be incriminating?

Too late now.

"He had a sword, I had a stick, and we fought."

"You *what?*" Rupert appeared to be looking her over for injuries. "How badly are you hurt?"

"Don't be absurd," she said, her knees wobbling as the aftereffects of the battle finally began to hit her. "He was toying with me. He could have killed me if he wanted to, but we only sparred for a few minutes. I asked what he wanted, threatened him with the full retribution of Crown justice, and he only laughed."

"He didn't say anything?"

"When he heard you returning, he disappeared."

"Of course he did," Rupert muttered.

"You were in a swordfight?" Coralynne almost shrieked in her ear, causing Batrice's heart to jump into her mouth for at least the third time that night.

"Yes." Batrice winced as Coralynne tackled her with a hug that nearly knocked her to the ground. "But I'm perfectly all right."

"Was it thrilling? Do you think he was a real highwayman?"

"I think he was amusing himself at my expense," she grumbled, "but..." She couldn't help a tiny smile just for Coralynne. "It might have been a little bit thrilling," she whispered.

"And the scholar?"

Batrice could hear the suspicion in Rupert's query and knew she would have to tread carefully for this part of her explanation. She couldn't exactly tell him they'd been alone in the woods together, let alone that his arm had been around her.

"I saw him dash off in the direction of the horses as soon as he noticed they were loose."

"And what was he doing before that? I know he wasn't in his bed."

Oops. She'd forgotten Rupert had been keeping watch. He would have known the moment Jamie left the fire. Which meant he probably suspected they'd been together. Could she redirect his suspicion? "Are you actually suggesting he was the one who turned them loose? That he purposefully stranded himself in the woods along with us?" Batrice asked baldly.

"Yes." Rupert wasn't pulling any punches either.

"Well, it's a ridiculous idea," she replied. "Can you give me even one logical reason for him to behave so absurdly?"

"I can." Rupert held her gaze accusingly. "You."

"Me?" Shock made her voice come out a bit higher-pitched than usual.

"Your connection with the Crown makes you a tempting target. He may have made assumptions about your importance or your fortune, and be looking to gain influence by compromising you in order to force a marriage."

Hah. Just went to show what he knew. Jamie had deliberately avoided compromising her, on multiple occasions.

"Well, you're wrong," she said, knowing that, as a denial, it was weak and would do nothing to convince Rupert of Jamie's innocence. "And I know for a fact he was trying to help tonight, not trying to compromise anything. Or anyone."

"Did you actually see him helping? Or did you see him race away from camp and assume that's what he was doing? He could have circled back. Could have been planning to rob you or kidnap you. He could have been the man you fought, who only disappeared because he heard me coming."

Jamie? The man in the cloak? Batrice couldn't help laughing. "The man I fought was a trained swordsman who recognized the sword form I was using and toyed with me as though putting me through my paces. His footwork was exquisite, and he both appeared and disappeared without so much as a sound. I assure you, he could have kidnapped or robbed me at any time he chose. It seems a bit of a stretch to surmise that a man who depends on us for transportation might have turned our horses loose and donned a disguise, all for the purpose of crossing weapons with a flustered debutante in the middle of the night."

Now that she put it into words, it sounded worse than absurd. What could the man have wanted? Why had he paused to spar with her instead of going after his objective? And why couldn't they seem to get through a single day—or night—of this journey without a new mystery being added to all the other unsolved ones confronting her?

But it didn't seem as though any answers would be presenting themselves. Rupert's unrelenting stare still transfixed her, and his next question reminded her of the dangers of speculating aloud while distracted.

"The sword form you were using?" he echoed. "Every time I think I have finally plumbed the depths of this assignment or fit it neatly inside predictable lines, you smash your way through those lines with a blithe smile and act as though I should have expected it to happen."

Batrice opened her mouth, frantically searching for an explanation that glossed over the truth without actually being a lie, but she was saved from her floundering by Coralynne's quick thinking.

"You've had fencing lessons?" Coralynne squealed, and even Batrice would have been fooled had she not only recently explained the origin of her unusual prowess. "That's so very thrilling! And terrifying! I used to dream of being in some nobleman's guard instead of being a maid, but of course, it wouldn't have been at all appropriate. Though it would be so very exciting to know how to defend one's self in the event of an attack, as you did."

"Ah. Yes," Batrice ventured. "It is. Exciting. And you're right, of course. Not appropriate at all. But, you know... brothers, and all that." She shot Coralynne a quick wink.

"That doesn't explain..."

Batrice was saved yet again from Rupert's inquiries by the sound of Mayhem's rather sleepy barking, which presaged the faint sound of horses. After only a few moments, all four of their carriage horses trotted tamely back into camp, led by John, who rode bareback astride the leader. And if Batrice hadn't been watching, she might have been too distracted to notice Jamie slipping back into camp behind them, looking exactly as he had the last time she'd seen him.

Did he appear mussed or out of breath enough to have been running through the woods in pursuit of escaped horses? Or could he instead have donned a hood and gloves and crossed weapons with her in the guise of a highwayman?

Shaking her head as if to rid herself of unwelcome suspicion, Batrice approached the lead horse and nodded to John. "Thank you," she said, with genuine gratitude. "I'm so glad you were able to find them. Could you tell how they were able to get loose?"

"Ropes cut."

He showed her the end of the lead he'd used to create makeshift reins, and Batrice shivered with sudden apprehension. Sure enough, the rope had been sliced cleanly, with a blade of some sort. A deliberate act of sabotage, and one that could have left them stranded.

But to what end? What did their unknown stalker stand to gain by leaving them without horses in the middle of the woods? Could it have been an attempt to gain another opportunity to search the carriage? Or something more sinister? Had they all been intended to disappear?

"Don't worry," Rupert said, and from his solicitous tone, Batrice knew he was addressing Coralynne more than anyone else. "We'll picket them here on the edge of camp, and John and I will stay up for the rest of the night. You'll be perfectly safe."

Coralynne smiled tremulously, nodded, and ducked back into the tent.

The moment she disappeared, Rupert turned to Jamie, who had approached the fire nonchalantly and held his hands out over its warmth. Goblin left his cozy spot by the flames to rub himself against Jamie's boots, which only made Rupert glare harder.

"Where were you?" Rupert demanded.

"Where was I just now? Or earlier?"

"After you left your bed. What were you doing in the woods? I know you left your blankets before the horses' ropes were cut."

Batrice held her breath. Jamie owed her nothing, and the only way to clear himself from Rupert's unspoken accusation would be to admit that he'd been with her—an admission that would practically confirm Rupert's suspicion that Jamie meant to compromise her.

Jamie's brown eyes lifted from the flames, which cast deep shadows on the planes of his face. He regarded Rupert calmly, without a trace of guilt or defensiveness. "I couldn't sleep, and I went for a walk."

"Alone?"

Jamie nodded, without even a glance at Batrice. "Alone. Whatever it is you think I've done, I have no more desire to be stranded in these woods than you do. Turning the horses loose while we're miles from help is a dangerous trick, and I've no need of a guardsman's training to know the potential consequences." Not only had he not betrayed her, he spoke mildly, as though unconcerned by Rupert's suspicion.

Batrice watched them both. One of her mentors in the acting troupe had impressed upon her the need to study body language in order to convey emotion clearly to an audience. Small cues could say more than anyone expected or even realized.

Jamie was not at all afraid. A scholar with no transportation of his own, he was all but adrift somewhere in the vast northern woods, facing an angry, suspicious guard in the middle of the night, yet he was relaxed, almost amused.

And not because he didn't know the dangers.

She studied him for a moment where he crouched by the fire, arms resting loosely on his knees. Only a few strands of his dark golden hair had escaped their tie to fall alongside his firm jaw. The strength in his shoulders wasn't really evident on a casual inspection, but his ill-fitting shirt and jacket didn't exactly draw attention to them. Just like his quiet manner didn't really draw attention to his keen intelligence. But he was capable of swift, decisive action, and he saw far more than he admitted to.

Heard more too. He'd known Coralynne was a novelist, when the only times he might have been privy to that information were the hasty words she'd muttered under her breath after rescuing Goblin, and the conversation she'd had with Coralynne while he was supposedly unconscious.

Could he have heard her that day? Had he even meant to reveal that he knew? Or was it a completely innocent conjecture as he'd claimed?

Most importantly, was she a fool to trust him? True, he hadn't betrayed her, so it was unlikely he intended to compromise her. And she didn't think she'd simply fallen for a pretty face and attributed to it myriad virtues he neither possessed nor deserved. Granted, it was a nice face. And, more importantly, as she'd told him so plainly, she liked him. Liked his sense of humor, and his quiet way of helping where it was needed. And yes, she rather liked the air of mystery about him. Mystery was a weakness of hers, almost as much as perfect hands.

He was easy to be with. Easy to talk to. But both of those could very well be by design. And now that she'd admitted there was possible reason for suspicion, it would be all the more difficult to forget it again. Almost as difficult as it was going to be to forget what it had felt like to rest, even for a moment, in the circle of his arms.

A shiver ran through her at the memory, and when she looked up, Jamie was watching her, as if he could read her thoughts. Had he been the man in the cloak? She was almost certain he hadn't set the horses loose, but she also had no idea what he'd been doing before she encountered him. Had he really heard someone else in the woods? Or had that been his excuse to don his disguise and attack while Rupert and John were distracted?

But why? Why go to such lengths only to cross weapons with her? She could ask him, but knew better than to imagine he would answer. Where Jamie was concerned, she had very little but questions, and it seemed unlikely she would ever gain the answers.

No matter how much she liked him, no matter how perfect his hands, she needed to set her attraction aside. Not because of Rupert's suspicions—but because it was the right thing to do under the circumstances. The only reward she would gain for continuing to hope was a broken heart.

CHAPTER 14

Coralynne slept, as evidenced by her continual snores, but Batrice doubted anyone else did. Her own eyes refused to close as her mind churned through the night's events. Every hour of wakefulness seemed to add even more questions and worries to the mounting number that continued to plague her.

She stopped pretending to rest the moment the first hints of dawn lightened the sky, and she was not the only one—by the time she emerged from her tent, the three men were already awake. Jamie offered her a silent nod that she pretended not to see, but he still helped her by building up the fire high enough that she was able to prepare a rough gruel for their breakfast.

The result was barely edible, but no one complained as they took turns eating from the single available pot. Mayhem devoured the last of it after Goblin turned up his nose, while Batrice carefully packed away the remains of their camping supplies, hoping fervently they would not need to use them. She wanted a bath and for the journey to be over. Only two more days of travel, by her estimation, should see them to her grandmother's house, a place she never thought she'd be glad to see.

They were underway before the sun rose above the trees. Coralynne occupied the first few hours of the journey quizzing Batrice about her battle the night before, and her sword skills in general, while Jamie seemed content to ruffle Mayhem's ears and look out the window. Goblin alternated between snoozing and batting at the glove Batrice had donated to the cause of his distraction, narrowing his enormous eyes into slits as he wrestled it into submission.

The three of them eventually fell into an awkward silence that lasted until they stopped around midday in a small village. John watered the horses and checked the harness, while Rupert procured a cold lunch. After eating, Jamie said he needed to stretch his legs and took off, leaving Mayhem to howl mournfully after him from where he was tied to the wheel of the coach.

Batrice watched him go from her seat on a bench outside the local pub. She must have looked wistful because Coralynne elbowed her sharply.

"You're pining over the highwayman again," she announced in a loud whisper.

"I suppose I am," Batrice admitted. "But I'm determined to stop."

Coralynne looked around as if to ensure no one was watching, then leaned closer and placed the back of her hand on Batrice's forehead. "Are you feeling all right?"

"No." Batrice smoothed out the wrinkles in her skirt and kicked at the dust. "I am most decidedly not all right. This entire trip has me... discombobulated."

"I'm so very sorry." Coralynne looked rueful. "And here I've been having such a grand time with all of our adventures. It's been so much more than I even dared hope when I decided I had to come with you. I dreamed of adventure, of course, but mysterious scholars? Highwaymen? Camping in the woods? Carriage wrecks, vandals, and thieves? If I wrote all of this into a novel, no one would think it remotely realistic."

"But surely we haven't experienced quite enough drama for a novel." Batrice summoned a smile for Coralynne's benefit. "First, we have to be abducted by sinister strangers and dragged off to a dark and mysterious estate."

"Oooh, good point." Coralynne nodded. "I shall have to invent a suitably terrifying locale for our fictional abduction."

"Wait until we reach my grandmother's house," Batrice returned dryly. "I believe you might find it appropriately inspiring."

Rupert approached them, then, with what appeared to be a map in hand.

"We're a bit behind," he said, "so I would ask your permission, Miss Reyard, to alter our plan somewhat. We were to have stopped at Kipworth tonight, but that would leave us traveling later than I would like. There is a smaller inn on a side road, a bit further from the usual route, but friendly to travelers. Takes us perhaps a mile out of our way, but I believe there is a shortcut from there to Peridale, and it would allow the horses a proper rest before we take up the final leg of our journey."

"We will do as you think best, of course," Batrice said coolly. "I am looking forward to sleeping in a proper bed, no matter where we find it."

Rupert seemed almost surprised at not being forced to argue and folded his map while he turned to Coralynne. "And... are you well, Miss Smythe?" he asked, a little hesitantly.

"I am very well indeed." Coralynne smiled warmly at him. In spite of the older girl's avowal not to be in love alone, Batrice had not seen much abatement in Coralynne's decided preference for the handsome guard, nor in her blushes when he showed her the slightest hint of attention. What would it take, she wondered, for the two of them to admit to their feelings for one another? Would they go on like this forever, both believing themselves in the right for hiding their affections, unwilling to take a chance for fear of disappointment?

The truth was, though, the situation would only get worse when they returned to Evenleigh. Once Coralynne's identity was known, and her "ruination" official, Rupert would declare her too far above him, and she would declare herself too far fallen for marriage.

If there was to be any hope for their romance, it would have to happen before they returned.

And as Batrice's own heart was lamentably entangled with an unavailable man, what would it hurt if she distracted herself by aiding another in finding true love?

Then perhaps she could stop staring after Jamie as though there was some power in her gaze to make him open up and trust her.

Her thoughts were interrupted by the arrival of another carriage, which rolled slowly into the village square and came to a stop. She watched with interest, and dawning delight, as the door opened to reveal the creaking, corpulent form of Sir Abner.

"Well met again, dear ladies," he said, offering them the shallow bob that was probably all the bow he could manage without either toppling over or losing his wig. "When I did not see you last evening, I thought perhaps our ways had finally diverged, but I'm delighted to see you again."

"The pleasure is ours," Batrice returned pleasantly. "We had a bit of a mishap, but all is well again. I hope your journey has been uneventful today."

"A bit too uneventful if you ask me," Sir Abner replied with a wink. "A spot of excitement might do me good, just as a moment of conversation with a pair of beautiful young ladies makes me feel ten years younger."

Coralynne giggled. "Perhaps we'll see you again this evening, sir."

"I do hope so, Miss Smythe, I do hope so. And where will you be stopping for the night? Getting close to Peridale, are we not?"

Batrice had just begun to wonder uneasily whether they ought to be discussing their route in the public square when Coralynne answered unconcernedly.

"Oh, we're taking a side route, I believe. Not making the usual stop at Kipworth."

"Oh? Well, that is good news. My own road takes me off towards Tavisham before we reach Kipworth, so we may find ourselves sharing a convivial breakfast once again."

Sir Abner said his farewells and stepped into a shop, after which Rupert announced they were ready to depart. Batrice almost protested that they should allow time for Jamie to return, but he reappeared before she could even get the words out. Almost as though he'd been listening.

"It's a fine day," John said suddenly, before any of them could return to the carriage. "If either of you ladies would care to ride on the box?"

"Oh, but could I?" Coralynne burst out, which left Batrice with little option but to smile at her enthusiasm.

"Of course," she said. "I'm quite sleepy, myself, and would prefer to be inside where I can doze away the afternoon."

It was a wretched lie, and as Rupert handed Coralynne up onto the box, Batrice felt her heart begin to pound with painful anticipation. The hours ahead of her could be nothing but awkward. Trapped alone in the carriage with Jamie, after what had occurred the night before, was the very last place she wished to be.

And also the first.

Drat her heart.

He gave her several miles to worry and stew before he spoke up.

"Are you angry with me?"

She didn't dare look at him, only continued to stroke Goblin's velvety head where it rested on her lap. "What is there to be angry at?"

"I lied about seeing you last night."

She was startled into meeting his eyes. They were somber, serious, and somehow darker than usual.

"I thought it was what you would prefer," he continued, "but I've been known to be wrong, so I wanted to apologize if necessary."

"Yes," she said dryly, "please do apologize for saving me from ruin and our entire party from the scene that would have ensued had you admitted to the truth."

"I didn't lie out of shame," he clarified, "or any desire to deny this… whatever this is between us."

"The only things between us," Batrice said briskly, "are secrets. I suspect we both have more than are strictly comfortable to carry around on a regular basis, and clearly, neither of us are ready to share the burden."

"People say that burdens become lighter when shared," Jamie said quietly, "but the same is not always true of secrets. Sometimes the weight only grows."

"And sometimes we use mystery to insulate us from reality," Batrice countered. "It's far easier to hide behind masks than to let anyone see the truth, or risk them finding out that we are nothing like we pretend to be."

Jamie looked back at her without flinching, but his hands flexed where they rested on his knees. "You've never pretended with me, have you?"

"Not nearly as much as I should have," she responded honestly. "You've offered me no direct truths and made no promises. You flirted with me, yes, but I've done the same, so I attach no blame to you for it. I simply should have known better than to let myself believe that you flirted for any reason other than the impulse of the moment. But you're easy to talk to, even when you're claiming to be a thief, and you invite confidences without ever offering them. It feels like friendship at first, until you realize how very one-sided everything is."

"I realize this comes as little consolation, but if you were any other debutante, I probably could have answered your questions," Jamie said. The plainspoken words stabbed her until he clarified with a crooked smile. "Most women want to know whether I prefer rain to sun, whether I own a carriage, whether I enjoy hunting, or prefer green to yellow. But you aim straight for the heart, Batrice, and whether I will or no, I have no choice but to protect it."

"Should I be flattered that you think me a danger to your heart?"

"I cannot recall the last time I had to work so hard to hide it."

His words were quiet but fervent, and Batrice was startled to realize that they sounded like the truth.

"I warned you already that I won't listen to your 'I wish it could be different' speech." As she always did, Batrice concealed her pain behind flippancy. "They're too easy to compose, and I could hear a dozen per evening if I wanted. Have already heard more than enough for one lifetime. I understand you owe me no truths, and I won't ask for them again, but I would prefer your silence to placing the blame on fate."

He acceded for a moment and stroked Mayhem's furry head.

"And if you had your way," he said at length, "how would this have gone, from the moment we first met?"

"No," she said, shaking her head, understanding now the wisdom in Coralynne's determination to never again be in love alone. "I won't give you that much. No more games, scholar. If you want my answer to that question, you're going to have to answer it first."

"Very well." His eyes lifted to hers, but there was nothing dark or somber about them now. They blazed hot, burned through her resolve, and left her shivering as she awaited his response. "If I had my way, our first meeting would have ended with an introduction. I would have asked to see you again. Wherever and whenever I could. But even then, there are things I would never change. I would never trade away my memory of you defending me when I lay nearly unconscious in the road, nor the moment when you declared I was a highwayman and you had every intention of overseeing my execution."

Oh, heavens, she'd really said that, hadn't she.

"I would have given anything not to scare you off that day when we walked to the village, and when I caught you in that maid's uniform, I would have kissed you until you had no doubt of how utterly bewitching I found you."

Batrice's mouth opened as heat flooded her cheeks. She probably should have been scandalized, but she found herself far more flattered than angry. And relieved. He might not be in love with her, but he really had wanted to kiss her. She hadn't imagined that part.

"I would have protected you from whoever has tried to harm you, kissed you again when we searched the woods, and when we encountered one another last night, I would have begged you for just one more moment, one more chance to be with you. The way you embrace life with passion and intensity draws me like a moth to a flame, and I don't want to let it go."

Though her brain was largely a blank at that point, Batrice noted to herself that if he really was no more than a flirt, he was *very* good at it.

"But that is where my wishes and reality would have collided unavoidably, because I'm a scholar and you're a lady. And there is no future possible for two such different people when, as you say, there is nothing between us but secrets."

Batrice focused her attention on Goblin, who was washing the back of her hand, to avoid a sudden attack of maudlin tears. She did not cry. Ever. Unless she meant to, which was an entirely different affair.

"That was quite a thorough exposition," she said, her voice only slightly hoarse.

"I can give you that much honesty at least."

"I almost wish you hadn't. It's one thing to suffer an unrequited interest, but entirely another to know your interest is returned but without any intention of doing anything about it."

"You would rather I trifle with you, knowing the entire time that I was toying with your heart?"

"No." Batrice blinked rapidly and looked out the window. "I think I would rather have gone on believing my interest to be blissfully one-sided. Which is, I realize, a bit absurd, but at least it would hurt less."

Why oh why had she ever thought it would be entertaining to experience a tragic love affair? Because right now, this was anything but entertaining. Although, she reminded herself, it wasn't actually love, or an affair. She'd only known the man for five days, which meant it was a ridiculous infatuation, even if it hurt like it was something more.

"I'm sorry that I've caused you pain," he said. "But I refuse to deny that I do wish things were different."

"My pain is hardly your fault," Batrice replied tartly. "I'm old enough to know that hasty, ill-judged attachments almost always end in heartache. And," she added, "I might as well admit to being a hypocrite. I also wish things were different. I wish I was not a fool, and I wish you were not a thief, but those are not the sort of wishes that come true."

He had no denial to offer. "I promise I will do my best not to make our situation worse, even if that means avoiding you as much as possible."

"Don't be ridiculous," Batrice said briskly, looking up at him and narrowing her eyes. "You will do nothing of the sort. The truth is, we're no different than two people who met at a ball and shared a dance. I have confessed that I am not entirely indifferent to you, and you've admitted to a degree of interest. But not enough to, say, send flowers or make morning calls. So we'll go our separate ways when this journey is over and only remember one another whenever our carriages break down, or we have burnt gruel for breakfast."

He looked troubled but didn't contradict her.

"So then, there's no reason for this to be awkward. Well, any *more* awkward at least."

"Can you forgive me?"

"What would you have me forgive?" she asked bluntly. "You've not apologized for thieving my belongings from a locked trunk, so why should you ask forgiveness for my heart, when I was so foolish as to leave it unguarded?"

"Because hurting you is the last thing I would wish to do. And I should have kept my distance. Intended to at first. But when you confronted that ridiculous marquess, I simply couldn't help myself. I wanted to know you."

She could have invented no more exquisite torture if she tried.

"Please," she said desperately, "no more. It is conflicting enough that I cannot tell whether or not you are truly a thief. We've established that we can mean nothing to each other, and I have no wish to continue reminding myself of the fact. Can we simply choose to be strangers, from here on out?"

"If that is what you wish."

She didn't wish it. She didn't wish it at all, but what choice did she have? Whoever he was, he'd chosen his secrets over her, and there was nothing she could do about it.

Perhaps this was what Lady Norelle had meant when she spoke of the realities of the life Batrice aspired to. She would always have to choose her secrets over the impulses of the moment. There would be no freedom to simply follow her heart, only her responsibility to the Crown and to the other people who would be relying on her.

Was she ready to give up her autonomy to that degree? Ready to make those hard decisions for the sake of a career that would make it difficult—if not impossible—to form deep connections or long term relationships?

It was a sobering thought, and the questions continued to plague her as the carriage rolled deeper into the forest. Farther from home, perhaps, but ever closer to the end of her journey, which couldn't come soon enough. She might have to deal with her grandmother, but she could rid herself of troublesome guards, worries about thieves, and one tiny, destructive puppy who was currently asleep amidst the shreds of the blanket from inside his once pristine and beautifully trimmed basket.

If only she could rid herself of Jamie so easily. He might be leaving them at Peridale, but she knew her memories would plague her long after his warm brown eyes and perfect hands were gone.

CHAPTER 15

*D*espite her distraction, Batrice noticed the difference as soon as they branched off the main road. The trees grew taller and closer together, and the path narrowed. Fortunately, they met few other vehicles, though there were deep ruts in the road that indicated it wasn't always so empty. It made for a slow, rough journey, and they pulled up in front of the inn just as night was falling.

Coralynne was drooping with exhaustion, and even Rupert was silent, so there were few words as they disembarked. Jamie disappeared immediately to make his own accommodations, and Batrice forced herself not to watch him go.

The inn, at least, was larger than she'd expected, and busier. When she inquired about rooms, the innkeeper was cordial but brisk.

"I've but one room," he said, "that you'll have to share with your maid, but it's large enough. Your men will have to sleep elsewhere. There's a bunkhouse out back for the staff with some extra beds if they're willing, for only the cost of meals."

It would be disappointing after the day they'd had, but at least it was the last night. Her grandmother would have more than enough room for them.

But it was odd to find so many travelers that far from the main road. Indeed, when she and Coralynne entered the common room for dinner, she noted there were more than a few roughly dressed men present.

After seating herself, Batrice glanced around the room and accidentally caught the eye of one of them. He looked away, but Batrice did not because there was something familiar about him. Something...

He looked like one of the men she'd seen the previous morning. One of the men she recalled thinking seemed strangely familiar.

It was too difficult to be certain. He was dressed the same as most of the other men in the room, in nondescript workman's clothing, and there was nothing remarkable about his face. But there had to be a reason why she thought she'd seen him before, and her heart pounded uncomfortably as she tried to study him without appearing suspicious. Could this be one of the men responsible for their misfortunes? The destruction of the coach, the threatening note, and their missing belongings?

Calling the innkeeper over, Batrice tried to make her inquiries as innocently as possible.

"You've a fine inn," she said pleasantly, "but I can't help but notice that you're quite busy for being so far from town. Is there some kind of fair, or other entertainment to bring so many travelers through this time of year?"

"We've nothing like that, here, Miss," the innkeeper said with a chuckle. "We're working folk, and the demand for lumber is up. We've had a steady supply of workers needing rooms for months now, plus some interest from investors hoping to capitalize on the rise in shipbuilding. Been good for me, and for the village, so I don't complain."

Was he no more than a lumber worker then? He might be using that as a cover, but it could also legitimately explain why they'd been traveling the same road for a few days. And as she had no clear memories of seeing him before the previous morning—only a hunch—Batrice settled back into her seat, feeling a bit disappointed. It would have been so satisfying to have caught the thieves herself and pointed them out to Rupert, but also alarming—to believe that the person or persons following them might have been able to anticipate their movements even after a change of plans.

She would simply have to continue watching the man in order to prove or disprove her suspicions, so she bent her head over her dinner, feigning interest in the simple stew as she kept a close eye on the crowd around her.

Batrice thought briefly about sharing her observations with Coralynne, but one glance was enough to confirm that it would be better to hold her peace. The poor girl was nodding over her bowl, far too tired to engage in anything like a rational conversation, let alone a discussion of the possibility that they were sharing an inn with a dangerous criminal.

Batrice had also been unable to bring herself to say anything to Coralynne about what had transpired between herself and Jamie in the coach. It was still a raw wound, still something she hadn't quite had a chance to come to terms with, and she couldn't imagine trying to explain it to anyone else.

After dinner, they readied for bed in near silence, Coralynne yawning so frequently that she had to give up trying to write and simply collapse into bed. Batrice tried to close her eyes and focus on Goblin's sleepy purr beside her, but she couldn't seem to stop seeing Jamie's smile, or hearing his voice telling her he was drawn to her, like a moth to a lantern, like lodestone to iron, like Mayhem to trouble, or like fleas to a...

That was quite enough of that. Throwing off her blankets, Batrice crossed to her trunk with her jaw set and her hands clenched. She would not drive herself to distraction over a man. Not even a beautiful one with a perfect sense of humor. Not even a golden-haired paragon with a gorgeous smile. Not even...

Throwing open the lid of her trunk, she dug into the bottom until her fingers located the nondescript bag she'd hidden between her underthings. It was rolled up into a compact ball, surprisingly small and light, and she'd wondered when she packed it why she'd bothered. It was a symbol of the life she'd left behind, the life she'd been trying to forget in an effort to become what Lady Norelle asked of her.

But she'd felt so free, almost weightless, when she'd dusted off her sword skills beside the fire. Maybe it was time to remember the joy she'd once found in driving her body to its limits in other ways as well.

The spangled tights and close-fitting suit would be scandalous by almost anyone's estimation, but to Batrice, they represented freedom. As she slid them on for the first time in ages and gathered her hair into a tail at the nape of her neck, it was like going home and remembering part of herself that she'd missed but hadn't been able to put a name to.

Her body was stiff at first, but it was almost a relief to fall into old habits and routines, stretching her muscles until they remembered what she expected of them. When she was warm and limber, though far less flexible than she'd once been, she began attempting more serious exercises. Nothing too loud, of course. It was a relief to find that she could still bend backwards until her toes touched her nose, still walk across the room on her hands, and even almost managed a flare without waking Coralynne. That one might need some work.

Once she'd tired of the exercises she could do without too many suspicious thumps, Batrice was still hungry for more, and was eyeing the door with steely-eyed determination when a sound at the window brought her whirling into a crouch.

A natural sound from a creaky old building?

A bird or a moth?

Or something worse?

Heart galloping from more than just the unaccustomed exercise, she remained motionless, almost ready to believe it had been nothing more than settling timbers when it came again.

A creak, a quiet snick, and then the window began to open.

She ought to have been afraid. Probably ought to scream, or make some other noise to draw the attention of someone who might come to her aid.

But suddenly, she was angry—furiously, blindingly angry—and refused to give the intruder the satisfaction. Whether it was the man she'd recognized downstairs, Rupert or John, or even Jamie, she wanted to know once and for all what face to assign to the shadowy someone who had stalked them since Evenleigh.

So when a dark-clad, dark-gloved arm appeared in the window, Batrice crept nearer, nearer, grabbed the arm in both hands, and pulled. Hard.

She was strong, but she was off to the side to avoid being seen, so her leverage was poor. Plus, he was wearing a laced leather bracer over his sleeve, so her fingers slipped a little, and she didn't manage to smack the would-be-intruder's face against the window frame as she'd hoped.

But the owner of the arm was startled enough to swear, in a harsh whisper that didn't seem familiar. Then he tore away from her grasp and began to make a hasty retreat.

Batrice probably should have let him go, should have considered his plans foiled for another night, but her blood burned in her veins and her fingers itched for something to be real, something that she could know for sure.

She grasped the window frame, hoisted herself up, and shot through the window feet first after him.

The rough shakes of the roof bit into her bare feet, which had spent too long safely encased in slippers and boots, but she barely felt the sting. The dark figure had too great a lead on her, and was quickly receding into the darkness on the other end of the roofline. Almost to the end, her quarry dropped onto his stomach, rolled over the edge, and disappeared.

Batrice followed, taking only a short glance before lowering herself to a window ledge and then flipping off it to the roof of a gable window below. Down the steep incline, then a front flip over the edge to the ground. Only after she landed did she wonder whether she shouldn't have attempted such a thing after such a long hiatus, but then she was off into the night on the heels of the swiftly fleeing figure in black.

He disappeared around the back of the stable, so Batrice made the hasty decision to sneak in through the front instead. She could pursue him out the back door later if needed, but this way she could confront him if he'd attempted to conceal himself inside.

It was darker than she expected once she slipped through the doors and closed them behind her. Horses shifted in their stalls, but none sounded the alarm, so she bent low to creep past the line of doors to the back. She was about halfway down the long aisle when something hit her from behind.

She was knocked to the floor, but rolled and came up ready, only to be struck from the side, her arms pinned and her feet kicked out from under her. Batrice fell to the ground heavily, barely managing to keep her head from hitting the floor. Her breath left her with a pained-sounding grunt and remained gone for a moment as she struggled to free her arms.

Panic began to build, but before she could draw in enough air to cry out, the arms holding her tightened, then stilled. The body pressed against hers drew back.

"Batrice?" The hoarse whisper made her heart sink as she recognized it at last—and realized exactly who she'd been chasing through the dark. Who had nearly knocked her unconscious on the stable floor...

Before she could make any reply, he lifted her off the ground and carried her outside, setting her down and releasing her as soon as they cleared the back door.

There was enough moonlight for her to see the incredulous expression on Jamie's face as she glared at him accusingly.

"It was you," she said softly, harshly. "It was always you. And you were going to try it again." She shook her head, unable to believe how badly she'd been taken in. "Was it all a lie? All of it except the thieving part? And what is it you want so badly that you've followed us all this way to get it?"

"What are you talking about, Batrice?" Jamie asked in a low voice. "And why are you running around in the middle of the night dressed like that?"

"Don't play innocent," she snapped, quieting her voice at the last moment as she remembered that it would be wise to avoid drawing anyone else's attention. "It makes you look a fool. You know exactly why I chased you out the window and off the roof. I'll ask you again, what were you trying to steal?"

"*Off the roof?*" She saw his eyes go wide, and for the first time was able to see past her anger and disappointment to realize that she may, in fact, have made a mistake.

His clothes were all wrong. He was wearing an untucked white shirt, with only half the buttons done up, his hair fell loose around his face, and his feet were bare. The man she'd chased across the roof had worn black, with gloves, boots, and a hood, not to mention the bracer. There had been no time for him to shed that much clothing between the moment he'd disappeared and the moment she'd entered the barn.

It could not have been Jamie.

Relief struck her so hard that her knees buckled and she dropped to the dirt behind the barn, or would have had Jamie not caught her before she could touch the ground... Caught her and pulled her into his chest with a groan that sounded almost as desperate as she'd felt at believing him the villain.

"Gods above, Batrice, are you all right?"

"I'm fine," she murmured into his chest, drawing a deep breath that smelled of hay and linen and... of Jamie. She couldn't identify the scent, only knew that it was his and that she was a fool because it made her feel safe when she was anything but.

"Come with me," he said, releasing her only to take her by the hand and draw her after him back into the barn.

"Jamie, I really did chase someone out here. Someone who tried to enter my room through the window."

He paused and looked back at her. "I've been awake, and no one else came in after the hostler left. Just you."

"Then he's still out there." She tugged her hand from his. "I need to know who's doing this. Need to find him and make it stop."

"He's probably long gone," Jamie said, "and it's not safe out there in the dark. What if I'd been him? What would you have done?"

She grinned. Not all of her training had been for show. One of the other acrobats had been a wrestler before he was injured and he'd shown all of them a trick or two...

"This," she said, praying she still remembered the moves. Grasping his shirt front as if in entreaty, she ignored his startled gaze to leap up and to the side, twisting at the last second to wrap one arm around his neck, cross the other one over the back of his shoulders and squeeze, using her body weight to yank him backwards at the same time. She turned as they fell, so they both landed on their sides, him gasping for air as she continued to flex her arm until it cut off his ability to breathe.

"Okay, okay," he got out, in a strangled voice. "I believe you."

She let go and got to her feet, wincing and letting out a yelp as she realized that running barefoot across a wooden shake roof had probably not been the smartest thing she'd ever done.

"Did I hurt you?" Jamie asked, rubbing his neck as he rose from the ground.

"No," she muttered, a little annoyed by his question when she had been the one choking *him*. "But I think there are splinters in my feet."

He let out a rough sigh as he approached her and looked down with some indecipherable emotion glittering in his eyes. "May I take you back inside?"

He hadn't ordered—he'd asked. Warmth struck through her middle and left her incapable of words. So she nodded.

Jamie swept her off the ground as though she weighed nothing, causing an outbreak of intense fluttering in her chest as he carried her back into the warm, dark interior of the barn and set her down gently on a pile of hay. "Wait here."

The fluttering only intensified when he disappeared for a moment that stretched into two, and then a handful more, before he returned carrying one of the lanterns that would have hung in front of the inn.

Setting it down in front of her, he didn't meet her eyes but instead grasped her ankle and lifted it gently, swearing under his breath as he saw what the roof had done to the skin of her feet.

She expected him to be angry. To berate her for risking herself, for causing herself injury, for not being mindful of her safety, or even for not calling for help. It was what Rupert would have done. But Jamie's lips quirked into a smile.

"Whoever he was, he must have gotten the fright of his life when you jumped out the window after him."

"But it wasn't enough." The rush that had carried her that far was wearing off, and she could feel herself begin to droop in exhaustion and disappointment. "He got away from me again. Just like he did in the woods."

"The man you fought?"

She nodded. "I just want this to be over. I want to know who's doing this to us, and I couldn't just sit around and wait for someone else to do something."

"Did you notice any identifying features?"

"No. Just that he was large, so I assumed it was a man. Dressed in dark clothes, with gloves and boots. And when he cursed after I grabbed him, the voice didn't seem high enough to be female."

Jamie chuckled briefly. "I'm still going to ask for an explanation of the outfit. Not that it isn't flattering, but it's certainly unusual."

Batrice felt herself blush, but she was too tired to come up with a convincing lie. And anyway, she was never going to see him again after tomorrow so what did she care what he thought?

"I spent several years with a troupe of actors and performers," she confessed. "My family disowned me, and I really didn't care because I enjoyed acting, and I loved acrobatics even more. Since I was forced to leave the troupe, my family has been trying to bring me back into the fold of gentility, but I may very well be hopeless. I enjoy the freedom of this"— she indicated her outlandish outfit—"a little too much. And tonight I was so upset after…" she paused, glanced his way, then looked back at the floor. "Anyway, I needed a distraction, so I was practicing in my room when the intruder showed up at the window. I couldn't let him get away again, so I followed him."

"I'm sorry this isn't over yet," he said soberly.

"If I only knew what he wanted."

"Would you give it to him?"

She scowled. "What do you think?"

"I think you would beat him over the head with it, then bury him with it stuffed in his mouth for good measure."

He surprised her into laughing. And it felt good, to share that laughter with someone who understood her.

"Do you need help to get back to your room?"

Batrice bit her lip and considered the roof she'd jumped from. "Probably? I don't know whether I can jump that high, or if there's anything I can use to stand on."

But instead of helping her up, he continued to crouch in front of her, and was silent so long she was forced to look up and meet his gaze.

It was a mistake. In an instant, she was snared in the depths of his eyes, unable to look away from the pain and concern she read there. His hand was warm on her ankle, and Batrice felt a tug, not a physical pull, but one that nonetheless drew her towards him until there was no sound but their breathing and the steady thud of her own heart in her ears.

"Batrice," he said, and her name had never sounded like that before.

His mouth opened again. "I wish…"

As much as it hurt, she had to ask. "Even knowing that I'm not really a lady, knowing that society would shun me if they found out about my past, you still wish?" She hated that her voice trembled with vulnerability, but the question was too important.

His fingers tightened around her ankle as his eyes grew bright. "More than ever," he said softly. "And yet it changes nothing."

"Oh, but it does to me," she said, and managed a sad smile for both of them. "I loved that part of my life and hate that I have to hide it. Knowing that someone else can accept that part of me... it means everything."

His mouth curved, matching both her sadness and her smile, and Batrice knew she would remember that moment forever—the softness of the hay beneath her, the sting of her wounds, the play of light and shadow on his face, and the empty ache of a heart she'd finally given up for lost.

"Will you allow me to help with your injuries?" he said at last. "I can't imagine it would be easy to get all the splinters out on your own."

It was a bad idea, letting him touch her. It would only remind her of why she'd fallen for him in the first place.

But tomorrow her journey would be over, and he would be gone, so she chose the memories over caution.

"Thank you," she said. "You may."

CHAPTER 16

*B*atrice never closed her eyes that night. She spent the hours before dawn listening for approaching footsteps while replaying those moments in the barn over and over, determined to hold on to them as long as she could. Jamie might be lost to her, but no one could take away the memory of his gentle hands washing the blood off her feet and carefully removing every last splinter before wrapping them in the strips of a shirt he could probably ill afford to lose.

She couldn't decide whether she'd been relieved or disappointed that he hadn't used the one he was wearing. But considering the almost overwhelming effect of his simple touch on her ankle, it was probably for the best that she be forced to only imagine what he might look like without a shirt.

Not to mention Coralynne would have noticed if she blushed every time she looked at him.

Batrice took care to be up and dressed before Coralynne began to stir, covering her bandages with her heaviest stockings and leaving her boots loosely laced. They were still uncomfortably tight and hurt with every step, but it was that or go barefoot, which was out of the question.

So she smiled brightly, pretended she wasn't ready to collapse from exhaustion, and found herself looking over her shoulder with every step down the stairs and out into a dark, cloudy morning.

It was the last day. They would be at her grandmother's house tonight, and then she would have the disapproving embrace of her family to help her forget everything that had happened over the past seven days. Jamie would travel on. Coralynne would write her novel. And everything would go back to the way it had been before.

Everything except her heart.

Which had been fractured anyway, long before she met Jamie. This journey had only widened the cracks and shown her the parts of herself where she'd been pretending everything was fine. Pretending to know exactly what she wanted out of life.

In reality, she had no idea. Only that she longed to fit somewhere, wished to belong to something bigger than herself. She thought perhaps she'd found that again with Lady Norelle and her network of Crown agents, but was that truly the life she was meant for? To forever be on the move, unable to form any attachments but to her job?

It was yet another sobering thought as she cradled a sleepy Goblin against her chest and waited for Rupert to help her into the carriage. But he seemed absorbed in reading a note of some kind and didn't even see her standing there, so she shifted Goblin to one arm, pulled herself in, and settled on the bench for the final leg of their journey.

The kitten mewed softly as she settled him on the seat next to her, for once not even protesting when Mayhem jumped in and wagged his tail tentatively.

Jamie followed the puppy, setting the basket on the seat and asking with his eyes whether she was all right.

She gave him a smile that was meant to be reassuring but probably came off as more of a grimace.

"I confess I am more than ready to be out of this carriage for good," Coralynne said brightly, as Rupert, who was apparently finished with his note, handed her in. She dropped onto the seat beside Batrice and sighed dramatically. "This trip seemed like a glorious adventure, and while it's been extremely exciting, it's also been exhausting."

"But you've gained so much material for your novel," Batrice reminded her, trying to sound encouraging. "And we have a whole day yet to come. Who knows what else might happen?"

Then she turned to Jamie and said in her most normal, pleasant voice: "Have you given much thought to the next stage of your journey? How do you plan to travel past Peridale?"

"I expect I'll walk until I can find someone to take me up," he said, shrugging nonchalantly as if walking alone for miles through the woods was a completely normal activity.

"That's quite unacceptable," Batrice said firmly. "I will ask my grandmother's groom to loan you a horse that you can ride until you are able to hire one. Any of the stables hereabouts will be well able to return it."

"And is your grandmother the sort of person to entrust her property to nameless itinerant scholars?" Jamie asked, one eyebrow raised in amusement.

"My grandmother is pretending to be at death's door," Batrice reminded him dryly. "By the time she has been sufficiently fawned over to fake a recovery, it will be much too late to question what has been going on in the stables during her indisposition."

"Perhaps," was all he would say.

The carriage rolled on slowly, carefully navigating the rutted track, stopping only for a brief midday meal before continuing their progress. It was early afternoon, under a gloomy gray sky, when the passengers heard a crack, and then felt an uncomfortable lurch. There was a grating sound before the carriage came to a halt, then silence.

"Ooh, Batrice, I do believe you were right!" Coralynne exclaimed, her eyes widening with excitement. "Something else *has* happened."

It wasn't as though she'd intended to wish yet another misfortune on them. Giving vent to an unladylike groan of frustration, Batrice didn't bother to wait for news. She pushed open the door, jumped to the ground, and found John standing by the carriage with his hands on his hips and a haggard look on his face.

"What is it? Can it be fixed?"

He looked at her, then at Rupert, who was only just riding up, with dark circles beneath his eyes that matched Batrice's own. She hadn't told him of her adventures the night before, for obvious reasons, but he looked to have gotten little more sleep than she had.

"It's the axletree," John said, looking oddly pale. "It's... snapped."

"Snapped?" Rupert dismounted hastily and dropped to one knee to look behind the wheel.

"Aye. But not just snapped..."

Rupert glanced up, and Batrice saw when some understanding passed between them.

"What is it?"

When neither of them answered, she strode nearer and bent down to take a look for herself.

Even she could see where the axletree had broken, with jagged splinters visible between the two halves... but not all the way across. On one side, the break was smooth, as neat and even as if the wood had been cut by the blade of a saw.

When she glanced behind her, Batrice saw the same knowledge in the eyes of her guard and driver—someone had deliberately sabotaged their carriage.

"We can't stay here," she said instantly.

"I agree." Rupert spoke up in unexpected support. "Let them have the carriage if that's what they want. I can escort you and Miss Smythe on towards your grandmother's house."

"How much farther?" she asked.

"Not completely certain, given our slow pace so far, but probably too far on foot," he told her grimly. "We're perhaps halfway. If you are willing to ride, we should still make it before dark."

"I am," she confirmed.

"I'll stay with the carriage." John's tone was firm, and it was clear that he wasn't asking for permission.

"Someone will need to return to our last stop for a cart to fetch the bags," Rupert reminded him.

But John remained obdurate. "Can't leave the royal coach unguarded. It's my job to look after it."

"Perhaps I could be the one to go for a cart." Jamie's surprising offer earned him a suspicious stare from Rupert, but it wasn't as if the guard had a choice.

After a moment of indecision, he nodded. "Thank you. I suppose that places us in your debt once again."

"No debt," Jamie said easily. "It's but a few hours ride, and I'm glad to be of service."

Batrice kept to herself the thought that it might be the most dangerous of their disparate tasks—wherever the saboteurs were lurking, it was likely to be on the road behind them.

While Rupert announced the plan to Coralynne and helped her out of the carriage, John unhitched the horses, and Jamie unloaded their luggage from the roof. Only after they'd gathered up their most necessary items and prepared to depart, did Batrice remember what they'd not accounted for in their plans.

"Drat," she said. "What are we going to do with Mayhem and Goblin?"

"Leave them with the coach?" Rupert suggested, his scowl making it clear that he wished both animals to perdition.

"And what if the thieves return?" Batrice protested. "John will have himself to look after, and we can't have them stealing Mayhem—he's a gift from the Crown to a loyal subject. And what of Goblin? Anyone who sees him may very well try to kill him."

"For good reason," Batrice thought she heard Rupert mutter, but decided to pretend she was mistaken.

"Cats can look after themselves," Rupert insisted, a bit more loudly. "We can try to take the pup, but that creature of yours will have to stay."

Batrice was on the verge of protesting when Jamie spoke up yet again. "I'll take Mayhem." At Rupert's incredulous look, he explained. "I've grown fond of him, and he's comfortable with me. It's possible he might even enjoy the ride."

"As you wish, scholar," Rupert said with a shrug. "As long as I don't have to hear it or see it, I don't much care what becomes of it." But he directed a grim stare at Jamie's back that made Batrice wonder whether he might not be telling the whole truth. He might have become more attached to the little beast than he was willing to admit.

Batrice was tempted to smuggle Goblin along with her but gave up the idea when she realized she would be balancing herself and a bag on a horse with no saddle. She rode well, but there was no sense courting danger when they were already in plenty of that. And Rupert was actually correct, much as she hated to admit it—Goblin could take care of himself, and as long as he stayed in the carriage, she could rescue him later.

When she saw that Jamie was about to mount up, bareback, on one of the carriage horses, Batrice couldn't help herself—she crossed to stand beside him and grasped his sleeve. "Be careful?" she said quietly. "Take good care of Mayhem, and yourself. Whoever did this is still out there, and I wouldn't want you to encounter them alone."

"I'll be fine," he said, but his voice was flat, and he refused to meet her eyes.

Confused and hurt, Batrice stepped back, and could do nothing but watch as he slung his bag over his shoulder, tucked Mayhem under his arm, and vaulted onto the horse's back. He deliberately avoided looking back as he wheeled his mount and returned the way they'd come at a canter.

Feeling as though he'd slapped her, Batrice wrestled her disappointment into submission and meekly accepted the reins of one of the carriage horses from Rupert. For whatever reason, Jamie hadn't wanted to say goodbye. And once she reached her grandmother's house, it was possible that she wouldn't be allowed to see him again.

Heartache threatened to crush her, but she resolutely beat it back. There was no time to be maudlin. Someone had sabotaged their carriage. That someone might still be coming for them. They would need to be alert and move as quickly as possible.

She could cry later, when everything was over.

It was a silent, uncomfortable ride. Coralynne was up behind Rupert, as before, with a bag across her shoulders. Batrice rode alone, her stained cloak wrapped around her shoulders and a makeshift pack slung over the horse's back. And riding behind her was the realization that someone might be following them. John could be in danger, and they still knew nothing of why they'd been targeted.

Her shoulder blades itched with apprehension, but all they could do was continue on.

Occasionally they would see a cottage or a bit of fence off in the trees, but for the most part, the woods remained unbroken, even extending their branches over the road in places to form a living green tunnel.

"Batrice, why does your grandmother live all the way out here?" Coralynne asked, keeping her voice low. "If she's that desperate for attention, and she's rich, couldn't she just move closer to a town?"

Rupert twisted in his saddle to look at her oddly, and Coralynne blanched.

"I'm sorry, Miss Reyard," she whispered meekly. "I didn't mean to sound so disrespectful."

"Oh, never mind that," Batrice said wearily, waving a hand. "Under the circumstances, don't you think he might as well know the truth?"

"The truth?" Rupert raised an eyebrow. "What could the two of you possibly be hiding that's worse than that cat?"

Coralynne blushed. "Are you certain, Batrice? Is it safe?"

"He'll find out eventually when we get back. Everyone will."

The other girl seemed to wilt and pulled away from the handsome guard in front of her. "Well, we weren't sure how to tell you but..." She shrugged helplessly and turned to Batrice.

"Rupert, Coralynne isn't actually a servant. She wanted to come along to write a book about our adventures, so she posed as my maid, but she's actually a friend from Evenleigh."

It was Rupert's turn to change color, and for a moment he was utterly bereft of speech.

"You..." he started to say, but he didn't get any farther into whatever speech he was planning. Before Batrice's horrified eyes, his head snapped to the side, his eyes rolled back, and he toppled off his horse to the ground.

"Coralynne!" Batrice cried.

"It wasn't me!" Coralynne tried to dismount, but got stuck in her skirts and tumbled off after Rupert with a shriek. The horse shied, right into Batrice's mount, which reared up, causing her to nearly lose her seat.

She hung on grimly until it settled again, snorting and shifting its weight, ears forward and head up as it stared into the trees.

"Is he all right?" She looked down at Coralynne, who had rolled Rupert onto his back. But even Batrice could see he was far from all right—a lump had already formed on his head, and was oozing blood.

"What happened? Why did he fall?"

"Something hit him," Coralynne wailed, her eyes wide with terror.

What could have hit him?

"Batrice! Get down!" But Coralynne's warning was too late.

A dark shape plummeted from the branches above her, catching her by the shoulders and knocking her from the horse's back. She twisted in time to prevent her attacker from falling on her, but he was too strong to throw off entirely, and she ended up on her face in the dirt, her arms held together behind her back.

"Get her up." The command was given in an unfamiliar voice, not deep but rough, almost deliberately so, and it was instantly obeyed. Batrice was hauled up by her arms, which felt as though they'd been nearly wrenched out of their sockets.

Coralynne, too, was yanked away from Rupert, though she struggled and hissed in protest. Within a few moments, they stood side by side, each of them held with their arms behind them, and a darting glance revealed that the man gripping Coralynne's arms wore a mask.

But it was a ridiculously tiny one, and Batrice knew the shape of that jaw. Recognized the hair cut and color. She took a moment to feel grimly pleased with her instincts as she confirmed that the man who held Coralynne's arms was the one she'd thought she recognized during their stops, not once but twice. Which meant that the one behind her must be his companion.

And the one who gave orders in that odd voice?

His face was hidden beneath a cloak as he emerged from the shadows of the trees.

Batrice glanced both ways down the road, hoping that for once another traveler would chance by, to stop whatever was about to happen, but the road remained empty.

"You've done well, girl, but the game is over," the man said, crossing his arms... his leather bracer clad arms.

Batrice's eyes narrowed as she stared into the shadows of the hood, hoping for a clue to his identity. At least it wasn't Jamie, she could tell that much. This man was shorter, and thicker around the middle, though his shoulders were narrower and his voice nowhere near as deep.

She should probably be embarrassed to realize that she'd stared at Jamie's shoulders long enough to tell the difference.

"I have no idea to what you are referring," she said, lifting her chin imperiously, "but you've interfered with a Crown-sponsored member of the Andari court. You've attacked a member of the Royal Guard and destroyed one of His Majesty's carriages. I think you'll find that Crown justice is swift towards those who disrespect the king's royal seal."

The man chuckled. "A fine show, little miss. But it's obvious you're not really going to your 'grandmother's house,' and your only value to the king is in what you carry. We know you have the basket. Hand over the formula and the goods, and we'll let you go free. Without the horses, of course, but undamaged, unless you continue to fight."

Hand over the *what*?

"You have waylaid entirely the wrong party," Batrice snapped, infuriated by the realization that every one of their misfortunes had been a simple case of mistaken identity. "I am, in fact, going to visit my grandmother, and I can't possibly hand over what you want because I have no idea what you are talking about."

One of the man's gloved hands dropped to his belt, where it landed on the hilt of an impressively large dagger. "You can stop pretending," he said, his voice sharpening. "Lady Norelle trains her agents well, but you're far too young to understand what you're dealing with. I don't know what she told you about the basket, but I assure you, I'm not the only one you'll find willing to kill for it, only the smartest and the fastest. Hand it over, and I might be convinced to leave you tied up, with a lump on your head so you can at least claim you fought me for it."

"For *what*?" Batrice was almost yelling now, so thoroughly overwhelmed with shock and rage that her control entirely deserted her.

Lady Norelle?

The basket?

Willing to kill?

What in the name of Andar was happening here?

"If that's the way you want it." The man whipped out the dagger. Batrice flinched, but he didn't throw it. Instead, he took three quick strides and pressed its shining edge to Coralynne's trembling throat.

"Give me the basket. I'll have the formula and the sample, or I'll slit your maid's throat and leave her to bleed out in the middle of the road."

For the first time in her life, Batrice felt herself grow genuinely faint. He wasn't joking. As a thin trickle of red trailed down to stain Coralynne's collar, and a terrified whimper escaped her lips, Batrice strained to regain her grip on reality. On sanity. On anything that would let her make sense of what was happening.

And her efforts left her, as they usually did, on the stage. Where she could hide behind a character who would know exactly what to do.

"Stop!" she shouted, allowing tears to form in her eyes and trail down her cheeks in an ever-increasing flood. Batrice Reyard never cried unless she intended to, but when she did, it was an awe-inspiring spectacle. "Please stop. Just don't hurt her. She doesn't know anything. I'll do whatever you want, but please don't kill anyone. I couldn't bear it if you killed anyone!" She dropped to her knees, which wrenched her arms a great deal, but it startled the man behind her into letting go.

Batrice remained on her knees in the dirt, sobbing hysterically. "I didn't know! She never told me! Just said I had to take it with me. The basket is in the carriage so please don't hurt us. Please!" She wailed her last please as loudly as possible, trailing it out into another round of sobbing and allowing her head to fall onto her knees.

"Oh, for the love of all, just shut her up, would you?" the dark-cloaked man hissed.

Batrice was yanked rudely to her feet, where a quick glance at Coralynne confirmed that her ruse had been at least partially successful—the dagger was no longer at her friend's throat, and she was now looking more startled than terrified.

Good. They would need to be ready to run when the moment came.

"The two of you stay here." The dark-cloaked man was already turning back the way they'd come. "Bind the guard. Keep the girls quiet. I'll find out if she's telling the truth."

A low whistle brought a bay horse trotting out of the trees. Without another word, the man mounted and rode off, somehow not disturbing his hood by even an inch, much to Batrice's disappointment.

"Come on." The man holding her arms jerked her towards the trees. "We're getting you off the road."

"We can't just leave my guard lying there," she protested with a pitiful sniffle. "What if he's run over by a carriage? Or eaten by wolves?"

The man tugging Coralynne behind him rolled his eyes behind his mask. "Blinkin' debutantes," he muttered. "There aren't no blinkin' wolves in these woods. And what, you think we're going to waste our breath saving a man who'd try to kill us the moment he woke up? Think again, girlie."

Coralynne burst into tears.

As soon as they entered the trees, the men pushed Batrice and Coralynne to the ground, but no longer bothered to hold them, probably because by now they were both weeping loudly.

"And shut up, the both of you, or we'll have to gag you."

Coralynne tried to be quiet, but her sobs, at least, seemed real, and well past the point of being contained.

Batrice allowed her own tears to ease gradually as she waited and watched for an opportunity.

Which came only a few moments later when a rustling started up in the brush.

"What's that?" One of the men drew his dagger and peered into the shadows.

"A bird? A squirrel? How should I know?" the other man complained.

"Sounded too big to be a squirrel."

"What, are you going to start complaining about wolves now, just like the little girl?"

"I know there are no wolves," the first man growled. "But there's something out there."

"We're in the *forest*," the second man drawled sarcastically. "There are a lot of things out there. Mostly bunnies. But we're practically on the road, and there are two of us with big shiny swords. If it helps, I promise I won't let the scary bunny eat you."

"You're an ass, Jerid," the second man snapped. "If something jumped out of these woods right now, I swear I'd feed you to it without a second thought."

The brush rustled again, louder. Batrice felt around her until her fingers landed on a rock that was large enough to do some damage, but small enough to be pried up from the forest floor.

When Coralynne saw her, she dried her tears on her sleeve and picked up a stick, which she hid behind the folds of her skirt.

"Well here's your chance," the first man taunted the second. "Would you like to go see what it is so you can offer it a nice dinner?"

"I'd like to bloody your face."

A blood-chilling yowl issued from the bushes, followed by an evil hiss.

Both men yanked their daggers from their belts and turned to face the sound.

Which was precisely the moment Batrice had been waiting for. At her nod, she and Coralynne crept up behind them, rock and stick held ready...

The brush parted.

One of the men screamed and bolted.

The other one jerked backwards, right into Batrice's rock. She didn't even really hit him, he just sort of folded up into a heap at her feet...

While Goblin sat down on the forest floor and began calmly washing his paws.

CHAPTER 17

"*H*ave I mentioned lately that I adore you?" Batrice breathed, scooping up her escaped cat and kissing him loudly on the top of his head. "Coralynne, help me find something we can use to tie him up."

They searched the unconscious man's pockets and found nothing but dried beef, a handful of coins and a disgusting handkerchief.

"Oh, bother it," Coralynne exclaimed, sitting on the ground and taking off her shoes. "We can use my stockings. They're ripped anyway."

So they bound the man's wrists and ankles with pink silk stockings, giggling helplessly as much out of shock as amusement. When his eyes opened, and he began to struggle, Batrice took off his mask and gagged him with it instead.

"They've been following us for days," she informed Coralynne grimly as she surveyed his now red face. "I saw him both last night and two mornings ago, and I could swear I remember seeing him before that as well. I just can't remember when or where."

"There were an awful lot of people at the inn that first night," Coralynne suggested. "Perhaps you saw him there in passing."

Batrice frowned and squinted at his fairly nondescript features before her gaze snagged on the silk stockings, and she suddenly remembered—there had been two middle-aged women in plain, dark cloaks. Women with heavy features, who kept their heads down over their plates...

"That's why I couldn't remember!" she exclaimed. "And that's how they've gotten away with following us for so long. They dressed as women! I suspect they changed back and forth to convince us we were seeing completely different people each night." It was embarrassing really, that she hadn't thought of it. She'd seen men play women's parts often enough on the stage that she ought to have been able to see past their clothing. It just hadn't occurred to her to watch for such a thing.

Some spy she was turning out to be.

"But why did they want a basket?" Coralynne asked.

That was the question, wasn't it? There was only one basket in the coach, and it had been placed there by Lady Norelle, under the pretext of sending a present to Batrice's grandmother.

Had that been a lie this whole time? Had the puppy been a cover for something else? A fluffy, ridiculous front for something far more dangerous?

Mind whirling, Batrice began to wonder just how betrayed she ought to feel. Their attackers had genuinely believed her to be an agent of the Crown in possession of valuable secrets. So this was either a mistake of epic proportions, or they had gotten that idea from someone who knew where Batrice was going and what she apparently carried. And who would have access to that information besides the person who prepared the basket the thieves were willing to kill for—Lady Norelle herself?

Batrice didn't want it to be true. Didn't want to believe that her mentor was capable of such a deception, but which was easier to believe? That a violent gang of thieves had identified the *wrong* basket-toting young woman on the way to visit her grandmother in the middle of the woods, or that a veteran spymaster had manipulated a trusting protégée?

It was crushing to realize how badly she'd been taken advantage of.

How naive she'd been. This entire time she'd believed herself the recipient of Lady Norelle's kindness, she'd been nothing but a target and a tool. A pawn in some dangerous game, pursued by enemies of the Crown across half of Andar without her realizing a thing.

But what about the basket could possibly have attracted so much attention? Surely not Mayhem. He was cute, perhaps, but not adorable enough to inspire anyone to murder.

There was nothing particularly remarkable about the basket itself, either—certainly nothing that could be mistaken for a state secret. Which led Batrice to yet another painful conclusion—her party may have served as nothing more than a decoy.

Had Rupert been in on it the whole time? Had John? Was anyone truly concerned about her safety, or was she merely expendable?

Her already bruised heart reeled under yet another blow, but there was no time to fall apart. The danger was real, and whether or not anyone else cared if she and Coralynne survived, Batrice cared very much about returning home in one piece to confront the ones who'd used her.

"I think," Batrice said slowly, "that the basket may have been nothing but a trap."

"A trap?" Coralynne echoed. "But for whom?"

"Bait, if you will," Batrice said wearily. "That's the only thing I can come up with. There's nothing in the basket but Mayhem, and no one wants to steal him. We were set up from the very beginning."

"Then..." Coralynne's lips began to tremble. "Did everyone else know? Did Rupert know?"

Batrice couldn't think of any way around it. "He must have," she said firmly. "Unless this was all a big mistake." But it made sense of so much that had puzzled her. Why he had insisted that she was mistaken about their belongings being stolen. He'd known thieves would be after them, and he'd wanted the chase to continue.

"But it wasn't a mistake, was it?"

She lifted her eyes to Coralynne's. Tried to think of something comforting to say. "No."

"I see." Coralynne's lips pressed together, and her jaw clenched. "Then what are we going to do now?" She pushed her hair out of her eyes and placed her hands on her hips. "That man will be back when he can't find what he wants."

She was right. They had to move fast. But where could they go?

"We'll have to try to reach my grandmother's," Batrice said decisively. Apparently, the thieves didn't believe she actually had a grandmother, so perhaps they wouldn't expect her to continue on.

Come to think of it, how had they known about her grandmother in the first place?

That was another question for later.

Batrice scooped up Goblin again and placed him in the hood of her cloak, hoping he would be content to ride there as they walked. The thief they left on the ground, where he was turning quite red from his efforts to communicate around the makeshift gag. Batrice judged from his expression that whatever he wanted to say would be entirely inappropriate for ladies' ears in any case.

They returned to the road to find Rupert just beginning to return to consciousness. His horse stood nearby, nibbling unconcernedly at the leaves of a bush.

Batrice ignored Rupert and took up his mount's reins. "We'll take the horse," she said firmly. "That will get us to my grandmother's faster."

But Coralynne didn't respond. She was standing over Rupert, staring down at him where he lay, blinking in confusion with blood running down the side of his face.

"What happened? Are you all right?" He sat up, but it clearly hurt because he let out a pained groan and clutched at his head.

"Did you know?" Coralynne demanded fiercely.

"Did I know? Know what?" He swayed a bit and tried to push to his feet.

"Did you know about the basket?"

His eyes widened momentarily, and he flinched, which was all Batrice needed to see.

All Coralynne needed too, apparently, because she slapped him, hard, on the uninjured side of his face.

"I didn't deserve that," she said, with quiet steel behind her words.

Rupert sank back to the ground and closed his eyes.

"I'm a soldier, Miss Smythe," he answered wearily. "And I had a job to do. I realize now that nothing has gone the way we planned, but I've still done my job to the best of my ability. I haven't always liked it, but part of my oath of service is to remain true to my mission in spite of my personal regrets. My opinion of my orders changes nothing."

Coralynne shook her head. "Maybe it doesn't change things for you," she told him, "but it does for me." She stood, turned on her heel, and walked towards Batrice.

"We should get out of here," she said.

Batrice mounted smoothly, grateful to have a real saddle with stirrups this time. She extended a hand to Coralynne, who struggled but eventually settled in behind her.

"Where are you going?" Rupert called after them. "You're putting yourselves in grave danger if you leave here without me."

"We're saving ourselves, Rupert," Batrice answered coldly. "You were the one who put us in danger in the first place, and I won't rely on you again."

"Don't do this, Miss Reyard," he pleaded. "You don't understand. This wasn't what was supposed to happen. We made plans to keep you safe."

"No," she said, turning the horse and riding it back to where he struggled to rise. "*You* don't understand. But we do, now. We understand that whatever calculations you may have made, they've failed. There are people out there who are willing to kill to get what they want. One of them threatened to slit Coralynne's throat."

Rupert's eyes slid to Coralynne, and he seemed to turn even whiter than he already was.

"So you'll have to excuse us if we're not in any hurry to trust you again. Whoever said there are no wolves in these woods was obviously mistaken."

Tugging the horse's head around, she tapped him with her heels and trotted off down the road.

They'd made it perhaps a mile when they heard the sound of galloping hooves behind them on the road.

Batrice leaped down and dragged the horse into the brush beside the road, getting them out of view just in time before a horse flew by. It was the man who'd fled from Goblin, probably terrified at having lost the pair of young women his leader had ordered him to subdue.

But he presented a very real problem—they couldn't stay on the road, for fear of discovery, and they couldn't ride through the woods. The trees and brush were too dense.

"I'm afraid we're going to have to go on foot from here," Batrice said softly, and bit back an unladylike curse at the thought. Walking was going to hurt. Her feet were still sore, and her boots still too tight around the bandages.

Bandages made her think of Jamie. Made her wonder whether he was all right, or whether he'd also encountered the thieves, but there was no time to dwell on his fate until they'd secured their own.

She helped Coralynne slide down, then followed, securing the horse's reins to his saddle and sending him off with a slap to the rump. He didn't go far before he began browsing on bushes again, which hopefully would distract him until they were a fair distance away—the longer until he was discovered, the better.

"All right then," Batrice said firmly. "We'll have to run when we can and walk when we can't. Otherwise, we may not make it to the house before dark, and I've no desire to be out here in the woods after nightfall."

Coralynne nodded her agreement. "I'll try to keep up," she promised.

And she did. They ran as best they could, dodging brush and clambering over downed trees for what felt like forever. When they couldn't run anymore, they paused to catch their breath, then ran again. Several riders passed on the road, but none stopped to search for them. They wished for water before they'd gotten far, but neither of them had carried any with them from the coach, so they simply kept on.

Batrice winced with every step and soon felt as though her whole world had shrunk down to nothing but burning thirst and the pain in her feet. But the sun was already low, and they could not have many hours of daylight left, so she gritted her teeth and put one foot in front of another, trying to pretend she didn't see Coralynne's exhaustion. They just had to keep moving.

Until Coralynne finally stumbled, with a pained cry, and declared she simply couldn't go any further. "I've twisted my ankle," she said softly, tears visible in her eyes. "It hurts Batrice. And I can't even move, I'm so tired. You'll have to go for help."

"I can't leave you out here alone," she protested. "What if they find you?"

"They're not searching the woods," Coralynne insisted. "The only one who'll be in danger is you. Please, just go, and be careful. I'll be fine until you come back for me."

"And if I can't come back?"

"Then I'm bound to be rescued eventually," Coralynne said, but Batrice could see her forcing herself to be brave. "Go on. It's our best chance, and you know it."

She did know it, she just didn't like it at all. From what the man in the dark cloak said, she didn't think he would know where to find her grandmother's house, considering that he didn't believe such a person actually existed. Hopefully, that meant they would be safe once they reached the Entwhistle estate. But the possibility remained that she was wrong. They could be heading straight into a trap.

But instead of voicing her misgivings, she crouched down and grasped Coralynne's shoulder. "I promise I'll come back for you," she said firmly. "I won't leave you here, no matter what."

"I believe you."

"You hide as best you can, and don't come out until you know it's safe."

Coralynne nodded, her eyes wide and her lip wobbling.

Batrice threw her arms around her friend in a quick hug, then leaped to her feet, and jogged off as quickly as she could.

Somehow, she made it Peridale, just as dusk began to fall, identifying the tiny village only by the hand-painted signs hanging above its shops. On her previous visits, she'd been confined to a coach, and had only seen the house at the end of the journey. She'd glimpsed little of the road coming or going, nor had she ever been allowed to explore the town. It would be necessary to ask for directions if she were to have any hope of finding her grandmother's house from there.

She used the coins taken from her attacker's pocket to purchase a roll and was able to wheedle a drink of water out of the shopkeeper, who surveyed Batrice's filthy and disheveled appearance with distaste.

"Can you tell me which road I should take to reach the Entwhistle estate?" Batrice asked of the woman behind the shop counter. "My... brother works there, and I've news for him."

The woman eyed her suspiciously. "There's no one in residence there, not for weeks. Th'old woman up and left."

What? Her grandmother wasn't even home? How was that possible? She was supposed to be at death's door.

Batrice nearly muttered something entirely unladylike at the prospect of yet another mystery, but it wasn't as though this changed her plans. No matter what had happened with her grandmother, the house wouldn't be entirely empty. There would be a skeleton staff, and some horses, she hoped. Someone who could help her rescue Coralynne. "My brother works in the stable, Mistress. Perhaps he's still here, lookin' after the stock."

"Hmph. Well, you take the left fork going out of town t'the north, then when you see a bridge, go right. Th'old house is set back a ways, but it's the only one on that road, so you can't miss it."

"Thank you..." Batrice started to say, only to be interrupted by a horrified screech. The woman pointed at her with rapidly widening eyes and mouth agape.

"Get out!" she shrieked. "Out! Out of my shop!"

Was it something she'd said?

"I'm sorry," Batrice said, "but I didn't mean..."

Whirling around, the shopkeeper grabbed a broom and swung it directly at Batrice's head.

She ducked, only barely fast enough, and as she did so, a faint mew of protest sounded right by her ear. An almost hysterical laugh threatened as she realized the cause of the attack—Goblin had woken up and poked his head out of her hood.

"It's just a cat," she said soothingly, hoping an explanation would placate the enraged shopkeeper, but when the broom swung at her head again, Batrice decided it wasn't worth the effort. All of that yelling was going to attract unnecessary attention, so she murmured a hasty apology and left the shop.

Keeping to the shadows and trying not to limp visibly, Batrice set out for the north road as quickly as possible. A woman in a stained hood was one thing, but a woman with a limp would cause comment. Anyone who saw her would remember her and could reveal her presence to whoever might still be chasing her.

But as soon as she was past the edge of town, the race was on. She ran until she stumbled from weariness, listening all the time for the sound of hooves or wheels on the road, afraid of what might await her, but more afraid to stop.

She almost didn't believe it when she finally stumbled onto the drive and saw the dark gray stone of her grandmother's house looming up ahead. Almost convinced herself it was a dream. But the lawns were neat, the paving stones were swept, and a single lamp burned in one of the front windows.

The rest of the house was dark.

Swallowing her misgivings, praying that she would find someone to help her, Batrice limped up the drive, dragged herself up the steps, and knocked on the front door.

CHAPTER 18

The door swung open under her hand, and Batrice was rather forcefully reminded of her words to Coralynne—that they had yet to be kidnapped by strangers and dragged off to a dark and mysterious estate.

Well, they'd taken care of the kidnapping part, and this certainly qualified as a dark and mysterious estate. All that was now needed was the black cloaked villain, who really ought to sweep into the room, twirl his mustaches, and declare that she'd stepped right into his trap.

Except that this was her grandmother's house, and her grandmother would most certainly never allow anyone to sweep, or twirl. She would consider an abduction to be vulgar and evict the perpetrator at once with a hearty denunciation of his ancestry and upbringing.

But where was her grandmother? Where was anyone at all, for that matter?

The entry hall was dark. No candle had been left burning, and no footman stood sentry to receive visitors. The furniture was not under covers, so it seemed unlikely that the house was completely empty, but it was not yet late enough for everyone to have gone to bed.

"Hello?" she called. "Grandmother? It's Batrice."

When there was no answer, she took a few more hesitant steps. Perhaps her grandmother truly was near death, and everyone stood vigil at her bed. Or perhaps she had simply retired to the drawing room for the evening. Batrice stepped carefully through the dark until she saw the drawing room door ajar, a faint light coming from within.

Breathing a deep sigh of relief, she made her way across the hall and entered the drawing room, pleased to see a fire crackling on the hearth.

"Grandmother, are you in here?"

"Ah, Batrice. Do come in, my dear."

The voice came from a deep wingback chair pulled up before the fire, but it was not her grandmother. And even though Batrice could see nothing of the chair's occupant, she froze, like a rabbit who'd scented a predator.

She knew that voice... and its presence in her grandmother's house should have been impossible.

A chill swept over her while her mind raced. Could there be an innocent explanation?

It was bad enough that she could match the voice from the chair with the mysterious man who had threatened Coralynne. But now that she wasn't seeing a sinister figure in a cloak, her mind supplied a different picture. A different person entirely. Someone who would have no way of knowing where her grandmother lived. Someone who had no reason at all to be anywhere but on the road to Tavisham.

She probably should have guessed. Even when she'd failed to recognize his voice, she should have realized the truth when the cloaked man mentioned her grandmother in the first place. He was, after all, the only person she'd told. How could she have missed this?

But she had, and now she was faced with a dilemma. She could still run. If she fled immediately, she might make it back out the door, but where would she go? Or, she could stand and face this down, find out why she'd been targeted and what her mysterious pursuers truly wanted. Only then would she be free to rescue Coralynne and ensure that Jamie had come to no harm.

Assuming she survived the confrontation. Because if the house had been empty for weeks as the shopkeeper claimed, the letter urging Batrice's visit might not have come from her grandmother at all. Had that letter simply been another small part of an utterly baffling plot?

Had her grandmother even actually left? Or had something worse happened?

"Why, Grandmother," Batrice said dryly, moving forward in spite of the urge to flee, "what a very deep voice you have."

"Yes, well." A dark form began to rise from the chair. "Some things are not so difficult to disguise with the right tools. A face is easily concealed. I can make my eyes look bigger or smaller. Change my teeth. My hair. Even my weight. But I've never been able to change my voice, more's the pity."

"What's pitiful," Batrice said scornfully, "is your apparent fondness for threatening innocent young women. What sort of a gentleman does that make you, *Sir Abner*?"

"Not a gentleman at all." The figure stepped fully into the light of the fire, and it was only Batrice's stage training that enabled her to conceal her shock behind a polite smile.

"I was about to congratulate you on the miraculous improvement of your gout," she said, "but it seems I must also compliment you on other fronts. You appear to have misplaced a great deal of yourself. Along with your age, your gender, and probably your name. Is there anything I've missed?"

The woman facing her chuckled in apparent amusement. "I'm impressed," she said, in a deep, husky contralto. "Most don't see through that particular disguise. Sir Abner is elderly, overlarge, and almost unbearably silly—three things that are often ignored or overlooked by others. Very few bother to notice the voice behind all the makeup."

"Sir Abner was kind," Batrice contradicted her tartly. "A difficult thing to overlook, even if it did turn out to be fake."

What else had been fake, she wondered, eyeing the woman's wide face, short, straight brown hair and broad, muscular build, while recalling each of their encounters along the road.

This could easily have been the person she chased across the roof, whom she'd foolishly assumed male because of his size and the timbre of his whisper.

Probably also the person who'd left her the threatening note, and destroyed the inside of the carriage. Sir Abner, and most likely his henchmen as well, had been present on both of those occasions.

And what of the swordsman?

No. At least, she didn't think so. He'd been taller. And most definitely male, she admitted to herself. The woman in front of her now had effectively concealed her obviously feminine shape beneath the corpulence of Sir Abner, and the cloak she'd worn in the woods. But Batrice had been momentarily held close by the man she'd fought, and his chest had been a decidedly *male* one.

"Where is my grandmother?" she demanded, and the other woman shrugged.

"The house was empty."

"And how did you even know to come here? The last time we spoke, you didn't believe this place existed."

"Your coachman told me everything," her opponent replied, with a small smile. "Seemed to think you really were visiting your dying grandmother."

"Did you hurt him?" Batrice demanded, taking a quick step forward.

"And what if I did?" the woman said lazily. "I doubt you're prepared to do anything about it. You're unarmed, limping, and your companions have all deserted you. I hold the upper hand here, so your wishes and demands mean less than nothing."

"Then now what?" Batrice asked, all too aware that the woman probably spoke no less than the truth. She was exhausted and overwhelmed by a situation that had spiraled quickly beyond her grasp. The fact that she had not yet given up probably said more of her stubbornness than her intelligence. "I assume since you returned to my coach and tortured my coachman, you've discovered that I was, in fact, telling the truth. We don't have any formulas, and the only basket amongst our luggage is a smelly chewed up mess from having been used to contain a particularly repulsive puppy for the past seven days."

"Ah, yes." The woman crossed the remaining space between them to stare down at Batrice with glittering dark eyes. "The puppy. I want to know where it is."

"Mayhem?" Batrice spluttered in confusion. "Why do you want him? He's cute, I suppose, but loud and destructive. He was meant to be a present for my grandmother."

"Didn't you ever bother to ask yourself why anyone would send an unwanted dog on a seven-day carriage journey?"

"Only five times a day," Batrice muttered, more to herself than her adversary. "And anyway, the dog isn't here. I have no idea where he is."

"Oh, but I think you do," the woman said softly. "I also think you know what I want. You've hidden it, but I'll find out where before the night is through."

"Really?" Batrice scoffed, using bravado to cover her fear. "So you think you're just going to torture me like you did John? It isn't like my grandmother leaves her house completely unstaffed. Someone will hear us eventually because I can promise you—I will *not* go quietly."

But the other woman chuckled. "No, I'm afraid you're wrong there. I've searched the house and the grounds. There is no one here but us. And this is where we'll stay until you tell me where you've hidden the formula. Or is it the powder itself? Don't tell me you never got curious and opened that ball to find out what was inside."

Powder?

The ball?

The silver ball on Mayhem's collar?

Batrice blinked rapidly as she thought through the past seven days. Moments she'd dismissed. Tiny hints she'd ignored. People she'd trusted.

Why *had* Lady Norelle sent Mayhem with her in the carriage, as a gift to an older woman she didn't even know, wearing an ornament that would make him a target for thieves? It didn't make sense, but Lady Norelle never did anything without a reason.

And why had Rupert never taken her seriously regarding the threats to their safety? Unless he expected the threats in the first place but had never had any intention of sharing that information with her.

Because he didn't trust her.

Because she wasn't his true mission at all.

Suddenly, his insistence on keeping the dog with him at night made sense. His urgency when Mayhem escaped. His suspicion of Jamie up until the very end. The moment he'd let Jamie leave with the dog while staring at his back like a man whose suspicions had been confirmed...

And suddenly she knew.

Her heart crumbled into tiny shards of pain as she put together all the rest of the clues and faced the truth.

The woman hadn't lied when she said she wouldn't be the only one after whatever she was trying to steal. Someone else had gotten to it first. Someone who'd started by stealing her face powder and Coralynne's pounce, believing them to be something else. Someone who even now had possession of that strangely important silver ball. And someone who had stolen far more than a collar, a dog, and a secret formula.

He'd stolen her heart.

She should have known. So many times, she should have known. When he recovered so quickly from the carriage accident, she should have realized his wounds had been faked, and that the entire incident had probably been staged. When he refused to answer any of her questions but was strangely willing to accept their hospitality on the road, she should have heeded her own suspicions. Or when he'd *admitted* to stealing from her, for the love of Andar, perhaps she should have believed him.

All those times he'd offered to care for the dog, hoping it would learn to trust him. When he'd taken the ball off the collar and played with it, had he been trying to learn its secrets?

She should have listened to Coralynne. Even to Rupert, in this case, but she'd been a fool—a blind, lovesick fool, and now she was going to pay for it because Jamie had gotten what he truly wanted. He was long gone, and he'd taken the dog with him.

"No," she said dully. "I never knew. I didn't try to open it because I believed it was exactly what it looked like—a silly, expensive bauble to decorate a silly, expensive dog."

"And where is the dog now?"

"I don't know." She surprised herself a little. She could have simply told the truth—that Jamie had taken him and was miles away by now. But what would be the point? Her only concern now was Coralynne's safety. Everyone else could go hang.

"I think you're lying," the woman said harshly, leaning in and grasping a handful of Batrice's hair. "And I've invested a great deal in this search, so I intend to find out the truth, and I can assure you I won't be gentle in my methods."

Batrice didn't hesitate for a moment but went straight for her eyes, fingers curved into claws.

Shrieking, the woman yanked hard, pulling Batrice halfway to the ground before jerking her around until her back was to her assailant's chest. While one hand remained twisted in her hair, the other produced a dagger, which she scraped across Batrice's cheek with a trembling hand.

"Do you want to fight me *now*, little girl?"

"I will always want to fight you," Batrice spat, shaking with rage as much as with fear. "It won't do me any good to cooperate when you've already decided I'm lying, and I can't tell you what I don't know. The dog is gone. Your prize is even now slipping out of your grasp, so if you want it that badly, why don't you go chase it instead of threatening me?"

Suddenly, an outraged yowl split the air.

The woman screamed and released Batrice's hair, while the dagger went flying across the room.

Batrice whirled to see Goblin, his tiny claws tangled in the other woman's hair, raking her face as he tried to scrabble his way to the top of her head. His victim flailed wildly, but couldn't get a grasp on him before he leaped from her head to the back of a chair and then to the mantle over the fireplace, turning to hiss at his opponent with his ears lying flat against his skull.

"That's..." The woman's eyes were wide and panicked. "*What is it?*"

"Haven't you ever seen a goblin before?" Batrice asked, valiantly holding back hysterical laughter. She's forgotten he was in the hood of her cloak. That was twice now he'd saved her life.

"Goblins aren't real," the woman said automatically, her eyes fixed on the still angry cat.

"Well, this one is." Batrice began edging across the room to where the woman's dagger had landed and slid beneath a table.

"Then I'm going to kill it."

A growl followed that pronouncement, but it didn't come from the cat. It came from the drawing room door, which still stood ajar.

And from the tiny, furry throat of a thoroughly riled Mayhem, who shot through the door followed by...

"I apologize for being late," Jamie said, stepping into the room with long, confident strides. "As it happened, there were no carts available."

"You!" Batrice and the other woman both spoke at once, then turned to stare at each other.

Batrice's gaze turned next to Mayhem, who was barking furiously at Goblin, but she already knew what she would find. The silver ball on his collar was gone.

The taller woman's eyes darted from the dog to Jamie, to Batrice, then back to the dog.

"Where is it?" she hissed.

"Where is what?" Jamie asked politely.

"You took the ball." Her voice was a barely restrained snarl. "I'm not leaving here without it, so either you tell me where it is, or I kill the girl."

"You won't get very far threatening *me*," Batrice informed her, trying to ignore the pain of that truth. "I'm the one he stole it from in the first place, so it's quite unlikely he'd be willing to hand over his prize in exchange for my life."

"Oh, but you forget, I've been watching the two of you for days," the woman gloated. "I don't think he'll be willing to watch you die."

"He's not your concern," Batrice said boldly. "*I am*, and I'm not willing to watch me die either. Plus"—she ducked to snatch up the dagger from the floor—"now I'm armed, and you're not."

"And what are you going to do with that?" The woman laughed. "Throw it at me like some pathetic festival performer?"

Actually, she'd been thinking about it. Her troupe had boasted a knife thrower who could toss daggers into fruit while it was flying at his head, and he'd tried to teach her a few tricks. Her aim was terrible, but if she could just distract the woman long enough...

Too late.

She hadn't been paying enough attention to her opponent's hands, and one of them swung back into view, now holding a long, narrow tube with the tip of crossbow bolt visible at the front. It was pointed directly at Batrice's chest.

"You've probably never seen one of these before," the woman said conversationally, "but then, few people have. It's a crossbow, of sorts. Spring loaded. Diabolical when you think about it, but the perfect weapon for spies and assassins. They can be hidden almost anywhere, kill a person within twenty paces, and the draw is light enough for a child to manage."

Batrice froze.

"Now, drop the dagger."

She dropped it. Obviously, she was going to have to think of something else.

And Jamie? He was simply watching, appearing as calm as he always did, his body relaxed and his arms at his sides.

"Now." The woman turned to look at him, lowering her weapon slightly. "Tell me what you did with the formula, or I shoot her in the head."

"All right," Jamie said.

"*What?*" The word burst out of Batrice before she could stop herself.

"You allow Miss Reyard to leave, with her cat. Once she is safe, I will tell you where I hid the ball."

The woman laughed. "Do you think me a fool? I'm not letting the hostage out of my sight until I have what I want."

"I know very well that you are not a fool, Noadiah."

She stiffened and stared at him as though he'd struck her.

Batrice stared from one to the other, fascinated and slightly horrified. Was there no end to the twists and turns in this plot? It was really too bad Coralynne was missing it.

"My mother told me to expect you," Jamie explained, with a faint smile. "Said you wouldn't be able to resist getting your hands on the powder once you learned of it."

"You're one of Kassia's brats?" the woman spat. "I should have known. You even look like your father. And your precious mother wouldn't have wanted her little mistake slipping out into the world, now would she?"

"No." Jamie's expression turned sober. "And if you had any sense, you wouldn't either. It's too dangerous. A substance like that could overturn every balance of power in the known world. Empires have fallen over less. And you've already proven that there are those willing to kill over it. Better if it never sees the light of day."

"You're too late," the woman said scornfully. "Do you have any idea how many players there are in this game now? How many are willing to spend fortunes or spill blood to gain even a tiny sample of Spark for themselves?"

"No," Jamie admitted, "but I know how far I'm willing to go to keep it out of their hands."

The woman he'd called Noadiah laughed. "Not very far, apparently, if you're willing to give it to me in exchange for the life of one simple girl. Your mother was a fool to send you."

Jamie didn't even flinch. "As I said, I know how far I'm willing to go. Do you?"

Her expression hardened.

The hand holding the crossbow swung up, and she pulled the trigger.

CHAPTER 19

Several things happened at once, so quickly that Batrice, to her eternal embarrassment, froze like an amateur in the throes of stage fright.

A hollow thunk sounded from the wall behind her, indicating that the crossbow bolt had narrowly missed her head.

The woman cried out in pain, dropped her weapon, and clutched a bleeding hand to her chest.

Jamie charged in from the side, grabbed Batrice around the arms, and knocked her to the floor, rolling them both out of sight behind a settee.

And a new voice intruded on the silence that followed.

"Thank you all for finally putting me out of my misery. That was painful to watch. But enlightening, so I suppose it was worth it."

Batrice was torn between curiosity over who had spoken and the inclination to simply lay where she was, her head tucked beneath Jamie's chin and his arms wrapped around her in a protective hold.

It felt like coming home... but, on the other hand, what was she thinking? She should be furious with him.

"Are you all right?" he whispered softly.

"I'm all right enough to be tempted to punch you in the throat," she whispered back.

"Would the two of you stop flirting and get up?" the new voice demanded irritably.

Batrice felt a chuckle rumble through Jamie's chest, but he loosened his arms and allowed her to rise. She pushed to her feet, not without a wobble or two, and valiantly resisted the urge to kick him while he was down. How dare he try to rescue her right after he betrayed her? If that was actually what he'd done.

She'd never felt so confused in her life.

Once she emerged from behind the settee, she glanced around the room and finally caught sight of the newest member of their little farce.

A man of middle age and moderate height, with a nondescript, completely forgettable face.

Forgettable if you didn't know exactly who he was.

"*Quinn?*"

She'd met him twice. Once, very briefly, in Camber, after the incident with the former Countess Seagrave and her mother—the incident that had led to Batrice's introduction to Lady Norelle. She'd met Quinn a second time at Evenburg, where he'd been introduced to her as one of Lady Norelle's associates.

There seemed to be some doubt amongst those who knew him as to whether he was a spy or an assassin, but no matter which title he was willing to claim, Batrice was utterly relieved to see a familiar face.

Until she remembered everything she had to be angry about.

"I officially hate you all," she announced grimly. "This was all a plot, and you deliberately used me as bait, didn't you?"

Jamie rose up behind her.

"I believe they did," he said calmly.

The older man glanced his direction. "You're in no position to complain," he said. "You almost botched this entire operation by failing to alert us to your presence, and when I instructed the guard to give you an opportunity, you nearly sacrificed everything."

Botched the operation? Batrice couldn't tell for sure, but it almost sounded as though Quinn was defending her. Berating Jamie for stealing what he wanted and leaving when her life had been in danger. She was grateful to know that someone had been concerned for her life at *some* point in this fiasco, but wasn't sure how Quinn had come to expect anything in particular of a man he'd never met before.

"Not everyone shares your priorities," Jamie replied, his voice a little harder, cooler.

"This work leaves no room for vulnerabilities. You shouldn't be in it if you're weak enough to abandon your objective over a threat to a single person. Makes you a danger to your kingdom."

Wait, what?

"You're upset that he tried to *save* me?" Batrice interjected incredulously.

"He knows what's at stake." Quinn didn't even look at her.

"I'm here because I was the only person available," Jamie said, not looking particularly perturbed. "I was pressed into service, not groomed for it. And as I said before, I know how far I'm willing to go. Even if the powder had escaped, it's not worth sacrificing my principles over."

"And if it had been used against your people? Reduced your own kingdom to fiery ruins?"

"How many sacrifices should I justify, then, in the name of preventing an atrocity that might never happen?"

The two men gazed at each other, neither one giving an inch until Noadiah interrupted.

"Oh, it will happen," she said calmly. "I can assure you of that. And no matter what happens to me, this isn't over. My men will track your every move until you reveal where you've hidden it."

Her men? Batrice almost laughed aloud. Did she mean the idiots who'd been outsmarted and overwhelmed by a pair of young women armed only with a cat? She couldn't imagine them being much of a threat.

But Jamie surprised her yet again by reaching into his pocket, pulling out the silver ball and holding it up.

"You mean this?" he said, grinning a little.

Noadiah's face fell. "It's a fake, isn't it?" she asked bitterly.

But it was Quinn who answered. "Did you honestly believe we would endanger the secrets of Spark by sending it across the kingdom in a carriage protected by a single guard?" He sounded almost offended.

Jamie shrugged. "Stranger strategies have proven effective. And it isn't completely fake. If you figure out how to open it, as I did, you'll find a note, courtesy of the Andari Crown."

"And I should just take your word for it?" she said contemptuously.

"Of course not." He tossed the ball in Noadiah's direction, but Quinn got there first, snatching it out of the air so quickly, Batrice almost didn't see him move.

"Enough," he said to Noadiah, in a flat, dark tone. "Consider your mission a failure and your welcome revoked. If you are found inside the borders of Andar again, the Crown will not be so courteous."

The woman clenched her fists so hard her knuckles turned white. "Understood. And since it is unlikely we will see one another again, give your *handlers*"—she invested the word with a healthy helping of scorn —"this warning: the rest of the world is coming. They know about Spark, and they will not want to be the last to possess it for themselves. Wars have been fought over less, so considering that Andar is tiny, and your military laughable, perhaps alliances should be reconsidered."

"So noted." Without even a pause, Quinn threw the ball right out the drawing room window. Shards of glass showered the carpet as Noadiah threw one last loathing look at Quinn and dashed through the door.

Batrice collapsed into a chair. "My grandmother," she announced, "is going to kill you. Unless..." She shot Quinn a horrified glance.

"She is very much alive," he said, sounding slightly irritated.

"Can't blame me for wondering," she muttered. "Not after all that talk about not abandoning your objectives over a threat to a single person."

"Any particular reason you're letting her go?" Jamie asked casually.

"It's not in my kingdom's best interests to detain her," Quinn replied. "If yours wants her dead, perhaps they should have sent a killer instead of a scholar."

Which was, of course, the moment Coralynne and Rupert chose to burst into the room. Rupert came through the door first and tried to shield her, but Coralynne shoved past him with an irritated glance that indicated they had not yet managed to patch up their differences, even if he *had* somehow managed to rescue her.

Batrice was quite proud of her.

"Oh, good!" she said brightly. "We're all here. Does that mean it's story time?"

"Heavens, Batrice, are you all right?" Coralynne dashed to her side. "I've been so worried."

Batrice pulled her down to sit beside her and hugged her tightly. "I'm quite well, thank you. No physical injuries at least."

"What's happened? How is your grandmother?"

Batrice eyed Quinn.

"If you want a story, you tell it, Miss Reyard."

If that's the way he wanted it.

"There was once a naive young woman who wanted desperately to belong somewhere," she began. "So she accepted a position with a respected member of the King's Cabinet in hopes of finding a purpose that suited her talents. Soon after, she received a letter from her grandmother, who commanded her family to attend her because she was dying. The young woman was sent off on a journey to her grandmother's bedside, with a basket of gifts to comfort her ailing relative. But all of it was a lie."

Coralynne gasped. "Batrice. What are you saying?"

214

"The young woman traveled for days through a dark forest, enduring numerous accidents and uncovering a series of mysteries that perplexed her greatly. She had no way of knowing that she'd been betrayed and that all but one of her companions already knew the truth—there was nothing at all the matter with her grandmother."

Rupert wouldn't meet her eyes.

"She'd been used as bait in a scheme to discover the identities of a group of foreign agents. These agents were planning to steal the secret formula for a weapon held by the Andari Crown." Batrice wasn't completely sure she had the details right, but it was close enough. "The weapon was in the form of a powder so dangerous, so explosive, its own creator was willing to risk anything, including his own life, to get it back." She couldn't look at Jamie. She would deal with him later.

"The young woman's mentor believed her safe. Thought a pair of guards would be sufficient to ensure that her charge remained unharmed as she traveled, but the mentor was wrong. The foreign agents were resource-ful, determined, and ruthless, and the young woman's life was repeatedly in danger. But still, no one would tell her the truth, so she was forced to find the truth for herself and nearly died for it.

"She was rescued at the last possible moment, but by a man who valued his mission more than her life, and in the end, she realized she had no idea who she could trust."

"I miscalculated," Rupert said unexpectedly. "We all did. Lady Norelle learned that someone in her office was trying to steal a state secret—a mysterious, explosive powder we'd found in the hold of a merchant ship. We needed to lure them out, and she needed to know if you were ready for more serious work. So she forged the letter from your grandmother and let it slip that the powder was moving north. We expected to uncover an Andari traitor, not an entire nest of foreign agents."

So she'd been right. She'd genuinely been betrayed. "That doesn't excuse the fact that you lied and endangered our lives, and for what? A test?"

"There should have been no danger," Rupert argued. "News of the discovery should have been confined to our own people, and they wouldn't have wanted to endanger their position by threatening you. We expected a theft, quick and invisible, except we would have been watching."

"Well, there *was* a theft," she accused, "and you saw nothing."

"Because we were watching the actual bait. We knew they'd try again when they realized they hadn't gotten what they wanted."

Mayhem. And the silver ball.

"Then why didn't you turn back when you realized you were wrong?"

"It was too late by then," Rupert explained. "And we were supposed to have more support. Lady Norelle sent another agent to watch our backs, but I didn't realize until today that she fell ill after the second night and was no longer following us."

"The old woman in the purple dress?" Batrice asked, discovering that she was not at all surprised.

Rupert nodded, looking grudgingly impressed.

"Even if I believe you..." That was by no means certain, and belief did not equal forgiveness. Not when so many questions remained unanswered. "None of this explains your rudeness," she said, with the prick of tears that indicated she'd been more hurt by it than she'd realized. "Why did you treat me so badly?"

"Orders," he said, folding his arms uncomfortably and looking at the floor. "Lady Norelle instructed me to attempt to bring out the worst in you. She said she needed to know how you would respond under pressure. She also said you had an over-romanticized idea of spying, and that you needed to know the truth about what that life would be like."

Batrice felt as though she'd been slapped.

Coralynne turned to Rupert with her brows lowered. "You... you... you were mean and rude and dismissive *on purpose?*" She sputtered incoherently, apparently unable to produce any further words to sufficiently give vent to her feelings.

"Don't imagine you're somehow special," Quinn interjected. "If working for the Crown is the life you want, you should know that sometimes you'll be used, and no one will apologize. Your safety will be considered, but you may never know the full truth of the maneuvers being made behind the scenes. You will have to accept that, along with the dangers involved."

"I understand," Batrice said finally. She was not going to cry. Batrice Reyard did not cry until she decided to. "So this was a test." She let that idea settle for a moment before a question slipped out in spite of her intention never to ask. "Did I fail?"

Rupert shrugged. "That's not for me to say."

She couldn't even look at Quinn, but he answered anyway.

"I will be reporting to Lady Norelle that you did reasonably well for your first attempt," he said, without any noticeable inflection to indicate that he had feelings about it one way or another.

"She did steal my horse and leave me to die," Rupert interjected.

Quinn's stare was flat. "A point in her favor as far as I'm concerned."

Rupert turned an interesting shade of red as Quinn turned back to Batrice.

"Unless you've decided against continuing in the service of the Crown, I would offer you another assignment," he said, quite unexpectedly.

Batrice wasn't sure how to answer. She felt battered—bruised as much in spirit as in body. Everything she'd believed had been turned upside down. People she'd trusted had lied to her, and her new life had been revealed as a fraud. Did she even know what she wanted now?

"What would that be?" she asked cautiously.

"There is one remaining foreign agent who I am recommending be escorted back to Evenleigh. Considering our mutual interest in preventing Spark from falling into the hands of anyone else, I believe he ought to be offered the opportunity to discuss an alliance with the Crown on behalf of his sovereign."

Her eyes shot to Jamie, who remained still, his gaze resting on hers.

"Are you asking me to escort this... *spy*, back to Evenleigh?" she asked.

"I am." Quinn's voice was so bland, she shot him a look of mild suspicion, but could read nothing from his face.

She had no immediate response. A part of her wanted to run, far away, and never see any of these faces again. She felt used, betrayed by the people she'd trusted most.

But she was the one who'd wanted to be a spy. Quinn was not wrong—that was not a life for the weak or the easily offended. She was going to have to be willing to grow, learn, and accept correction if she wanted to survive.

And, whether it made her a fool or no, she still wanted answers from the man who had not, in the end, betrayed her as quite as badly as she'd first believed.

"I'll do it," she said.

It took several days for them to be ready for the return journey. Fortunately, Lady Entwhistle's house was large enough for them to mostly avoid each other, which seemed to suit everyone.

While the carriage was being repaired and the horses rested, Batrice occupied herself with sleeping, thinking, and occasional chats with Coralynne, who had numerous questions whenever she wasn't scribbling in her journal. She flatly refused to discuss Rupert, however, and declined to so much as stay in the same room with him, even for meals.

Rupert himself nearly disappeared, and gave Batrice little chance to determine his true character. How much of his behavior had been a lie? Was he genuinely as difficult and disapproving as he'd pretended to be?

Or had that been an elaborate pretense enacted only on Lady Norelle's orders?

John, on the other hand, was frequently around the house and turned out to be an even better actor than Rupert. A member of the king's guard, he'd feigned diffidence for the sake of their ruse, though in truth he possessed a naturally garrulous and friendly personality. When Batrice conveyed her disapproval of his deception, he shrugged, grinned, and went back to playing Battlements with Coralynne, who proved to be an unexpectedly keen student of strategy.

It wasn't until the evening before their departure that Batrice finally found enough courage to seek out Jamie and confront him with what she'd learned.

"Sit," she commanded, when she walked into the kitchen and found him with his hair loose and his shirtsleeves rolled up, pouring himself a cup of tea.

"Would you like one?" he asked, holding up an empty cup.

"No, thank you." She seated herself at one end of the worktable in the center of the room, determined not to be distracted by his hands, no matter what they were holding or how perfect they might be.

Jamie drew up another chair just around the corner of the table and settled himself, not looking noticeably nervous.

Which was most terribly unfair. Batrice's knees were shaking with the effort of facing him again.

"Is Jamie your real name?" she asked, as soon as he'd set down his cup.

He curled one hand around it and seemed to stare into the steaming surface of the tea. "Yes," he said finally, with obvious reluctance. "And no. My full name is Prince Jamison Reule Ranolf. Fourth son of His Majesty King Elgard Reule and Her Majesty Queen Helena Ranolf of Isernia."

Batrice could only stare. A spy was bad enough, but this was so much worse than she'd ever imagined. And where in the world was Isernia?

"You're..."

"I'm still Jamie," he said.

"A prince!"

"My kingdom has more chickens than people," he told her, raising his eyes from his cup. "Most outsiders have never heard of Isernia because we're too tiny to bother with. My father serves as his own steward, and Mother visits every new baby in the kingdom before they're a week old. I wasn't joking about my three older brothers having a fondness for sharp objects—they're the head of the guard, the commander of the army, and assistant to the royal chef."

"And what are you?" His answer seemed terribly important. How much of what he'd told her had been lies?

He reached out and placed a tentative hand over hers, while she tried not to show how much it affected her ability to breathe.

"I didn't lie to you, Batrice. I really am a scholar. I enjoy books and studying, and alchemy in particular, as it's our kingdom's primary reason for existence. My mother is also an alchemist, and she took me on as her apprentice when I was twelve."

"That isn't all you study," she accused. "You were the swordsman I fought in the forest that night."

He ducked his head and grinned. "Yes. I've had to become competent at that as well. But I didn't lie to you that night either. We were being followed, and I suspected someone had loosed the horses in order to distract your guards and attempt an attack. I decided to pretend to attack first to throw them off."

Her eyes narrowed as she considered his story. "And you admit the thefts were you as well."

"Yes," he acknowledged. "But I told you so at the time."

"And the note? Searching the inside of the carriage?"

"Not me," he insisted. "I needed to recover the powder, but I never wanted to scare you. Those had to have been Noadiah, or one of her men."

Batrice decided she believed him. He'd been visibly upset when she first mentioned the note, and destroying the inside of the coach had been the work of someone both violent and impatient, neither of which described Jamie.

"Who is Noadiah? Is she from your kingdom?"

Jamie grimaced and settled back in his chair. "I've seen her from a distance, but never actually met her before. She's a mercenary, of sorts, but I don't know where she's actually from. She speaks four languages that I know of, and she's traded with us before, primarily for information, which is a valuable commodity when you're small and vulnerable to attack. But she found out about a collaborative experiment Mother was working on with an exiled Erathi enchanter."

Andar had only recently learned of the magical history of the kingdoms at their borders, and of the existence of such people as mages and enchanters. Erath in particular had been a mystery for hundreds of years, until their exiled king, an enchanter himself, had returned to restore his people to their former home.

Batrice had always found those stories fascinating but had never dreamed she might someday encounter a person who had experienced magic for themselves.

"Then..." She couldn't quite keep the curiosity and excitement out of her voice. "Magic is possible in Isernia?"

"Oh, yes." Jamie seemed almost startled by the question. "Alchemy is deeply reliant on magic. But in this case, we think they relied on it too much. My mother and her partner were working on ways to create a rich, dense soil that would grow crops even in small gardens or rocky conditions, such as the mountains of Isernia. We think they overcompensated in a few areas, and accidentally created the compound that's come to be known as Spark."

Batrice leaned forward and put her chin in her hand. "What does it do?"

Jamie took a sip of his cooling tea. "As it's created with magic, it has an enormous amount of potential, but it doesn't require magic to be activated —only heat and water. We've discovered that with a little too much heat, the resulting explosion can be powerful enough to blast through solid stone."

Her eyebrows shot up. "So, you accidentally created a weapon of war while trying to grow vegetables?"

"It does sound bad when you put it like that."

"And now you're trying to keep the secret out of unsafe hands."

"Essentially." He leaned back and raked both hands through his hair. "Andar first learned of it when a merchant smuggled an alarming amount of the powder into one of their harbors along with a shipment of untaxed silk. We believe it was taken from Mother's partner, who disappeared shortly after their accidental discovery. We've been unable to make contact with him, or his family, ever since, and Father is afraid he may have been kidnapped for his knowledge."

"Could he make this compound on his own?"

"We aren't entirely certain," Jamie admitted. "Initially, we considered it unlikely. Even if he remembered every step of the process, it requires alchemy as well as enchantment, so he would have needed to find an alchemist who could recreate Mother's work. But unless he's somehow created more, we can't imagine how that merchant could have come by the amount he had in his possession. And if the formula itself were to get out?" He shook his head. "All that talk of war was no exaggeration."

"How did you even know the powder was here in the first place?"

"Rumors. And an offer from Noadiah to acquire the powder and sell it back to us at an exorbitant price."

That explained most of what had been bothering her. But there was still one thing she didn't understand.

"Why send you, specifically? Why would they risk a..." She stumbled over the word. "A prince?"

"Batrice, being a prince doesn't make me any better or less expendable than any other man," he said, with quiet sincerity. "In Isernia, we all take on many tasks. In this case, I'm the only one who could identify the powder and contain it safely." After a pause, he continued. "I'm also the only one who is gifted enough with languages to pass as Andari without causing comment."

She thought he was probably being honest with her. It was too strange and preposterous of a story for him to have made up, and besides, Quinn had seemed aware of his identity, at least in some respects. He would be a fool to lie about details she could confirm with Quinn later if she chose.

But a scholar prince who was also a spy? And an alchemist to boot?

All of his evasions now made perfect sense. And his regrets. It wasn't as if he could have told her the truth about his origins or his purpose, noble though they were, and there was no amount of mere attraction that could have overcome the differences between them.

But at least he hadn't truly lied to her or betrayed her. He'd come to Andar on a mission of such grave importance she shuddered to contemplate the consequences for failure, and it was no part of her nature to resent him for doing his duty to his kingdom. No, the blame for lies and betrayal lay elsewhere. As for Jamie, he'd flirted, and she'd flirted back, and now they would agree to go their separate ways with no hard feelings.

The wound in her heart could not be laid at his door.

"Thank you," she said finally, starting to stand, needing to take this knowledge and her broken heart elsewhere to begin to deal with them. "I appreciate you answering my questions. Perhaps someday I'll be able to sort out the fact from the fiction in all of this, and come to terms with my own place in it."

"Batrice, please wait." He caught her fingers, holding them gently enough that she could have pulled away, but firmly enough that she knew he wanted her to stay. Apprehension froze her in her place.

"I was happy to answer your questions. I wish I could have answered them honestly from the beginning, but I hope you now understand more of why I couldn't. Please believe that I never wanted to hide from you."

"But it's a lucky thing you did," she said, sitting back down and feigning a calm that couldn't have been farther from the truth.

"It is?" His brow furrowed in surprise.

"Of course." She tried on a smile. "I'm glad we met, glad we were able to be friends for a few days, but can you imagine if we'd become more than friends? It's going to be hard enough for me to say goodbye as it is, so it's probably for the best that we were never truly anything more than acquaintances."

"Acquaintances?" he said softly.

"Yes." She nodded firmly, decisively.

"Batrice." He leaned in until it was almost uncomfortable not to meet his eyes. "Batrice, please look at me."

She tried. His gaze was too heated, too intent.

"Batrice, can you forgive me?"

"What do you think you need forgiveness for?" she asked tremulously.

"For letting you see my heart when I wasn't free to offer it to you," he said, and his bluntness startled her into staring back at him.

"Your heart?" she repeated, not daring to believe she'd heard him correctly.

"Yes. My heart." His grin suddenly filled with mischief. "Or don't you believe that princes have those?"

"I... yes?" She swallowed, not sure where this was going.

"Batrice, I told you that I was a scholar of the unexpected, and that is as accurate a description of alchemy as I can give you in a single word. It's less a science than an art, even on the best days. I never know quite how my work is going to go—whether it will blow up in my face, or create something new and beautiful—and that is part of why I love it.

"But the truth is, the most unexpected and beautiful thing I've ever encountered is you."

She blinked. She couldn't possibly have heard him right.

"And now that you know the truth—about me and my mission here—I'm free to say things I couldn't say before."

"Stop," she demanded, leaping to her feet and pulling her hand from his. "Don't say another word. Not even one, unless you really mean it. Unless you're ready to accept the consequences."

"And what are those?" He stood and took a step towards her, with a tenderness in his eyes she almost couldn't believe was real.

"Jamie, I won't have my heart broken again," she said fiercely, her voice wobbling a little. "And you... You're the friend I never knew I'd been missing, and I've already fallen. I've fallen so hard that I don't yet know how to pick myself back up. So don't give me hope. Don't offer me everything I've ever dreamed of unless this is real, and you're truly free to offer it to me."

He came closer, closer, until she could feel his warmth even though they weren't touching, and his hand lifted to cup her jaw as if it were infinitely precious and fragile. "Batrice, what are you afraid of?" he asked gently.

"Everything," she whispered. "I'm afraid of you being a prince and me being a... an actress. I'm not ashamed of anything I've done, Jamie, but I'm afraid you will be. That your friends and family would despise me if they ever found out. I'm afraid that I'll fall for you even harder only to discover that there was never any way for us to bridge the gaps between us. And I'm afraid that I'll find myself falling alone, with no one to catch me."

"Then let me fall with you," he said simply, and before she could answer, he moved in closer, took her face gently between his hands, and kissed her. Once, lightly, gently, perfectly.

The kiss stunned, elated, and remade her, gathering all her broken pieces together and fitting them perfectly into place.

"Oh, yes," was all the eloquence she could manage as he wrapped her up in his arms, pulled her into his chest and tucked her beneath his chin.

Batrice decided almost immediately that it was her favorite place in the world—a place where she felt safe in every way that mattered.

"I'm sorry that I'm a prince," he whispered.

"You should be," she murmured into his shirt. "The nerve of you. Here I was hoping I could seduce you by proposing to support your scholarly habit with my acting skills. Now I have nothing to offer. Especially now that we know I make a terrible spy."

"I should be the one to worry," he told her. "What will your family think when they find out you've brought home a man who regularly singes his eyebrows off?"

Batrice laughed. "My family will be so surprised I brought home anyone at all, they'll forgive you anything. But…" She pulled back, leaving her hands on his shoulders. "Do you really want to meet my family? That is… are you sure…" She had never in her life had so much difficulty with words.

"I'm very sure, Batrice," he said, tucking a strand of her hair behind her ear. "I love you."

Her eyes flew wide.

"And I've never said that to any other woman in my life. Because I had no idea a woman like you could exist. I love that you're not afraid to say what you think. I love your sense of humor, the way you laugh, your determination, and your enthusiasm. I love that you're willing to chase a villain across a roof in the middle of the night and that you're not afraid to defend yourself when necessary. I even love that you rescue hairless cats."

"That's good," Batrice said, almost giddy with the knowledge that he loved her. "Because I'm taking Goblin home with me."

"And what of Mayhem? Aren't you afraid of hurting his feelings?"

She made a face. "I'm thinking of leaving him for my grandmother. To distract her from the pain she'll be experiencing when she finds out what we've done to her house."

"Or we could take him with us when we go. After all, if it wasn't for him, we might never have met."

Batrice groaned. "I suppose I love you enough to put up with that wretched creature if you truly wish me to."

Jamie laughed and dropped his forehead against hers. "We should probably return him to Evenleigh. He was, after all, the key to unraveling a plot to steal state secrets. Perhaps your king would consider offering him a full-time job."

"You're right. I shouldn't sneer at him too loudly," Batrice said with a sigh, "He turned out to be a better spy than I am."

"If it helps, we really don't have much demand for spies in Isernia. But there's a raging demand for princesses who don't mind getting their hands dirty."

Batrice couldn't help the huge smile that spread across her face.

"Are you accepting applications from former actresses with a tendency to cause more trouble than strictly necessary?"

"It's the only kind of application I'm interested in."

"Then you may kiss me again," she said, and didn't wait for his response before she stood on her toes and claimed a kiss for herself. The experience was so very nearly perfect that she kissed him again, and then it really wasn't very clear who was kissing whom, only that kissing Jamie was possibly the best idea she'd ever had.

"Do we have to go back?" she asked breathlessly, when they ended the kiss more out of a need to breathe than any particular desire to stop.

"I would beg you to elope," he said, grinning, "but in our case, it might cause an international incident."

"How very disappointing." She sighed. "Wait, what if we went back, discussed your alliance with King Hollin, and *then* eloped?"

He dropped a kiss on the tip of her nose. "I've heard Isernia is beautiful this time of year."

Her smile was wicked, but she didn't care. "And I've heard it has an unusual number of unmarried princes. Perhaps we should visit."

"Not," he growled, "until we're safely married. My brothers can't have you."

After a peal of delighted laughter, she kissed him again, and knew that she had finally found what she'd been looking for since the day she left home—a place where she truly belonged.

EPILOGUE

atrice lifted her hand to knock on the door in front of her and paused.

She lowered it again, bit her lip, and squeezed her eyes shut.

When she opened them again, the door was still there. That trick hadn't worked on audiences either, but one never knew.

She'd been avoiding this meeting ever since returning to Evenleigh with Jamie, but the time for avoidance was over. This was her last opportunity to get answers, or maybe just her last chance to come to terms with her disappointment.

Either way, she couldn't leave until she faced Lady Norelle again, so Batrice pressed her lips tightly together, straightened her spine, and knocked.

The door flew open.

"There you are," Lady Norelle said briskly, her hand still on the doorknob. "I was just about to hunt you down, in case you were thinking of sneaking away without answering any of my messages."

"I wasn't. That is, I hadn't…"

Lady Norelle raised one eyebrow.

"All right, fine. I thought about it," Batrice grumbled. "But I didn't do it, so I believe I deserve some credit for overcoming my baser impulses."

"Congratulations," her former mentor said dryly. "Since you're here, why don't you come in and sit down."

"I don't have long."

"Do you really think that carriage will be leaving without you?"

Batrice chuckled in spite of herself. "An elopement with no bride does seem a bit pointless. But I shouldn't keep them waiting too long, so perhaps we should be brief. What was it you wished to discuss?"

Lady Norelle walked around her desk and took a seat behind it, leaning back in her chair and gazing thoughtfully at Batrice. "You are angry with me," she said matter-of-factly. "I understand, as I am thoroughly angry with myself, but I had hoped for a chance to explain how the situation came about and ask for your forgiveness where my mistakes put you in danger."

That was not at all what Batrice had expected her to say.

"I... yes?" she said. "I mean, I would like that as well."

"Thank you." Lady Norelle crossed her arms, and suddenly looked a great deal older, and more weary, than Batrice had ever seen her look before. "Batrice, you know some of my history. Enough, I believe, to understand what I mean when I say that I fell into my present position almost by accident.

"I was neither born nor trained to advise a king, let alone to engage in intrigue or espionage." Her grimace was dark and pained. "I became a mother, of sorts, far earlier than I expected, and once I began accepting responsibility, it seemed natural to take on more.

"At first, I only needed to give practical advice. I helped make sure everything ran smoothly and provided much needed"—she coughed and shot Batrice a pointed look—"feminine wisdom where it was lacking."

Batrice couldn't help laughing a little. It was true that the king did tend to have male advisors, all of whom seemed to be of similar ages and dispositions.

"But it didn't end there." Lady Norelle rose from her chair and paced towards the window. "I won't lie and pretend that I don't enjoy my life, or that I'm not well-suited to it most of the time. But, in recent years, as Andar has engaged in deeper and often more complex relationships with other kingdoms, I find myself frequently wondering whether I've wandered well beyond my depth and capacity."

Despite her hurt, Batrice found her admiration for her mentor rising once again. It couldn't have been easy for a woman of Lady Norelle's age and experience to admit such things. Or for her to continue to strive in the face of her own sense of doubt and inadequacy.

"Spark terrifies me," Lady Norelle said bluntly, turning from the window to face Batrice. "I simply didn't understand what was at stake at first. I believed it would prove troublesome, especially after I discovered that one of my own, trusted people must have sold information about its existence. But as to the rest?" She shrugged. "I thought all I had to do was root out the identity of someone willing to sell secrets for money. Someone who'd promised to acquire a sample in exchange for payment. But I will-fully ignored the depths to which such a person might be willing to sink. I wanted to believe it was merely a momentary lapse. A temptation, possibly regretted, easily confronted."

"So, you really did believe I'd be safe."

"I would never have willingly put you in danger," Lady Norelle said fiercely. "If you believe nothing else, I hope you can believe that. But my plans were formed around unmasking a single traitor, one I couldn't believe to be capable of violence. It had to have been someone close to me. Someone I knew, and I let that blind me to the possibilities."

"I understand," Batrice said, and she did. That part, at least, was easy to forgive. "You expected a coward and a sneak thief, and instead, you got a nest of international spies willing to kill."

Her mentor nodded. "We still have no idea who the traitor is, and now this discovery has thrown us headlong into a battle we're ill-prepared to fight. Especially considering that we don't know who our enemies are, or how they might choose to attack."

"Then you agree that there could be war?" Batrice's eyes widened as she grasped the import of what Lady Norelle was saying.

"We simply don't know. And it's the not knowing that weighs the heaviest."

Her expression shifted then, to something warmer, and the spymaster became the mentor once again. "But that's not really what you need to discuss with me, is it?"

Batrice let out a long breath and shook her head.

"You feel as though I betrayed you," Lady Norelle continued, "not only by placing you in danger but by choosing to test your mettle in the field."

"You instructed Rupert and John to lie to me. It was as if I were in a play, but I was the only one who didn't know it was all fake."

Lady Norelle crossed the room to lean back against her desk directly in front of Batrice. "Yes. It was. And while I will forever regret the ways that I placed you in danger, I cannot and will not apologize for testing you as I did."

Again, not at all what Batrice had expected to hear. And yet...

"As I said, I had no training for this life, Batrice. But I've come to recognize some of its dangers, its traps, and its pitfalls. I've seen the regrets of many in my employ and seen the toll this work takes on those who devote themselves to it. It's hard, lonely work. It requires you to place blind faith in those you work with, and accept that you will never know the whole picture of which you are a small part. Sometimes you'll be asked to follow a plan even when it looks foolish, but sometimes you'll be required to improvise, and you must have the wisdom to make that choice under great pressure, in only a moment's time."

Batrice thought she understood. "You put your faith in someone who betrayed you, and in doing so, placed everyone else around you in danger.

You wanted to find out whether I would break. Whether I could be trusted to make the right decision, even when I felt alone."

Lady Norelle nodded. "It seemed more important than ever. And if you couldn't accept the need for us to test you in order to determine whether you were worthy of our confidence, this could never be the life for you anyway."

Batrice met her eyes soberly. "Thank you for explaining," she said. "I think until now I didn't truly appreciate the weight of your responsibilities. And if it helps, I still admire you for everything that you've accomplished, and for being so very uniquely yourself in the midst of it. You've inspired me, and I'll always be grateful for that."

"But?" Lady Norelle asked, a hint of a smile curving her lips.

"But this isn't the life for me," Batrice admitted.

"I think the handsome fellow waiting downstairs with a carriage was my first clue," her mentor replied cheekily.

Batrice grinned, then sobered briefly. "I think perhaps I was more angry with Rupert than with you. Even now that I know about his orders..." She almost couldn't put her feelings into words. At least, not very polite ones.

"He was an ass," she blurted out. "To Coralynne and to me. And then, after he admitted he was only acting, he disappeared and refused to speak to Coralynne again, so I've had no opportunity to find out whether he's actually a decent human being or whether he's just truly horrible."

Though given how he'd treated Coralynne, she was inclined to believe the latter.

"I can't speak to his interpretation of my orders," Lady Norelle said. "All I can tell you is that he requested leave the moment he returned, and I granted it."

So Batrice would probably never know for sure.

And neither would Coralynne.

Who continued to insist that she was well, and perfectly content with her lot in life. Since returning to Evenleigh, she'd taken up residence in a tiny set of rooms with a maid for company and begun work on her next novel. As a reward for her part in Batrice's misadventures, the Crown had insisted on covering Coralynne's expenses for at least two years, which should give her time to establish herself comfortably in spite of the rumors of her failed "elopement."

Whenever Batrice expressed regrets over how their journey had ended, Coralynne always said, "Just because things didn't turn out the way I hoped, doesn't mean they didn't turn out perfectly in the end."

And she did seem happy, so Batrice was happy for her. Even if she still wanted to kick Rupert's shins on her friend's behalf.

"I suppose that's it then," Batrice said, rising from her chair.

"Except for one thing." Lady Norelle stood and threw her arms around Batrice in a warm and motherly hug. "I hope you will be able to forgive me and find the adventures you always dreamed of."

Batrice returned her embrace, feeling suddenly as though she were about to lose something precious.

"There is nothing to forgive," she promised. "How can I be angry when I've finally found where I was always meant to be?"

Lady Norelle smiled at her and brushed at a suspicious glimmer of moisture in her eye. "Then get along with you. And write to me occasionally so I will know whether to send one of my spies to threaten your new husband."

Batrice laughed. "Thank you. For everything."

With that, she was shoved out the door—feeling lighter than she had in weeks—to descend the stairs to the courtyard in anticipation of yet another journey.

This one, however, she approached with a great deal less dismay.

She was leaving for good this time. Walking away from this life that had once seemed to be everything she'd ever dreamed of, to pursue another that she'd never even dared to hope for.

She, Batrice Elanza Reyard, was about to elope with a charming and handsome prince, who would carry her off to his castle where they would live happily ever after.

Or at least, that was how she'd presented the notion to her parents.

In reality, she was running away with her best friend Jamie to have adventures and blow things up in the name of science.

Which, to Batrice, seemed like the happiest of all possible endings.

Or beginnings, depending on how you looked at it.

So as she emerged, laughing, into the bright, mid-summer sun to throw herself into Jamie's waiting arms, that was exactly how she chose to imagine it—as a new beginning for them both. And as she melted into his kiss, it was as if the curtain was rising for the last time on a play with no stage, no audience, and no rehearsals—only the two of them and the life they would build together.

Unexpected, unscripted, and perfect.

THANK YOU

Thank you for reading! I have loved writing this series and getting to know its characters and I hope you have enjoyed going on this journey with them. For more of their adventures, check out the rest of the series, or sign up for my newsletter to be the first to find out about new releases.

http://kenleydavidson.com

If you loved Path of Secrets and want to share it with other readers, please consider leaving an honest review on Amazon or Goodreads. Not only do I love getting to hear how my stories are impacting readers, but reviews are one of the best ways for you to help other book lovers discover the stories you enjoy. Taking even a moment to share a few words about your favorite books makes a huge difference to indie authors like me!

THE ANDARI CHRONICLES

The Andari Chronicles is a series of interconnected fairy tale retellings that evoke the glittering romance of the originals, while infusing them with grit, humor, and a cast of captivating new characters. *If you enjoyed the world of Andar, be sure to check out the other books in the series:*

Recommended Reading Order:

- *Traitor's Masque*
- *Goldheart*
- *Pirouette*
- *Shadow and Thorn*
- *Daughter of Lies*
- *Path of Secrets*

http://kenleydavidson.com/books

ALSO BY KENLEY DAVIDSON

FAIRY TALE RETELLINGS

THE ENTWINED TALES

A Beautiful Curse

ROMANTIC SCIENCE FICTION

CONCLAVE WORLDS

The Daragh Deception

The Concord Coalition

http://kenleydavidson.com/books

ABOUT THE AUTHOR

Kenley Davidson is an incurable introvert who took up writing to make space for all the untold stories in her head.

She loves rain, roller-coasters, coffee and happy endings, and is somewhat addicted to researching random facts and reading the dictionary (which she promises is way more fun than it sounds). A majority of her time is spent being mom to two kids and two dogs while inventing reasons not to do laundry (most of which seem to involve books).

Kenley is the author of The Andari Chronicles, an interconnected series of fairy tale retellings, and Conclave Worlds, a romantic science fiction series.

She also writes sweet contemporary romance under the pseudonym Kacey Linden.

kenleydavidson.com
kenley@kenleydavidson.com

ACKNOWLEDGMENTS

I'd like to officially speak up in support of the idea that writing a book while moving is a bad idea. That said, I somehow finished this book while moving, and I'm still a little confused as to how and when all those words got written.

Mostly, though, the book happened because I have a fantastic support team. I owe flowers and a year's worth of pedicures to Tiffany, for taking my kids on adventures while I was writing, and something equally awesome but slightly less girly to Jeff, for giving me space to write in a season where there was very little space of any kind.

I'm also incredibly grateful to my proofreader, Theresa, who does an absolutely stellar job of making my words shine and finding all the places where my fingers tend to trip when I'm typing too fast.

And thank you most of all to my readers, for sticking with me during the extended gap between *Daughter of Lies* and *Path of Secrets*. It's been a long year, but I hope you'll find this book was worth the wait.

CPSIA information can be obtained
at www.ICGtesting.com
Printed in the USA
BVHW032032140121
597880BV00009B/112

9 781712 597309